Abby's Crossing

Abby's Crossing

Darryl Harris

Covenant Communications, Inc.

Cover images: *Covered Wagon* © JillLang, *Young Woman Standing by a Field during the Civil War* © JayBoivin, courtesy istockphoto.com.

Cover design copyright © 2016 by Covenant Communications, Inc.

Published by Covenant Communications, Inc.
American Fork, Utah

Printed in the United States of America
First Printing: January 2016

21 20 19 18 17 16   10 9 8 7 6 5 4 3 2 1

ISBN 978-1-62108-832-5

Dedicated, first of all, to all the Shoshoni
Indians and soldiers who died in the 1863
Battle of the Bear River. To the descendants
of all those who survived. To the hearty
descendants of the men and women who
settled Franklin, Idaho. And to the miners and
and freighters of Bannack City.

Acknowledgments

My profound thanks to the people at Eschler Editing with whom I have the great luxury of working, and to the editors at Covenant Communications. I would also like to thank my wife, Chris, for her patience. And, of course, thank you to my readers.

Chapter 1

WATER FLOWED FROM AUTUMN-DAPPLED MOUNTAINS, dragging rocks and gravel along the creek bottoms, then frothing and rushing until they were unseen in the turbid runoff.

Abby heard the rushing water before her group reached the crossing. Aspen, cottonwoods, sagebrush, and grass lined the creek bottom, and they rose before her as the wagon rumbled over the road. A suspended drizzle filled the air—it wasn't as thick as the cold rain that had drenched the area for the past week, but it still clung to the earth, the air, the turning leaves, and mostly, to Abby's skin.

Her friend Winny now broke a long period of charged silence. "I don't like the sound of that creek, Isaac." Winny sat on the edge of the wagon seat, gripping whatever she could take hold of to keep seated. "I told you we shouldn't have come today. The runoff from the storm has swelled the creek like a puffed bullfrog."

Isaac's face was still red and lined from the anger he'd kept inside for miles. His hat was pushed so far down on his forehead Abby wondered how he hadn't developed a headache. He lashed out at Winny. "I'm well aware of your hesitance, Sister Davis. I'm also aware that it has little to do with crossing this creek or with the runoff."

Abby sat next to Isaac with her son, Yahnai, squished between her and Winny. She was glad there were two people between Winny and Isaac.

"Well," Winny said, "as long as you're aware, why don't we just discuss it? Stop the wagon, and we'll have a nice, long conversation."

Isaac cracked the lines, and the horses lunged down the slope toward the water.

Abby turned to her outspoken friend, but Winny looked past Abby, glaring at Isaac. Shaking her head, Abby said, "Winny, I'm marrying Isaac, and honestly, it's not your concern."

"Such a proud, stubborn man," Winny hissed, looking at the crossing ahead.

Above the growing roar of the creek, Isaac shouted, "I'm an experienced horseman and am quite capable of bringing my intended safely to the doors of the Endowment House." The horses slowed to keep the wagon from pushing them down the steep slope. Impatiently, Isaac cracked the lines again.

The incline caused Abby to plant her feet more firmly on the baseboard and put a protective arm around Yahnai. "I don't like the look of the creek either," she muttered, turning to Isaac, trying to appear more faithful than she felt.

"We'll be fine." Isaac looked at her with eyes that spoke of his forty-six years of experience—eyes streaked with stubbornness and determination. "Trust me."

Abby did trust him. But she also knew he could be wrong.

"She shouldn't even be your intended," Winny shouted. "You're old enough to die in ten years and leave her alone with a quiver full of children to raise."

"Winny, hush!" Abby looked over at her friend, who wrapped an arm around Yahnai as well. The Indian boy's black hair glistened in the moist air and sunlight, and his dark eyes looked to Abby like obsidian stones. She wasn't sure whether the fear in them belonged to him or whether it was her own fear reflected in his gaze.

Isaac clicked at the horses. They pressed forward to the swirling, foaming water.

"Today's not a good day to cross," Winny yelled. "It's too deep. Can't even see the bottom. Let's go back to the settlement and wait for the creeks to go down."

Isaac focused on his horses, clenching his teeth as if his life depended on the strength of his bite. His eyes narrowed like he was aiming at a target, dodging all warnings.

"Mama?" Yahnai said, looking at Abby with definite fear. He wrapped his arms around her waist.

Isaac bellowed at the horses again. They pinned their ears back, a sign they could hear Isaac's commands and feel his slaps, but they had their own intuitions to confront. The horses' response didn't suit Isaac. He reached for his big leather whip and jerked it out of its holder. The whip cracked loudly in the heavy air. Once, twice, three times. The whip scorched the rump of each horse, and they snorted, lowered their heads, jumped, and plunged into the water, taking the wagon and its passengers with them.

Water splashed onto Abby and chilled her. She could only imagine how the horses felt as the cold swirled around their legs, brushed the undersides of their bellies, and splashed up their flanks.

A dead thud accompanied the sharp lurch that halted their progress. The impact was so strong that Abby's tight grip on the wagon seat was loosened in a split second. She felt herself being hurled out of the tipping wagon, along with Yahnai and Winny. Freezing black water covered her. The shock took her breath away. She dug her heels into the rocky bottom of the creek and found she could stand, but the force of the stream was strong, and she had to lean against it. She saw quilts and luggage and tents being swept downstream. For a second or two, she couldn't see Yahnai. His head bobbed to the surface. She exploded toward him, swimming downstream a few feet. She grasped him by his neck and stood again.

He coughed and wrapped his little arms tightly around her neck. "Mama!"

It took all of her strength to let him wrap his legs around her waist and not be thrown off balance by his added weight. "I've got you."

The boy sputtered and coughed again, spitting water out of his mouth. He'd been a good swimmer ever since she'd known him, but he'd been thrust into the water unexpectedly. He was probably as shocked as she was.

She could see Winny close by, churning toward the embankment. She reached it and pulled herself to safety, collapsing momentarily in the willows.

"Winny! You all right?"

Winny nodded, water streaming from her dress. "I'm sorry to lose my temper, Abby, but I told you. I told him." She pointed at the wagon, which had flipped to its side. The horses were thrashing, kicking, jerking at their harnesses. Were they to break free, they'd run all the way to Mexico.

Abby couldn't see Isaac as she pushed her way to shore with Yahnai, one cautious step at a time. The roar of the creek was almost deafening. Just as she was about to panic and call out his name, she saw him holding on to the wagon, looking down at the water. His hat was missing. Abby gasped; her lifelong fear of injuries—wounds and blood—came into play. Blood streamed from Isaac's forehead and into his eyes. Even from this distance, Abby almost fainted.

"Isaac?" she yelled. His response was weak. He looked in her direction. His mouth moved, but she couldn't hear his voice.

"Yahnai, stay right here with Winny," she said, handing him off.

She ran upstream and hurled herself into the creek again, a few feet above the wagon to allow for downstream drift, and with one anxious step at a time, she made her way toward Isaac. In water above her waist, he reached for her. She looked away from his bloody head and took his hand. It was cold and shriveled but strong—the hand of a farmer, a settler, a man who had built his life through years of hard labor. That strong, cold hand trembled. As Abby looked at him, she saw not just hurt in his eyes but fear too. And embarrassment.

"Can you make it to shore?" she asked.

He spoke in short, painful gasps. "I'll try. . . . You'll . . . have to . . . help." His thinning hair clung to his scalp, and his eyes drooped more than usual. He looked worse than she'd ever seen him. He looked even older.

"What happened to you?"

"I fell . . . under . . . the horses. . . . They . . . trampled me."

She wrapped her arm around him and tried to lend him strength, to heal him with her thoughts if it were possible. "I'll help you. Don't worry."

"My head . . . my ribs . . . my legs . . . maybe . . . one of them . . . is broken."

She couldn't see how badly his body was beaten, but as he leaned into her, he trembled and coughed then groaned and nearly collapsed. She said, "We've got to get out of this water. We'll freeze to death." He nodded weakly, and she added, "Hang on to my hand."

He wiped blood from his eyes and nodded again.

She tugged on his hand and took the first step. The force of the stream worked against them. In her judgment, the horses had missed the safest part of the crossing. They'd gone too far left, where the water flowed over large rocks. The overturned wagon was blocking the whole crossing, but it also revealed the safe path they should have taken.

She was suddenly aware of Winny, who reached for her with an outstretched hand. With Winny's help, one step at a time—with Isaac grimacing in pain—they reached shore. Yahnai reached out to help.

Isaac collapsed in the willows, shivering. "My . . . leg . . . it's killing me. . . . I can't stand."

Abby shivered too. She looked at poor Isaac, shielding her eyes from the afternoon sun. Blood still gushed from his forehead. It made her weak in the knees. She was afraid to pull up his bloody trousers and look at his leg. There was a possibility that a bone might be protruding out of Isaac's skin. She turned away, feeling her vision begin to blur.

"What do we do now?" Winny asked as she knelt by Isaac's side and began dabbing at his bleeding head with her soaked skirt hem. "Stubborn old man."

"Enough of that," Abby said. "You're no less stubborn than he is, you know."

Abby assessed Yahnai's fear, Winny's anger, and her own confusion and worry. She stood for a moment, arching her back, rolling her shoulders, wrapping her arms around herself, searching for any surge of warmth, trying to stay calm. She took deep breaths. The wind flattened her wet dress against her body. She took her wet bonnet off and let the water in her hair stream down her neck. The horses had calmed down, their thrashing and tugging useless. The wagon was still on its side, water coursing around it. Some bedding had disappeared altogether. Some had been caught by brush and rocks. Their luggage was gone too.

"I'm cold," Yahnai said.

"Me too," she answered. Abby hugged herself. Yahnai and Winny knelt next to Isaac, shivering as they tended to him. Winny had ripped a section from her slip and pressed it against Isaac's head. Abby weighed her options. Building a fire was out—she had no matches. The twigs, branches, and logs lining the creek were soaked anyway. Somehow, somewhere, they needed shelter. They could die from exposure if they had to spend the night here, and Isaac could die from loss of blood or shock. There were few options. She could cross the creek and run south to the nearest settlement for help. She could run north, back to Franklin, which was farther away. Or she could wait. Perhaps there would be another traveler on the road, despite the weather.

She bowed her head and said a prayer in her heart. *Please, Lord, help us.*

Settling on the idea of heading back to Franklin alone, she squeezed as much water from her bonnet as she could and then did the same with her skirt.

Yahnai pointed south, across the creek. "Someone's coming."

Abby closed her eyes and listened. Above the roar of the creek, she detected only the honking of geese overhead, going south for the winter. Nothing else.

"Wagons," he said, insisting.

If Yahnai were right, Abby hoped it would be settlers. It could be anyone really—miners on their way to the gold discovery up north or trappers or traders or Indians.

From the creek, Isaac's brown horses whinnied their distress. Suddenly Abby perceived a faint rumble. Yahnai was right. Within a few seconds, on the hill overlooking the creek, mules and heavy wagons came into view.

"See?" Yahnai said.

"Freighters," Winny said. "What would they be doing here this time of year?"

Abby placed one hand over her heart as she watched the wagons descend. With the other, she gripped Yahnai's hand. Thanks to her prayer, help was on its way. But why did it have to be freighters? Freighters—teamsters, mule skinners, bullwhackers, or whatever you called them—had a lock on the lowest rung of the frontier social ladder, a full notch below buffalo skinners. Almost as bad as soldiers. Freighters had no compunction about cursing their animals with a vile stream of profanity. They could do it for ten minutes straight without repeating themselves. In fact, they were doing it now, loudly enough to be heard over the noise of the rushing water. She wished she could stuff cotton into Yahnai's ears.

There were five tandem wagons with big wheels and spokes, groaning under heavy loads. Each was big, bold, and brawny, three or four times the size of Isaac's wagon, each pulled by eighteen mud-caked mules. There was a smaller mess wagon following along like a mouse follows an elephant. All descended toward the creek crossing, mule skinners cracking their whips, which echoed like infantry picket fire.

The wagons stopped. Winny waved at them, her face bright with gratitude.

Abby held her breath, hoping they would offer help. Several rough-looking men stared at the shivering group from across the creek, surveying the strange scene before them. Most of the men held their whips as if they were a badge of honor. Some had rifles resting in the crooks of their arms. She watched as three men mounted ponies.

The first mule skinner to cross the creek rode his coal-black horse right at her. He dismounted and ambled closer, casting a monstrous moving shadow. He planted his feet wide and made himself as tall as he could, which was about three inches taller than she was, minus his filthy circus-barker hat. He had red hair, and his clothing was stained with mud, food, and tobacco juice; he smelled like an overworked horse.

Behind the redhead, the other two riders crossed the creek. Yahnai inched behind her wet skirts, and Abby hoped he was out of their sight. She never knew how people would react to seeing an Indian boy with a white woman. She smiled at the redhead as pleasantly as she could. His look was intimidating, one of impatience, recklessness, carelessness, and somehow full of entitlement. She asked, "Would you please help us?"

The redhead drew his revolver, a big one. His finger was on the trigger. He nodded at Isaac's two brown horses as if they were contagious.

Abby reminded herself to breathe.

"You plow chasers are blockin' the crossing," he said. His voice scratched from his throat like a trapped cat.

The statement angered her. "Can't you see what happened? We're freezing to death. My man has a broken leg. He's over there in the willows."

"I guess I could just shoot yer horses to start with," the redhead said.

Abby turned toward Winny, hoping for some sort of support. If this man shot Isaac's horses, Abby didn't know what she'd do. But Winny was still caring for Isaac, too far away to hear the conversation.

She turned back to give the disrespectful redhead a good scolding, but he was flat on his back. Another mule skinner stood over him, steely blue eyes glaring down at the rude man. It had happened so fast Abby could barely comprehend it.

"That's no way to talk to a lady," the golden-haired man growled. "I swanny, you do that again, and I'll knock you so hard you'll see tomorrow today. Where'd you leave your manners?"

The redhead quivered like a trapped rabbit. "I didn't mean no harm, boss."

The golden-haired man didn't drop his anger. "I see quilts and luggage strung downstream. You fetch everything. Get in the water if you have to. Then you'll know how these folks feel. Take all their stuff to the freight wagons for now. I don't want you within a hundred yards of these women. Got it? You mess up again and I'll send you down the road."

"Got it, boss," the redhead said. Quick as a cat, he jumped up, stroked his greasy red beard, mounted his black horse, and crossed the creek.

Abby reached back to Yahnai, who still clung to the back of her skirts. Even though this "boss" seemed kind and polite, she didn't want him to see Yahnai. She didn't trust him enough for that.

The golden-haired man motioned to the other rider who had crossed the creek. This mule skinner had dark brown hair, a full beard, a barrel chest, and a thick neck.

The boss told the barrel-chested man, "Tell the boys to unhook those horses and lead 'em out of the creek. Pull that wagon out and fix it. And keep Cad away."

The barrel-chested man tipped his hat at him and then at her. "Yes, boss."

The golden-haired man came nearer. In three long, fluid strides, he stood in front of her. He moved like the cougar she'd seen prowling the canyons above Cache Valley, confident and in control. He was taller than the redhead but not quite as husky as the barrel-chested man. He was young, perhaps not much older than Abby. With his square jaw, tanned skin, and golden hair—as gold as the frost-tinted leaves on nearby aspen trees—he was strikingly handsome.

"Ma'am, I'm sorry about Cad. He's got the manners of a pig. A bully sometimes. A waste of good food. But he's a hard worker when he puts his mind to it."

She hadn't expected such politeness. There was concern in his face. She didn't know what to say for a few seconds. She liked his voice. It was low and folksy and as comforting as hot stew on a cold day.

"Things like that annoy me," he added, his shoulders straight and thrown back.

"As you can see," she began, pointing at the creek, "we've had an accident. Isaac is hurt. When we hit, he fell forward, right under the horses. He's bleeding. He might have a broken leg. Please help us."

"Yes, ma'am, certainly. Be happy to."

Abby gestured toward the willows but let the man walk ahead of her. She took Yahnai's hand firmly in her own and followed. The man was going to help them, so she had to assume he would accept the sight of her son. Now her task was to leave no question as to where and with whom Yahnai belonged.

The man squatted next to Isaac. He didn't touch him, just clasped his own hands together and asked, "Gonna live, old-timer?"

The pain had rendered Isaac white as store-bought china. Between moans, he tried to catch his breath. "Yes . . . thank you for stopping. . . . My leg . . . my leg . . . is it broken?"

Abby turned her head and moved between Isaac and Yahnai as the mule skinner sliced Isaac's pant leg open with a knife. She didn't look but still felt queasy.

The man said, "It sure is. Just lie still until we get your wagon fixed up. I'll get a fire built and warm you up. And some wool blankets."

Isaac nodded while he took deep breaths.

The golden-haired man stood and yelled again at his sidekick. "Fetch a dozen or so wool blankets. And some matches and dry tinder. And be quick about it. There's an injured man here. Everyone is soaked and freezing."

The man responded immediately, militarily, with a snappy salute. "Yes, sir."

Abby admired how the men responded to him with prompt respect and obedience. She looked at the man and wondered. He seemed too young to be able to command so well.

"Those wet clothes have y'all chilled to the bone," he said, hovering over her like an angel. "We'll warm you up as soon as we can."

"Thank you," Abby said. The man had charm to burn. His warm voice, gentle but lively eyes, and the comfortable grace of his movements immediately put her at ease. He made her feel like a fine lady to be taken care of. She felt a tad warmer already.

"I go by the name of Scooter. Where y'all from?"

Abby nudged Yahnai behind her again, grateful that the man hadn't taken note of the boy yet. "Franklin settlement. Just a little north."

Scooter pulled a face. "Don't y'all know three bands of Shoshoni are camped just west of here? They can be bold and saucy at times. For all we know, they might jump out of the brush at us now, thicker than grass burrs."

Abby faked a quiet assurance. "I know where they're camped, but they won't bother us." She wondered where the man was from. He had a distinct Southern accent.

The man looked to Abby's side, and she knew he'd seen Yahnai.

"They don't bother you? Something to do with this boy you're hiding?"

She looked back at Yahnai, scolding him with her wide eyes. "Yes," she answered simply, not wishing or feeling any need to explain. "What about you? Why are freight wagons taking this route with all the Indian trouble lately?"

The golden-haired man didn't seem very worried—just calm, confident, and competent. "All my boys are well armed. We can take care of ourselves."

Abby scanned the mule skinners, shocked by all the weapons they carried. Some were unhitching Isaac's horses; others scrutinizing the wagon. What might happen if one of them saw Yahnai? She picked him up and held him in her arms.

The barrel-chested teamster arrived with dry tinder and matches. Next to Isaac, he lit a fire, small at first but building. The teamster kept feeding it with more dry tinder. Orange flames began licking at the sky. More tinder, more flames.

Winny snuggled closer to the fire, knelt, and said, "I hope the wagon's fixable."

"Don't worry. My men know how to fix wagons." Turning his eyes again on Abby and pointing to Isaac, he asked, "Is this man your father?"

Winny chuckled and quickly covered her mouth.

Abby glared at Winny and inched toward the flames. "No. We were on our way to Salt Lake City to be married."

He returned a puzzled stare. With a soft edge of scorn, he said, "Then I'd say fate has smiled on you. I'd hate to see a young beauty like you marry an old man."

Abby frowned at his audacity. As was proper, she moved away. But his words stirred up something uncomfortable in her. She couldn't claim it was just the impropriety of the words. He'd only reiterated what Winny had been saying for months, but it was the first clearly stated support for Winny's argument. As he spoke, she recognized a niggling sense of relief now that their trip to Salt Lake City had been delayed.

She pushed the feeling aside and rubbed her hands up and down Yahnai's arms. His sheepskin coat and wool shirt were merely damp now, and he'd stopped shivering. Every choice she made was really for Yahnai and her future children.

As the flames built, Abby looked at her son and saw that he was paying little attention to her. He was looking at Scooter and smiling shyly.

Scooter approached and crouched until he looked Yahnai in the eye. "Hello, young feller. My name's Scooter. What's yours?"

The boy looked down at first and then at the fire.

"Tell him," Abby said, but Yahnai shook his head. She stroked his soft hair, loving his shyness and worrying about it all at once. "It's all right. He's helping us."

The boy spoke, but his voice was still aimed at his feet. "Yahnai."

"Nice to meet you," Scooter said. "Want to shake hands?"

Abby gave him a gentle push. "Shake hands with him. He's here to help us."

Scooter extended his hand. Yahnai shuffled his feet, twitched from head to toe, and then slowly, very slowly, raised his hand.

Scooter took his hand and gave him a friendly handshake. "Nice to meet you."

Abby noted how loosely Yahnai's hand gripped Scooter's and how loosely his arm followed his hand.

"Y'all can do better than that, I bet," Scooter said. "Squeeze my hand. Tight. You've got a big hand. Try it."

Abby watched a smile spread across Scooter's face as Yahnai apparently tightened his grip. The smile thrilled her and made her want to giggle like a young girl. She covered her mouth and focused her gaze on Yahnai instead of the handsome man.

"How old are you?" Scooter asked.

Yahnai shrugged again, so Abby said, "Tell him." Yahnai didn't have many opportunities to meet new people, and she relished the attention this kind man was offering. It was good for the boy—to practice his English, manners, and all of the things she'd tried to teach him over the past two years since he'd come to her home.

"Six," the boy said.

"You go to school?"

The boy nodded.

"Learning to read? Learning to count?"

The boy nodded again.

"My men are unhitching the horses from the wagon. How many horses?"

"Two," the boy said without looking up.

"See those mules hitched to my big wagons across the creek?"

Yahnai looked at Abby. She smiled and heard Scooter ask, "How many mules are hitched to one wagon?"

The boy raised a hand, pointed his brown index finger, and began to count. He squinted and concentrated as he counted. "Eighteen."

"You're a smart boy," Scooter said. "Here's another question. My men have unhitched the brown horses. They're bringing the horses to the back of the wagon. What will the men do with the horses now? And that big chain?"

Yahnai paused but answered, "Get the wagon out of the creek."

"See, there, you knew," Scooter said. "You are a smart boy. Do you think the axel is broken?"

Abby looked toward the creek where the men were working as Yahnai shrugged. The wagon creaked and slapped the water as it fell upright once more. One of Scooter's men waved his hat high in the air.

"Not broken," Scooter said after the signal. "That's good news."

Abby stepped forward and put her arm around Yahnai, her heart flush with gratitude. This man had saved them from a disaster, and if that weren't enough, he had shown her quiet, sometimes awkward son great kindness. He didn't have to be kind to Yahnai. She knew plenty of people who should have shown the boy kindness but didn't. This man could have ignored or dismissed her son without any thought. Abby let herself look at Scooter, his blond hair catching the afternoon sunlight and rushing around his face in the breeze. Because of him, they were safe, dry, and warm.

Scooter smiled at Yahnai. "What's the name of the man with the broken leg?"

"Uncle Isaac."

"We need to get him home, don't we? Where's home?"

The boy pointed north. "Franklin. Up that way."

"Well, then," Scooter said, standing to his full height again. "Let's go home."

He looked at Abby, and she felt herself blush.

Chapter 2

ISAAC HAD HEARD THE FREIGHTER talking to the boy, but he hadn't followed the conversation very well. Just wisps of it now and then, muffed out by the roaring creek and the commotion of the mule skinners. He awoke when two men lifted him into the wagon bed, pain searing through his body.

Abby's soft hands spread blankets over him. Her gentle touch soothed his pain. He wanted more than anything for her to hold his aching head in her lap and nurse his wounds. But Isaac knew his place. He was there to marry and provide for Abby—and give her more children. His desire was to give Abby whatever she wanted.

Abby jumped down from the wagon bed. If Isaac had felt strong enough, he would have called for her and asked her to stay with him. He had to believe she would stay if he asked. Clearly, Yahnai was the center of her world. Abby was a mother now and needed stability. It didn't matter what her nature might have been before she became a mother—wild and impetuous enough to marry outside of the Church and move so close to Indian territory only to be left a widow and then saddled with an Indian boy.

He shivered despite the blankets. Winny climbed in the wagon and sat near Isaac's head. He groaned. His pride had already taken a beating, and he had no desire to be there with Winny Davis. Though she would be Christian about the whole thing—no gloating or mockery—she also likely saw the incident as support for her position against his marriage to Abby. Winny would share her thoughts with Abby, he was sure. Isaac didn't understand Winny's protests to the marriage. He couldn't understand why a woman of God wouldn't see that age has no hold on eternal marriage. He would take care of Abby and give her the children she longed for. What more could a woman want?

"She can't stand the blood, you know," Winny whispered. "Don't feel too badly that she's not caring for you."

Isaac's eyes fluttered as he looked at Winny; his head ached. Winny was kind, in the end, which made her feelings toward his marriage even more confusing. He could see the edge of her torn hem just above his sight line, blurred and blue. As he thought of his wounds again, he remembered his leg. He knew it was bad—worse than the mule skinner had let on. Concern spilled into his mind. How could he provide for Abby if his injury was any sort of permanent?

Guilt and shame hammered inside his head. He almost wished Winny would yell at him the way she had done as they approached the creek. Instead, her Christian silence pierced his soul. Winny had been right. The day had been ruined by his mistake. Now he was on his way back to the settlement, flat on his back. No marriage to Abby. Instead, there was a kind of helpless, crushed torpor in the air, and he had created it. His judgment had been off. He should have examined the creek crossing more closely.

Now, to make matters worse, Abby was sitting on the wagon seat next to a teamster—a young one, with golden hair thick as a horse's mane.

Isaac Jacobs watched the handsome Gentile smile at Abby, and he prayed she wouldn't forget all that he had to offer—a covenant marriage. She wouldn't fall for a Gentile again, would she? After all she had been through? Doubt stole into his thoughts as Winny wrapped a piece of fabric tightly around his leg. This time, the fire of pain burned hotter than before and brought near unconsciousness with it.

Chapter 3

ABBY COULDN'T STOP SHIVERING. BEING wrapped in a cocoon of wool blankets helped. So did being seated between Scooter and Yahnai. Winny sat in the wagon bed and cared for Isaac. Isaac yelped, and Abby looked back.

"Just working on his leg," Winny said. "It's not good. He's lost a lot of blood."

Abby looked away. "Thank you for caring for him, Winny. I just can't bear it."

"Of course," Winny said. "But out here you need to learn how to handle blood."

Abby shuddered. "Maybe. But not today. My stomach can't take it."

Scooter, lithe and relaxed and confident, was in firm control of Isaac's brown horses. The horses were behaving—relaxed, anxious to please. Their ears were neutral, paying attention to every sound coming out of Scooter's mouth and every command he issued from the leather lines in his hands.

With every bump in the road, Abby's shoulders touched Scooter's. His warmth was inviting. She couldn't ever remember touching any man that way—other than her late husband, Evan Browett, and perhaps Isaac—so it was an odd feeling. Their shoulders did touch, but their eyes met only occasionally. When they did, he returned a look that was mutually respectful, confiding, sympathetic, and understanding. She was impressed with the way the golden-haired man had talked to Yahnai. He was different—very polite, a pronounced Southern accent, a gentleman.

She worried about Isaac. He had moaned and groaned with every bump and every rut. But now the moaning had quit. The silence alarmed her. She twisted in her seat. "Isaac, are you warm enough? We'll be back at the settlement soon."

Isaac didn't answer.

"I think he's asleep," Winny said.

Isaac was flat on his back, breathing low. His face had turned a shade of gray. His head had quit bleeding. The cold weather had helped that at least. Abby felt sorry for him. Not only did he have a broken leg, but his plans had been disrupted, and she knew how he liked to stick to plans. No trip to Salt Lake City. A disaster for him, but she felt more relaxed than she had in days. She began to wonder if perhaps Winny was right. Seeing him so old and vulnerable in the water made her think about all of the things Winny had been saying for months. Having already endured one husband's death, was she ready to volunteer to endure another? Perhaps she did need more time to think.

Abby asked, "Is it normal for someone to sleep when they're in so much pain?"

Scooter smiled. "It's a nice way of saying he's unconscious."

The statement alarmed her further. "What can we do? Should we drive faster?"

Scooter replied, "He's better off this way. Don't worry. I've seen this kind of thing before. We'll revive him when we get to your settlement."

Abby nodded, relieved. She wondered about Scooter's background. What did he mean, *I've seen this kind of thing before*? She supposed that as a teamster he'd probably had more than one opportunity to care for a man trampled by a horse or a mule or a bull.

She looked back at Isaac and then at Winny. Scooter may have been accustomed to seeing a man trampled, but Abby certainly wasn't. She wondered what Winny thought of all of this and knew exactly what Winny would say if she could. *Everything happens for a reason.*

Winny would probably say this was proof that Abby and Isaac were not a good match. She'd been saying it for months. Abby could almost hear her voice again. *He's more than twenty years older than you. You won't be happy with him.*

"Isaac is a good man," Abby said. "I want him to be well."

"He will be," Scooter said. "How far do we have to go to reach your settlement?"

"Not far," she said. "We'd only been on the road for about an hour."

"We'll have y'all there in no time, then. These horses are still a little skittish, but they know they're headed home."

His accent intrigued her. He had to be from one of the Southern states, where the Civil War was raging. He didn't know much about Cache Valley, but he knew there were Indians around. How he became the boss of these freighters she didn't know.

"Surely your wagons aren't hauling freight to Franklin," Winny said, wrapped in her own cocoon of blankets. "We've always hauled our own supplies from Salt Lake."

"We're headed to Bannack City up yonder, where gold was discovered."

Abby hummed her disapproval. Precious metal discoveries were regarded as bad news in Utah Territory. All it meant was more Gentiles and worldly contamination. At least Bannack City was way up north, in Idaho Territory.

Winny said, "Oh yes. We've heard about it. We've seen miners passing through."

Scooter swelled up like a bullfrog. "What I have in my wagons will be worth a lot of money."

"I thought the freight route went through the Malad Valley," Winny said.

"I think the Cache Valley route is shorter and faster. I reckon I'm the first to use it."

"Well," Abby said, "we're fortunate you came along when you did. You got us out of a bad situation, and I thank you for that."

He turned and gazed at Abby again. "What you wear is a mite ordinary. I have a shipping crate with women's dresses. You sure would look good in yellow."

Abby blushed, feeling it improper that he was looking at her clothing. She was dressed in a threadbare green shift that women in Salt Lake City would have thrown away long ago. Her bonnet didn't even match. But the dress was sturdy and sewn from wool cloth. It was drying out just fine. A more expensive dress might have been ruined. "Save it for Bannack City," she said. "People here don't need such luxuries."

Scooter chuckled and then nodded at Yahnai. "How'd you end up with this boy?"

The question surprised Abby. In Franklin, everyone knew how she had become Yahnai's mother two years ago. When strangers passed through, they looked at Abby with the question in their eyes, but they probably assumed Yahnai was a half-breed, created through unspeakable acts that no one ever asked about. She knew the other residents of Franklin explained the situation in hushed voices, probably after Abby left the room. She wondered if Scooter had sunken to the deplorable assumption and had the audacity to ask the question that might afford an uncomfortable answer.

She wondered what he thought of her as she turned and glanced at Yahnai, who had nearly fallen asleep. He leaned against her, his head bobbing up and down with the jostling of the wagon. It didn't matter what anyone thought. Yahnai was her son now, no matter what circumstances surrounded his birth. He was the one thing in her life she was certain of. "He was brought to me by one of the Shoshoni chiefs."

"How'd that happen? Why would a Shoshoni chief give *you* a child?"

Abby sighed at his incredulous question, her memory troubled, her heart protective of the little boy she loved. She looked off to the east, to a line of hills and mountains and to a canyon that held the worst of her memories.

"I'm just curious, ma'am. I know everyone has their past and their secrets. If it's a subject best left alone, I can respect that."

She glanced at him, wondering again what his life had been like before that moment. What had brought him there with this mixture of curiosity and respect, and what secrets were in his own past? Somehow, his statement eased the tension in her neck. Then it loosened her tongue. "I came to this valley more than two years ago. My husband and I were among the first settlers of Franklin. His name was Evan Browett. Shortly after we built our little log house, he was all alone up a canyon cutting corral poles when two renegade warriors killed him." Pain ripped at Abby's heart all over again, just mentioning the incident. She had hoped her pioneer spirit and her religious beliefs would result in a happy and somewhat prosperous life. But decisions had consequences. Poor judgment led to tragedy. She was glad today had not ended in tragedy as well.

Scooter was quiet for a moment. When he spoke, his voice was hushed and reverent. "I swanny, Indians did that? I'm so very sorry."

Abby hung her head as she accepted his apology. She still thought about Evan every day and dreamed about him nearly every night. No one could replace him. Not even Isaac Jacobs. Isaac dove in and helped her in every way possible since Evan's death, and he seemed to accept Yahnai without a question. Ever since she'd agreed to marry Isaac, she'd felt as though she were betraying Evan's memory. But what was she to do?

Scooter asked, "Not to pry, but how did you end up with the boy?"

"One of the Shoshoni chiefs felt so bad about me losing my husband that he came to see me with a little four-year-old boy on the back of his pony. An orphan. He gave him to me." With one hand she smoothed Yahnai's black hair and cuddled him. "He's mine forever—except for a few weeks every winter."

"Every winter? Why is that?"

"So he can learn his Indian heritage and genealogy. He's expected to memorize things. Chief Sagwitch comes by in January and takes him to their camp."

Abby had visited the camp each of the past two winters. There, she learned about the Shoshoni way of life, and it touched her soul like a rich strain of music. These people had a beauty in their culture that white men couldn't understand. That beauty was imbedded in her now, a permanent fixture. She'd even attempted to learn the Shoshoni language. Her last visit had been cut short by the intervention of another chief, Bear Hunter, who disliked white people.

"Let me get this straight. You are a widow, raising an Indian boy, all alone?"

"Oh, I'm not alone. Winny has been a tremendous friend." Abby turned back to look at her and smiled warmly.

Winny responded, "And Isaac provides occasional food for Abby. Fixes things around the house. Expects her to marry him."

Abby sighed. Everything was still bubbling in Winny, just waiting for a chance to get out.

"I wondered about the old man," Scooter said, tilting his head back toward the wagon bed. "Why do y'all have to go all the way to Salt Lake City to get married? Is that the only place they allow old Mormon men to marry young Mormon women?"

Abby frowned, thinking he must be a joker of some sorts. "Obviously you're not a Mormon, and you're not from these parts."

"I was in Salt Lake only long enough to realize there's a fortune to be made hauling freight to Bannack City. And I'd consider being a Mormon if I were fifty years old and Brigham gave me permission to marry an eighteen-year-old beauty like you."

"I'm older than you think," she scoffed. "I'm twenty. Besides, there are no men my age in our settlement that I would consider marrying. Yahnai needs a father, and I need a husband. We were headed for the Endowment House, where our people are married for not only time but for all eternity."

"You want to be stuck with an old man for eternity? That's a long time."

She didn't like the way the conversation had turned and felt that this teamster beside her had been cut from the worst cloth in Winny's proverbial quilt—they matched each other perfectly. Abby inched away from Scooter so their shoulders would stop bumping. "*Stuck* is the wrong word."

He laughed. "Yeah, well, maybe trapped is better."

Abby squeezed Yahnai a little tighter, and he shifted closer to her. All of the warmth she had been feeling seemed to fade, and she pulled the wool blankets tighter around her. She hoped Isaac would heal quickly. He might be significantly older, but she realized in a flash that he was also significantly wiser than the companions closer to her age. Some sacrifices were worth making.

Chapter 4

FOR ALL THE IMAGINING HE'D ever done in his life, Scooter never imagined meeting such a stunning young woman on the road to Bannack City. He couldn't help but stare at the blonde Mormon girl so he could store away the memory. Her traveling companion more closely fit his perception of Mormon women—ruby-faced and plump. But the woman sitting next to him was a gem of gems: tall but not too tall, slender but not too slender, skin as smooth and sweet as cow's cream. Her natural, wholesome beauty didn't need the paint of a saloon girl. She reminded him of a curious cat with her slender white neck, sleek yellow hair, and the kind of hypnotic green eyes that started wars. Half the time she seemed unaware of how good she looked, and half the time she seemed a little bashful about it. She moved with a kind of agile economy, strong and athletic. Wet clothing and all, she had swept the Indian boy off his feet, thrown him effortlessly into the wagon, and then hopped in herself as if the wagon were flat on the ground.

Why a young beauty like her would consider marrying a man twice her age was beyond his imagination. Where he was from, old horses waited at the glue factory gate. Why she would adopt an Indian boy was also beyond his imagination.

He aimed to tease out details about her. "You haven't told me your name."

"I'm sorry. It's Abigail." Her head was tilted up and away from him. Her throat curved and sloped gently to her shoulders with grace and beauty, but if she'd been warming up to him before, she'd returned to acting chilly.

"I suppose friends call you Abby," he said, hoping she'd count him as such. It seemed the bond they'd just forged at the crossing warranted a first-name basis.

"Abigail, to you. Abigail Butterfield Browett."

The Butterfield name sounded familiar. The Butterfield Overland Mail Company was now known simply as the Overland Mail Company. It operated out of Salt Lake City and in every other major thoroughfare in the West. His eyebrows shot up in pleasure at the thought that the two of them might have something in common. "Butterfield? That was a big name in the overland stage and mail delivery business."

"That was my father's cousin. John W. Butterfield."

He wondered how she provided for herself, being single. "You inherit any of John W. Butterfield's money?"

"Of course not. He was a distant cousin—very distant. Wouldn't even know me."

He couldn't shake his curiosity. If family money wasn't the answer, then perhaps old man Jacobs was. "The old gentleman back there will take some time to heal. Will you be taken care of until then?"

"Mormons take care of each other," she said. "Isaac and I will reschedule the trip as soon as he heals. You have a real name?"

He smiled, pleased that she'd finally asked. "David Perkins."

"From where?"

"St. Louis."

She studied him for a moment, which made him uneasy. He hoped she couldn't see through his fib. He hadn't gone by his real name—Jesse Kemp—since he left Virginia, not St. Louis. But his mother had nicknamed him Scooter as a baby for the way he scooted around the floor. That part of his answer was true.

"Never been to St. Louis," she said. "I've heard it's a bad place."

"In what way?" he asked.

"An utter disregard for God's commandments," she said sharply.

He closed his eyes. Every Mormon he'd met seemed to have a low tolerance for the kind of behavior he'd seen in St. Louis. "You may be right about that," he said. He could tolerate such behavior better than the average Mormon, but when drink and women made a man rude and sloppy, Scooter figured it was time for that man to leave the saloon.

Except for the rattling of the wagon and the clopping of the horses' hooves on the soft road, they rode in silence for a while. He tipped his hat back and looked ahead. Tiny brown pinpricks blended into a cluster of small buildings. As they drew closer, he could also see flat fields recently stripped of their harvests.

"I see your settlement," Scooter said. He looked back at Isaac, whose skin was even paler than before. "Unless you've got a good doctor, your man may never walk behind a plow again. Then who'll take care of you?"

She folded arms across her chest and gave him a defiant look. "Bones mend. Bodies heal. And I have faith. Isaac will be fine." But there was worry in her eyes. "When we get there, pull right into the town square, next to the corrals." She stirred her boy awake. "Look, Yahnai. We're almost home."

Franklin was not the first Mormon settlement Scooter had passed through in the sparsely populated Cache Valley. It looked similar to the hardscrabble settlements of Wellsville, Providence, Mendon, Logan, Richmond, and Smithfield. All had looked as though they'd been built in some kind of a burst of Mormon pioneer enthusiasm by people who somehow believed in a promising future. If the future meant prosperity of any kind, prosperity looked to be twenty or thirty years away.

There was nothing much to see. To protect themselves from Indians, the settlers here had built their dour-looking small log sanctuaries in a large rectangle facing a town square. There were more than twenty homes on each side, not too close to each other but not far away either. Each home looked to be pretty much identical—same vintage, same construction, same type of logs hewn from trees out of canyons similar to the one where the Mormon girl had lost her husband. The largest structure was a log meeting house located right in the center of the square near the corrals. Probably used as a school and a church. There were herds of cattle and horses and sheep and pigs and chickens. He could smell wood smoke curling from nearly every cabin.

The return of the sodbuster's wagon caused a big hullabaloo. Settlers swarmed around him, more women than men, curious as to why he was driving the team. They wanted to know why their friends were wrapped in blankets. Why the old man was flat on his back in the rear of the wagon. They shuffled in place and clucked and pursed and fussed, quickly and clearly understanding the gravity of the situation.

Winny jumped from the wagon as soon as it had stopped, and she brought back with her a man whose neck was thicker than his head.

"The gash in his forehead is bad," Winny said to the man. "It's laid back some of the skin. The leg will need to be set."

The man jumped into the rear of the wagon, looked at the sodbuster's cuts and bruises, and grimaced. "Yahnai, fetch Brother Stanley. Be quick about it."

When the Indian boy hit the ground, a brown-and-white dog jumped up and down and licked the boy's hand. Abby's dog, probably.

"Come on, Riddle," Yahnai said. The boy darted through the converging crowd and then ran like a deer.

Scooter climbed out of the wagon and stood for a moment, rolling his shoulders, stretching his back, trying to work out the stiffness. He wondered if the Mormons would mind if he camped nearby. The creek crossing incident had cost him time, and now night was not far off. He hoped to make it to Bannack City and back to Salt Lake before winter clogged the passes with too much snow.

The way people bustled around to help the old man gave Scooter the impression that Isaac Jacobs was an important man in this Mormon community. Abby had climbed from the wagon, and she hovered near the action, her eyes locked on Isaac.

"He doesn't look good, does he?" Abby asked as Scooter approached her.

He didn't, but Scooter wasn't about to tell Abby that. "Is this fellow you call Brother Stanley the doctor here?" he asked instead.

"Casket maker," she said. "But he's good at setting bones."

The answer struck Scooter as funny. He wondered briefly if old man Jacobs would die. At least the casket maker would be handy for a proper measurement. He would have said the joke aloud, but Abby stared at Isaac with concern so deep it lined her face. He bit his tongue for her sake.

The man with the thick neck regarded Scooter with probing eyes. "So this is the man who rescued you?"

"I apologize," Abby said. "This is Mr. David Perkins. His freight wagons will be along shortly. Mr. Perkins, this is Carl Davis. Winny's husband."

The man extended a thick, meaty hand at him. It had been his experience that Mormons squeezed the hand more vigorously than other men during a handshake. Carl Davis's handshake was just that, firm and vigorous.

"Pleased to know you, Mr. Perkins," Carl said.

"Likewise. I go by Scooter, if you don't mind."

Just then Yahnai returned with John Stanley, who quickly examined Isaac's leg. The casket maker grimaced and told the men of the settlement to take the injured man to his cabin. Isaac groaned the whole way, as if being carried in a sling made of several woolen blankets was even more jostling than the wagon ride had been.

"He's awake," Scooter said as they formed a small procession of curious people moving toward the cabin. "It's a good sign."

"Yes." Abby's face relaxed. "Thanks again. I don't know how to repay you."

"You're welcome," he said. "I'm glad we could help. Anything else I can do?"

"Not unless you're good at making crutches."

The girl's humor made him laugh. "Will the folks around here mind if we set up camp just outside the settlement?"

"Not as long as you stay far enough away from the town square so the children can't hear your men when they curse."

There was that low tolerance again. He wondered how many children there were in the settlement. Herds of them, if these Mormons were like the others he'd met. He'd already seen several gawking at the wagon as he'd pulled into the square. He supposed that people who valued children so much had a right to shield them from the world whenever possible. "Agreed," he said. "We'll stay near the river bottom."

"Abby's good at doughnuts," Winny said. "We'll make a large batch and bring you a treat later tonight. We need to thank you for your kindness."

"Umm," he said. "I know the men would appreciate it. I'd be beholden to y'all."

Yahnai seemed to know all about doughnuts. A happy smile came over his face.

"You like doughnuts?" Scooter asked the boy.

The boy nodded.

"Better than candy?"

The boy shrugged.

"When you come to my camp tonight, I'll give you some candy. I have a lot of things in my wagons to sell to the miners up north. Candy included."

"Say thank you," Abby said.

"Thank you," the boy replied.

Somehow the sodbuster raised an arm. He spoke in short bursts, still in pain but not enough to keep him from expressing an opinion. "Doughnuts?" Isaac Jacobs said weakly. "Just remember . . . the settlement . . . only has a limited supply . . . of wheat. . . . The Indians . . . expect us . . . to practically feed them too. . . . We have to make . . . our supply last . . . until next summer."

"I'm sure we can spare a little," Winny protested. "We owe Scooter and his men that much for helping us."

The casket maker moved near Isaac's feet and began directing some of the other men to stand at his head. "Take a deep breath, Brother Jacobs," he said. "We're going to pull on your leg and shoulders to straighten out that bone. Brother Davis, hold on to his shoulders. Have the teamster help you."

The casket maker handed Isaac a small stick. "Bite down on this."

Scooter moved into position with Winny's husband. He placed his hands on the sodbuster's shoulders. So did Carl Davis. Fear gripped Jacobs's eyes.

Abby crossed her arms and squeezed herself.

Scooter looked down at the old man's face, which was now red and beaded with sweat. "If this doesn't work," he told Isaac, "we can always stretch you using your team of horses. I reckon that would hurt worse."

Abby stomped her foot, and Scooter looked at her. Her glare was nasty enough to cancel the offer of doughnuts.

When the casket maker gave a powerful tug on Jacobs's leg, the sodbuster gave out a mournful howl and bit hard on the stick, but Scooter wasn't worried about the old man. His mind was still on Abby.

Chapter 5

ABBY'S CABIN HAD BEEN BUILT by Evan Browett before he died. Only one photograph decorated its sparse interior. It was of Evan, his likeness captured in Salt Lake City just prior to their engagement. She had placed it opposite her door in a stained pine frame three or four times the actual size of the photo so that she saw it every time she walked in. Her cabin was not unlike all the others—log walls chinked with mud, bunk attached to the wall, planked floor, and a fieldstone fireplace built low in the center of one wall.

Yahnai had already built a fire that popped and spurted orange embers by the time Winny arrived. Winny's look from the moment she stepped inside told Abby where the conversation would head—her decision to marry Isaac. It was the same thing she'd heard for weeks, even months, only now it would be supported by the morning's events.

Isaac might be old, but there was a far more complicated problem with David Perkins. He was not a member of the Church. She'd been down that road before. Evan Browett had not been a member. He'd died before he actually accepted the Church, shattering her dreams. She'd vowed that wouldn't happen again. Isaac was worthy to enter the Endowment House. Her second husband would be a member, even if he were twice her age. Isaac Jacobs—despite all his faults—fit the bill.

Abby expected Winny to start in as soon as she arrived, but she didn't. Instead, she talked about the weather and the harvest and how happy Carl was that they'd returned home safely. Under Yahnai's watchful eye, they rolled the dough out on her sawbuck table. Yahnai used a mason jar to cut circles of dough and a small bottle to cut out the holes. Each time he snuck a piece of raw dough into his mouth, she mildly scolded him. But each time he disarmed her with his cute, mischievous smile.

Winny bustled her way past Abby, their skirts brushing; then with a small piece of dough, she tested the heat of the fat in a large iron pot that hung over the fireplace. "I suppose we could let Isaac have this first doughnut, especially if it's burned."

Abby tossed her head and said, more sharply than intended, "You don't need to pick on the poor man. Not now. Not after what happened today. "

Winny riveted large hazel eyes upon her. She looked as though she were plotting something—composing an argument in her head. "I've already said it all, haven't I?"

Abby smiled and laughed in spite of herself. "Yes, you have. Several times."

"All right," Winny said, holding stock still. "But Abby, can you tell me that none of this seems like a sign to you? A sign that you're not meant to marry Isaac?"

"And he that seeketh signs shall see signs, but not unto salvation." Abby rolled bits of dough into a ball and slapped it down so hard her palm tingled.

"And she who doesn't seek to know God's will may end up going against it."

It was the one part of Winny's argument that stuck in Abby's heart like a thistle. She hadn't received a burning confirmation—or even a quiet, peaceful one—that marrying Isaac was the right thing to do.

Winny drew the test doughnut out of the pot. "The temperature's just right. Let's fry our doughnuts. We've got a crew of anxious men out there surrounding a campfire."

Yahnai's eyes opened wide as saucers. "Can I have the first one?"

"Yes, but stand back so you don't get burned," Abby said. She carefully placed the pieces into the pot, one by one. They quietly watched the dough react to the boiling fat, bubbles rising up around the edges, slowly browning the doughnut. Abby liked the silence and hoped it would last a bit longer.

Winny started in again, her tone blunt. "Abby, you know I like Isaac. He's a nice man, one of the best in our settlement. It's just that he's not the right man for you."

"You've told me that before. I know how old he is. He's losing his hair, and his eyelids droop. Enough. You sound just like the *mule skinner.*"

"You say the word like it's a shameful profession," Winny said.

Abby shook her head. "Just think about the first mule skinner we saw today. He crossed the creek and, right off, wanted to shoot Isaac's horses. He was *disgusting.*"

"Our golden-haired boy waiting for doughnuts is not disgusting. He's dreamy."

Abby laughed. "Then you marry him and leave me alone."

Winny snorted. "Me? I've got Carl and two children."

Abby and Yahnai cut more doughnuts. She separated them and laid them out to be the next batch to put in the pot. Winny looked at her and smiled, expecting her comeback.

Abby said, with emphasis, "And I've got Isaac."

"But he doesn't have you," Winny countered. "Not yet. Let him find a droopy-eyed, forty-six-year-old widow down in Logan or among all those new members of the Church that keep swarming into the Salt Lake Valley."

Abby finally chuckled, though just a little.

Winny said, "Come on, laugh. You've grown so serious around Isaac. It's almost as if you are already as old as he is. We used to laugh together all the time. I miss that."

Abby knew Winny was right. She tried to laugh, just to satisfy her friend, but only a half-muted chuckle came out. This was serious stuff they were talking about. It had to do with the rest of her life.

Winny gave her a slanted look. "So now what?"

"I guess we wait until Isaac's leg heals, and then we try again."

Winny stiffened, and Abby could feel her friend trying to exercise self-control. "Well, waiting is good. And prayer is good. And confirmations are good."

Waiting wouldn't make her decision any less practical. Abby doubted that waiting would change her mind at all. Even though she hadn't received confirmation that marrying Isaac was the right thing to do, she hadn't received any indication that it was wrong. So she would choose for herself until she was inspired to do otherwise.

"Too bad Scooter's not a Mormon," Winny said. "He'd be mighty fine to have around. I'd trade a dozen Isaacs for just one Scooter."

Abby glanced at Yahnai. She had to agree with her friend's observation, although she wasn't about to admit it. When Scooter had smiled at her, she'd felt all fluttery, like a young school girl all over again.

She said to her son, "Yahnai, run over to Brother Jacobs's cabin and tell him, if he's awake, that I'll be there to check on him in just a few minutes."

"Can I have a doughnut first?" the boy asked as he put on his sheepskin coat.

"Here you go," she said. "Be careful. It's still hot."

Yahnai pulled the door open, nibbling at the doughnut, and left.

Winny didn't let up. "Scooter is so *mysterious*. Where did he get the money, at his young age, to start up a freighting business?"

Abby shifted her weight indignantly from foot to foot, thinking. "I don't care how mysterious he is. His lifestyle is so different than ours. Take your fantasies somewhere else. Besides, he'll be on his way tomorrow, and we'll never see him again."

"Except when he passes through on his way back to Salt Lake," Winny said.

Abby shook her head. "You don't give up, do you? I'm not even going to think about it. Besides, he probably has a girl. You know how men like him are. You don't have to use much imagination to know what's going on between the women who work the dance halls in Bannack City and the miners and freighters."

"I think you're jumping to conclusions." Winny shrugged. "He struck me as different."

"Just because a man is charming and handsome doesn't make him good. I don't need a problem like him in my life. My parents taught me something long ago that applies here. When the character of a man is not clear, look at his friends. His friends are rough, so you have to conclude that Scooter is rough too."

"Something about him makes me doubt it," Winny said.

"So you're receiving inspiration on my behalf now? You, instead of Isaac?"

Winny eyed her with a critical squint.

Abby felt stifled in the now too-warm house with Winny going on about things Abby didn't want to discuss anymore. Out the window she saw Yahnai returning. He walked without a care, and Abby wondered if he had checked on Isaac at all. She put on her coat, turned on her heel, and grasped the door.

"I'd better check on Isaac. I'll be right back."

Abby went out into the cool evening weighing her friend's words.

Chapter 6

OTING A CLOTH-COVERED BASKET AND bundled up against the cold, Abby strolled to Scooter's camp in the dark with Yahnai, Carl, and Winny. There was a smell of cold air and damp earth. A full moon in a partly clouded sky illuminated a cluster of tents and the night herder in the Muddy River bottoms. She hoped the night herder was the redhead and thus wouldn't be huddled around the campfire with the other men. She found Scooter and his men sitting on logs finishing their supper of beans and bacon. She turned her gaze back to Isaac's cabin for a moment. When she'd looked in on him minutes ago, he'd been resting comfortably, nearly asleep from a strong dose of laudanum.

"Anyone for doughnuts?" Winny asked.

Scooter was the first to stand. The campfire revealed a freshly shaven face. His men stood too, looking anxious. Their body language varied. Some tipped their hats, some nodded enthusiastically; others looked quiet and reserved.

Winny said, "My, my, Scooter. You've shaved."

Oscar—who had a full beard that covered a round, boyish face—pantomimed gestures of shaving with a razor. Laughing, he said, "He stood by a busted mirror for an hour divorcin' his whiskers."

The statement gained a round of chuckles from Scooter's men. Oscar's voice matched his bulk. It was deep, and the words were half swallowed by his heavy chest.

"He even broke into a case of toilet water," another mule skinner added.

"He got to that cologne before we could drink it," Oscar said with a snort of laughter. "He's all ragged out in his fancy doodads too."

Abby edged closer, trying to gain a whiff of the cologne.

Scooter's face reddened. "Don't pay any attention to these roughnecks."

"Did you say doughnuts?" Oscar asked. "The cook's coffee is thick enough to plow, but we're glad to share. Would you folks like a cup?"

"No, thanks," Carl said with a polite wave.

"Hello again, Yahnai," Scooter said. "Did you help make the doughnuts?"

Abby looked down and watched Yahnai nod his head and give Scooter a grin.

"If we hadn't watched him, he would have eaten them all," Winny said.

Scooter laughed. "Well, that proves he's a growing boy."

Yahnai smiled as Scooter asked, "Remember what I promised you?"

Yahnai nodded. "Candy."

Scooter reached down and produced a small paper sack. Yahnai's eyes widened.

"There's some hard rock candy in there. All kinds of flavors. It's all yours."

"What do you say, Yahnai?" Abby asked.

"Thank you," Yahnai said.

"Sit by the campfire with us." Scooter gestured them all toward the gathering.

Abby's eyes were trying to adjust to the campfire's light. She scanned the men, one by one, looking for the redhead.

Scooter sensed her concern. "Everyone's here except Cad. I've assigned him sentry duty. He's still sulking over the way I pulled him to the ground. He'll sulk for another day or two, and then he'll go back to being the same old obnoxious Cad."

Scooter's use of the word *sentry* made her wonder about his background. That, and the way his men used salutes occasionally. The mule skinners converged on her, looking for their promised treat, but Scooter held them back until Yahnai took the first doughnut. After that, the pastries disappeared rapidly. Scooter touched his doughnut to his lips and looked at her in an extra gesture of politeness. She sat on the log next to him. He smelled of smoke, but she detected the heavy scent of spicy cologne and behind that the musky smell of a man.

"Thanks for the treats," Scooter said.

"You're welcome," she said. "Thanks for helping us today."

"Look at us," Oscar said, "diggin' into these doughnuts like a wolf after guts."

"Mind your language," Scooter said. "You're in the company of ladies."

Abby said nothing but appreciated the comment.

"I'm curious." Winny broke in. "How'd you get started in the freighting business?"

A keen look brightened Scooter's eyes. "I was offered a job as a teamster by Ben Holladay's people hauling freight from St. Louis to Salt Lake City."

In the back of her mind, Abby remembered a connection between Ben Holladay and Alexander Doniphan, a man who had befriended the Mormons in Missouri.

One of the mule skinners fed the fire. The flames rose higher, and orange coals popped. The heat reached Abby, and she spread her fingers out toward it.

Scooter continued, "I figured, why haul freight for Holladay when I could make money off the Mormons myself? I had some family money to invest, so I went into the freighting business. After I sold my freight in Salt Lake, I heard about Bannack City. So I bought some goods from the Mormons, and here I am."

"Why, you're gonna be as rich as Ben Holladay in a few years," Winny said.

Abby held a low opinion of men whose goal was to make a profit off Mormons. But she had to admit that Mormons needed goods from St. Louis, and she also had to admit she liked the smell of the spicy cologne.

"Well," Scooter said, "there's no doubt hauling freight to Bannack City is going to be profitable. Afterward, I'll buy a good business, settle down, and raise a family."

Abby glanced at him, and their eyes met. She blushed and looked back at the fire.

"What's in your wagons?" Winny asked.

"Liquor strong enough to make a jackrabbit spit in a bobcat's eye," Oscar said.

As the mule skinners laughed, Abby wondered how much liquor some of the men had consumed this evening—or would consume after she and her companions left.

"Lots of shovels and picks," Scooter said on a more serious note. "I've heard that miners are using elk horns as gads and hand pikes for digging up there. Of course, we have food too: bacon, beans, flour, salt, dried vegetables, and just about anything you can imagine stored in a bottle or a can. Miners are going to be holed up in Bannack City for the winter, and they have to have something to eat besides a little jerked meat."

"You've got a big crew," Carl said. "Where did you get them?"

Oscar raised a hand. "Let me tell it."

Scooter didn't object.

Oscar spoke in jesting quips. "When I first saw Scooter in St. Louis, he looked bumfuzzled as a duck in the desert. He had posted himself in a big chair in front of a restaurant, opposite a hurdy-gurdy dance and gambling hall. His sole purpose was to intercept prospective mule skinners that might emerge from that den of iniquity so flat broke they would want to go to work." Oscar's laugh rumbled in his chest.

Abby bristled, wondering where Oscar would take the conversation. Not inside dance and gambling halls, she hoped. For Yahnai's sake, and hers and Winny's. Yahnai played with the fire using a long stick, but she knew he was observant and could hear more than she might think. She placed a protective arm around him.

"As for me," Oscar continued, "I left my last dollar at the poker table. Scooter had been sitting propped up in his chair with his feet on the rung. He dropped down to the boardwalk when I came along. You'd a thought we were best friends when he greeted me. I didn't look much like a mule skinner, but he said if I wanted a job, I could have one. Never in my wildest imagination did I think I'd be one of those men crackin' a whip at a bull or a mule."

"You never had any experience at all?" Carl asked.

"Nope. Scooter trained us all."

"And a bunch of greenhorns like you all made it to Salt Lake?" Winny asked.

"All but one," Oscar said. "One was killed by Indians. He was on night watch, and the Sioux caught him. Boy named Tommy. Scooter made us all take an oath."

"What kind of oath?" Abby's face clouded with uneasiness. She didn't like talk about death. Nor did she like talk about hostile Indians.

"We swore we'd kill on sight any full blood of the Sioux or Cheyenne or any other Plains Indian we came across." Oscar folded his arms as though the oath were still intact.

Abby drew Yahnai close to her again, wondering if the oath applied to the Shoshoni and to children. The declaration confirmed Abby's suspicions of the mule skinners.

Oscar's eyes glittered with malice. "And I would've done, if I'd had a chance. I swore I'd have my vengeance, or my name ain't Oscar. I'd a sent a Sioux hoppin' over the coals of hell if I would've had the chance. Tommy was a good boy."

The camp fell silent as a tree full of owls, except for the popping of the fire.

Abby squirmed. Yahnai looked at her with alert eyes, a look that confirmed he understood at least part of the conversation. She wondered if she should say something.

Carl solved the dilemma for her. "There are no Sioux in these parts. I hope you don't do anything to rile up the local Indians. We have to live with them, you know."

Scooter nodded his understanding and quickly changed the subject. "I understand there's not many white folk between here and Bannack City."

"That's correct," Carl said. "We're the last settlement."

Scooter asked, "Why are you so far away from Salt Lake City?"

"It goes back several years," Carl said. "Our militiamen, tracking horses stolen by Indians, discovered Cache Valley in 1851. Our people drove two thousand animals into the valley in 1856 to see how they would winter, but only four hundred survived. That didn't give Brigham Young much hope for expanding into the valley."

Abby couldn't relate to the events. She had been baptized a member of the Church in 1850, at age eight, while crossing the plains with her parents. In 1856, she was fourteen years old, living in the southern portion of the Salt Lake Valley.

Carl continued, "But the next year we petitioned Brigham Young to be allowed to settle the valley, and he agreed. But the leader of that first group, Peter Maughan, constantly complained to President Young that the local Indians demanded too much livestock and flour as rent for the land. Despite conflicts that included stolen livestock, more settlers poured into the valley. Franklin was settled four years later by sixty families, including Abby, Winny, and me."

Oscar said to Abby, "Scooter tells me Injuns got your husband."

The circle went quiet again.

Oscar added, "If I'da been here, I'da hunted 'em down for ya."

Abby appreciated Oscar's sympathy and his offer of protection. But she wished these men would all take a cold bath and wash the hatred off them. She didn't hate Indians, not even after what they had done to Evan—and they shouldn't either. The conversation had taken a bad turn. Besides, she was tired. She'd had a long day, full of unexpected trauma and events.

She stood abruptly and said, "It's time to get my boy into bed."

Scooter stood just as quickly, another act of politeness. "Let me walk you back to the square. Do you mind?"

Abby didn't know what to say. She caught sight of Winny grinning at her. Winny spoke for her. "She wouldn't mind. Carl and I will take Yahnai with us."

Abby felt a blush come over her but didn't object. She took Yahnai's hand and gave him to Winny.

"Good night, Yahnai," Scooter said.

Yahnai smiled. "Good night, Scooter."

As they wandered slowly away from camp, Scooter told Abby, "We'll be leaving at sunup."

In a flash, Abby felt a pang in her stomach. She wondered if she'd ever see him again. The pang surprised and confused her. She turned toward him and saw that he was staring at her, his blue eyes looking hopeful in the moonlight. "Have a good trip," she said, her voice getting caught in her throat.

"I understand we cross the Bear River about twelve miles north of here."

"Yes, within a half mile of the Shoshoni winter camp I told you about."

"Have they begun to gather there yet?" Scooter asked. "Three of their bands were camped not far from where you were stuck in the creek crossing."

Another pang hit her stomach. She wondered if Scooter's men would provoke the Shoshoni. "I'm not sure. Maybe you'd better steer clear of that area."

He nodded an agreement. "But that's probably not possible. We have to find a crossing where the water is shallow. I'm told that's the best place."

"Of course," she said. She knew too well how important a safe crossing could be.

"Have you ever seen the north country around the Snake River plain? And above that, Deer Lodge, near Bannack City?"

"No. That's a long ways from home."

His voice dropped in volume. "Neither have I, but they say it's worth seeing."

She looked away, feeling butterflies in her stomach, but no matter how she tried to avoid looking at him, somehow her gaze always found his face once more.

"Well, good-bye, then," she said, knowing all this had to end. "And thanks again."

"Yes, ma'am, you're welcome. Good-bye, then," he said.

They had taken their time strolling and enjoying one another's company, but now they had arrived back at her cabin. She turned and walked reluctantly to her home. She almost tripped on the little steps leading to her door. She could hear the golden-haired man's voice telling her good-bye once more as she opened her door.

The interior was lit only by the dim flames in her fireplace. She saw Yahnai sitting on his bed. There was enough light to see the photograph of Evan Browett. It was staring back at her.

Chapter 7

ABBY CLOSED THE SETTLEMENT'S WELL-WORN copy of *Oliver Twist*. Every morning for the past two months, ever since the accident at the crossing—page by page, chapter by chapter—she had been reading and explaining the book to Yahnai. Within minutes she expected Chief Sagwitch to arrive, and she would lose Yahnai for a few weeks. Strong apprehension coursed through her concerning the camp this year. Troubles between whites and Indians had escalated since that day Scooter rescued her from the creek. Contract mail carriers and miners traveling from Bannack City to Salt Lake had been killed by the Shoshoni. Colonel Connor's soldiers were making forays into Cache Valley, leaving everyone as tense as barbed wire. It was a different atmosphere than a year ago.

Yahnai sat opposite her on a bucksaw table, dressed in traditional rabbit-fur leggings and jacket, answering her questions. She framed him with a longing stare. "So now that the story has ended, what does Oliver have to be thankful for?"

With uncertain eyes, Yahnai shrugged his shoulders.

"Come on, tell me."

He ventured a guess. "That he doesn't have to beg for food?"

Abby smiled at him. "Yes, and more than that, Oliver is now part of a family. Mr. Brownlow has adopted him. Oliver is going to live happily with a family out in the English countryside."

"Oh yeah."

"So here in Cache Valley, who is Oliver?"

Yahnai's eyes brightened. "Me!"

"Right!" Abby smiled. "And why is that?"

"My real mother and father died, and so did Oliver's."

"And who adopted you?"

"You, Mama."

She brushed her thumb down the side of his face. "You won't forget about me while you're at the camp this winter, will you?"

"No. I'll think of you every day."

Abby heard footsteps crunching on the hardened snow outside. Someone was coming for Yahnai. She cringed. But she'd made an agreement with Chief Sagwitch.

Yahnai heard the footsteps too. He craned his neck and looked at the door.

"Stand up," she said. "I want to see how you look in your new sweater."

Yahnai's sweater was deep blue. She'd knitted it herself, a thing her mother had taught her. It matched the blue on the Union flag.

"I like blue," Yahnai said. "Did Oliver have one like this? It's warm."

Abby laughed at Yahnai's question, but she cringed again as she heard a rap on the door. "No," she answered. "Oliver didn't have one. You are the privileged one."

A gush of January arctic air swooshed in when she opened the door. It revealed the presence of Isaac Jacobs, standing there on two good legs, with Riddle. Isaac was leaning forward with a burlap sack in his hands. Abby's eyes were drawn again to the scar on his forehead. His limp was hardly noticeable nowadays, and he rarely complained about his leg or his ribs.

"Good morning, Abby, Yahnai," Isaac said, his breath blowing steam.

Abby and Yahnai returned the greeting.

Isaac extended the sack toward her. "I brought you some vegetables: carrots, potatoes, and big head of cabbage." He had a twinkle and a longing look in his eyes.

She accepted the sack. It was heavy and smelled musty, but it was another example of how Isaac continued to care for her.

Isaac took off his hat and curled the rim in his hands. "You have a glow about you, as usual. Have I ever told you that an unmarried woman is like a one-tined fork or half a pair of scissors? We could leave for Salt Lake City tomorrow if you wish."

Abby swallowed hard, trying to manage a feeble answer. He'd made that suggestion almost daily since his leg had healed. Winny was right. Abby had prayed night and morning for the past two months, asking God if she should marry Isaac. All she got was confusion and emptiness. And she'd worn out all the excuses she knew how to make. She hadn't shared those feelings with him yet. She didn't want to hurt him. Perhaps she was to blame. Maybe she wasn't worthy of an answer just yet. Maybe she just had to pray harder, try harder for an answer.

"What do you think?" he asked.

"Not in this weather. And I'd worry too much about Yahnai, being that far away."

Isaac put his hat back on his head, pulling it on firmly until a gust of wind couldn't have budged it. "I came to tell you that Sagwitch is here," he said, looking half asleep and disappointed, with those droopy eyelids. "I know you're expecting him."

"Tell him we'll be out in a minute. I need to bundle Yahnai up."

Isaac rubbed his throat and then brushed absently at his coat. "I can bring more vegetables if you need them. You might give the boy a few carrots. Tonight, perhaps you and I could dine together on the potatoes and cabbage. We could invite Carl and Winny."

She smiled patiently. "We'll see."

Isaac's shoulders drooped, but he gave her a weak smile anyway.

Abby closed the door and returned her attention to Yahnai. He looked handsome in the blue sweater, but it wasn't enough. Outside, the temperature was just a few degrees above zero. The sheepskin coat she'd made was large enough to cover the sweater. Under his leggings, she had dressed him in long underwear.

"Will you be warm enough?" she asked as she bundled him in the coat.

Yahnai nodded his head. "I'll be fine, Mama."

"I'll put some carrots in your pockets," she said. Tears came to Abby's eyes, and she wiped at them with her sleeve. She hated the thought of walking by the school for the next few weeks listening to the children sing songs and recite their numbers without Yahnai. She wondered what it would be like for him at camp without her. Her misgivings increased by the minute. "Give me a hug to last me until you get back. And a kiss."

Yahnai turned his face upward and stood on the tips of his toes. She stooped over and kissed his copper cheeks and then his lips and gave him a prolonged hug.

"*Suuntsaa'.*"

A wide smile broke on Yahnai's face. "*Suuntsaa'.*"

"Now say it in English."

"Love you," the boy said.

A lump caught in Abby's throat. She kissed him again, took his hand, and then went outside, knowing how horribly empty her home would be without Yahnai.

Chapter 8

AGWITCH AND HIS INTERPRETER HAD already gathered a crowd in the middle of the town square by the corrals. Of course Isaac was there, but so were Bishop Preston Thomas, Carl, and a handful of other men, admiring Sagwitch's pinto pony, talking, laughing, and showing as much warmth to the chief as possible.

Riddle barked at the distinctive rattle of a wagon, and Abby couldn't help but look to see if the approaching wagon was Scooter returning from Bannack City. But it was only a farm wagon, a settler probably returning from observing livestock roaming the Muddy River bottoms.

Sagwitch's pinto had a thick coat of winter hair, and in the frigid air, smoke came out its nostrils. Abby approached the interpreter, who gave her a neutral look.

"Last winter my son was in your winter camp for a month," she said. Abby took a long, deep breath. "That's too long. I know that's what I agreed to, but with all the unrest, I am concerned for his safety. I want him back in a week. Tell Chief Sagwitch that."

Both the interpreter and Sagwitch were about the same age, which was not as old as Isaac but a lot older than Abby. Sagwitch's skin, a deep copper color inclining to red, didn't show much in his winter garb. The first time she saw the chief, he'd been dressed in a simple breechcloth held on by a belt. Today his shoulders were all but concealed by a heavy necklace of giant grizzly bear claws. He wore rabbit-fur pants, a jacket, and an elk-hide cape. He stood straight as a willow next to his horse.

From the interpreter's tone, Abby felt he had not sensed her distress and was doing a poor job conveying her feelings to the chief. She regretted not being fluent in the Shoshoni language. Sagwitch gave his answer, using sweeping gestures.

The interpreter told Abby in broken but understandable English that she must remember the conditions of accepting the child. Yahnai must spend time to embrace and appreciate the history of *newe,* the people. He was now old enough to begin the task of memorizing that history. It was his duty. Abby had heard all this before. Oral history was so important that children were expected to stay awake while it was recited. If one fell asleep, the storyteller stopped speaking and ended the session.

"With what's happened lately, will my son be safe?" she asked with a glare.

Sagwitch took on a confident look. He answered Abby face-to-face, eye to eye, expressing no fear and making no apology. Even in a different language, she took his meaning. She'd offended him by questioning Yahnai's safety and well-being.

With the same confident look, the interpreter explained that white soldiers did not fight in the winter when conditions were bad. Besides, he said, the camp on the Bear River was so large soldiers would not dare attack it. The terrain provided protection from enemies. All of Sagwitch's warriors were in the camp and so were warriors belonging to the bands of Bear Hunter, Sanpitch, and Lehi. Days earlier, other bands had joined them for a special warm dance ceremony, and they were not far away in case they were needed. He said her worries were unfounded and that she should sleep well at night.

Abby turned a deaf ear to the chief's logic. She had pondered these things for a long time, and she didn't care if she offended him. "I want my son back here in a week."

The interpreter shook his head and said there was no point in asking. He was certain Sagwitch would not change his mind.

Abby gritted her teeth as she wiped Yahnai's nose, which had begun to leak.

When she finished, she turned to Sagwitch. "How about two weeks?"

Sagwitch shook his head, evidence that he understood some English. He abruptly mounted, and the interpreter hoisted Yahnai up on the pinto behind Sagwitch.

"Don't worry, Mama," Yahnai said, looking down at her. "I'll be fine."

With his arms wrapped around the chief and in his winter garb, Yahnai looked neither sad nor afraid but excited to see his young friends at the annual camp. He was young and didn't know the meaning of fear.

She held his leg as if that would keep him near. "Do you have plenty of food? I want my son to have enough to eat."

The interpreter's eyes dropped a little. As he mounted, he told her that the Shoshoni camp had baskets full of berries, chokecherry cakes, roots, and pine nuts, along with clay pots full of dried salmon. But counting the elderly, women, and children, there were around five hundred people in this year's camp. They would have to ration their food carefully. Rabbit drives had been somewhat successful, but hunting wild game such as deer and elk had not been very productive because of competition—not only from settlers and miners but also from immigrants on the Oregon and California Trails. He said that some men would arrive in a few days for the regular allotment of flour and wheat.

With that, Sagwitch kicked the pinto's ribs.

Abby reluctantly released her grip on her son's leg and said, "*Suuntsaa*."

"*Suuntsaa*," the boy replied with a little wave of his hand. "Bye, bye, Riddle."

Abby waved, but the tightness in her stomach didn't ease.

Chapter 9

As Abby cleaned her cabin in late January, she listened to the soft crackling of logs burning in her fireplace and the occasional laughter of bundled-up school children playing outside in the town square. Thinking of Yahnai, she broke out into a hymn and gazed at the pictures on her log walls, pictures that Yahnai had drawn in school. He was a decent artist for his age. He'd drawn the meeting house, her two horses, and their dog, Riddle.

Outside, Riddle barked. She regretted having only one window. There were new sounds out there, and Riddle was barking at whatever produced those sounds. The commotion pulled her toward her wall like a magnet. She placed her hands on the logs and pressed her ear against one. Faintly, she heard the rattling and clinking of wagons and the popping of whips.

Freighters!

She threw a coat over her shoulders and rushed out the door. Under a gray sky spitting small flakes of shimmering snow, she saw familiar strings of mules and freight wagons coming from the north. And then she saw him. The golden-haired teamster.

"Scooter?"

Even from this far away he was surprisingly familiar, as if he were an old friend. As he approached, pointing at her, she found it impossible not to return his disarming smile. He waved. She waved back as he drew near.

"Well, howdy, Abby. It's me, your favorite mule skinner. How are you?"

She smiled, watched Riddle lick his hand, and said, "Why, this is a total surprise."

His mouth curved into a big smile, his breath turning to vapor. "The surprise is that you are out here in the cold, not warming yourself by a fire."

She tossed her head and brushed her hair back with one hand. She'd stepped out without wearing a bonnet.

He stepped closer. "Should I address you as Mrs. Isaac Jacobs?"

She blushed and shook her head. "I'm still Abigail Butterfield Browett."

His brows lifted significantly. "Does this mean your sawbones doctor whacked off Isaac's leg?"

Abby looked away for a second or two, met his gaze again, and then laughed. "No, it healed—not perfectly, but he gets around just fine."

He leaned toward her, seemingly caressing her with his eyes as they gently searched her face. "Let me guess. You didn't make the trip because of bad weather."

She giggled as if he had uncovered a secret. "Yes, that's it—the weather. Come spring, perhaps we'll make the trip."

"Your mind is not set, then?"

She looked away. "I don't know for sure."

Scooter tipped his hat at her. "Well now, isn't that interesting?"

Wrapped in a heavy gray coat, Oscar joined the happy reunion. He tipped his hat at her. She returned Oscar's kindness with a warm hello and then cast her eyes toward the wagons and the other men.

Her concern was immediately detected by Scooter. "By the way, don't worry even one second about Cad. His banishment is still in effect. He's not to come around you. He's way in the back of our wagons, and he'll stay there too."

Abby accepted the explanation but wondered if Scooter treated anyone who crossed him that way. "Just passing through?"

Worry came to Scooter's face, as if he had a problem. He said with an edge to his voice, "We stopped to warn your settlement. We saw Indian men on horseback just a few minutes ago. They're headed this way. I didn't like their looks."

Abby immediately knew who it was. "That's Bear Hunter. He's one of the Shoshoni chiefs." Of all the chiefs, she liked the feisty Bear

Hunter the least. But he would have news of Yahnai. She began to muster up the courage to talk to him.

Oscar said, "Don't you think you ought to warn the settlers?"

Abby shook her head. "No, there's been talk that Bear Hunter would come today, so our minutemen already know. He's here for more wheat and flour."

"We passed by the Indian camp," Oscar said. "It's a big one. Lots of mouths to feed."

"And your boy is there?" Scooter asked.

Abby's voice went small. "I wish he wasn't, but he is."

"You should have kept him here and taught him the white man's history."

"I told you before," she said. "This is a condition of his adoption."

Scooter returned a disapproving frown. "Is taking all the wheat and flour the Shoshoni want a condition of the adoption too?"

"We're on Shoshoni land. It's a form of rent."

"I swanny, Indians can work just the same as your people. Why don't they raise their own wheat and grind their own flour? They can hitch their horses to a plow, same as you folks. Would they take the last that you have and let you starve to death? Who benefits most when they take your wheat, the adults or the children, like your boy?"

"They gather seeds and berries and all sorts of stuff, in season," she explained. "You'd be surprised what you'd find in their camp."

"Trade, then," he said. "Give them flour for dried berries or something."

Scooter's look remained one of frustration. He bit his lip and then turned to face the north, the direction where he'd seen Bear Hunter. "I think it would be a good idea for me and my men to stick around while Bear Hunter is here. There are no settlements between Bannack City and Franklin. My mules haven't had much to graze on. Will you please ask your men if they'd be willing to sell me some of their hay? I'm not like the Indians. I'll pay for what I receive—in Bannack City gold. I'd be beholden."

Abby's reaction was mixed. Would his presence provoke Bear Hunter? Would a man like Cad, a hothead, put the chief in the sights of a long rifle and pull the trigger? And what would Isaac think? On the other hand, was he saying this to help protect her and the other settlers?

In the end, she felt herself give in to his request. She trained her eyes on the village square. "I'll run over and ask Bishop Thomas about the hay and make certain he knows about Bear Hunter."

She found Bishop Thomas at the granary, the tightest log structure of the settlement, helping Isaac and Carl grind flour from the wheat supply and fill containers for some of the settlers' wives. Abby told the bishop what Scooter had seen.

Isaac returned an angry look. "Bear Hunter? No Mediterranean pirate ever levied tribute with more regularity and persistency. We've got to draw a line."

Bishop Thomas returned an annoyed look, saying, "I suppose we must."

All the men murmured about the Indians for a few moments. When the murmurs died down, Abby mentioned Scooter's request for hay. None of the men objected, so the bishop told her he would assign some men to deliver it right to Scooter's wagons.

She was about to leave when she saw Bear Hunter and two companions ride into the square. They were fully armed, as though rifles, bows and arrows, tomahawks, and knives were the tools of their trade. Each led a packhorse, and all the horses stepped sprightly on the frozen turf, making sharp clipping sounds.

Bear Hunter rode an iron-gray stallion with a thick neck. Light snow swirled in a slant of light, salting his hair and lining the creases of the red blanket wrapped around him. He had piercing brown eyes set deep and close together in hooded sockets. Those dark eyes seemed to scorch the earth before him, radiating a fiery clarity that forecast his reputation for unblinking severity. He came straight into the square. He didn't look to the left or to the right. He didn't wave or even acknowledge anyone. He was being tactical, as if he were the most important chief among the Shoshoni nation.

When Bear Hunter arrived at the granary, she approached him, looking up, twisting her bare hands together in nervous anxiety. She had no idea what to expect. She could feel his hostility. His posture spoke of remote, impersonal indifference. She felt his toughness. He was just as ready to turn his fury inward as outward. She gathered every ounce of courage she had and spoke. "Have you seen Yahnai? Is he well?"

The intimidating face staring back at her was thick and weathered and pompous. He was here to impress, not to please. It was obvious that he had more on his mind than a six-year-old Indian boy who had been adopted by a white woman—against Bear Hunter's wishes. He was more intent on seeing the chief of the white men in her settlement. His fists were wrapped tightly around the reins, his elbows were kinked outward, and from his lofty perch on the horse, he gave everyone in his path a beady and threatening gaze.

Riddle growled.

For a few seconds Bear Hunter didn't respond. His eyes locked on Bishop Thomas, but the bishop motioned for Bear Hunter to answer her questions. The Indian gave a disapproving frown. He was known to speak English well enough to get by, but he still didn't say anything.

Abby looked up at Bear Hunter and repeated her questions. He glared back at her as if to reinforce his toughness and superiority. Finally he changed his look to neutral and acknowledged her. He answered in short, clipped sentences. Yes, he'd seen Yahnai. The child was well. Bear Hunter had seen Yahnai playing with other children. He'd been in the same teepee with Yahnai on occasion as stories of Shoshoni history were told.

"Was he wearing his blue sweater?"

Bear Hunter gave a curt nod and then gestured at Bishop Thomas. Abby took it that the conversation was over. She had pried all the information about Yahnai that the chief was willing to spend time talking about. She slowly walked away, her mind focusing still on Yahnai. From a distance, she looked back and saw more evidence of Bear Hunter's overt hostility. He was making demanding gestures—chin tilted up, chin tilted down, thrusting one arm in the air and then the other, fingers pointing up, fingers pointing down, even shaking his fist. His body language said, *Give me what I want, or I'll burn the whole place down.* Soon the bishop, Isaac, Carl, and a few other settlers busied themselves filling sacks.

Abby hurried to where Scooter's men had circled their mules and wagons beside the Muddy River.

When she found Scooter, he asked, "What did your men say about the hay? I'm determined to stick around. I didn't like the looks of Bear Hunter."

"They'll deliver you some hay," she said. "They said the price would be fair."

"Thank you," he replied. "My mules are famished." Smoke began to curl up where the camp cook had built a fire. With gentleness in his voice, Scooter made another request. "It's too cold to ask y'all to sit around a campfire with me and the men. May I call on you this evening?"

Scooter's steady gaze made her feel uneasy but flattered as well. She wondered how to make his visit seem proper in the eyes of other settlers, especially Isaac. After all, she was still his intended wife. She thought about the appropriateness of his calling on her. Certainly they couldn't be alone in her cabin.

He waited for her answer.

She smiled faintly. "Yes, of course. I'll arrange for a dinner at Winny's so we can thank you again. Give us about three hours to prepare."

"Yes, ma'am. I'll look forward to it."

Their conversation was interrupted by a commotion at the granary. Indian war cries pierced the winter air. Abby and Scooter stared at each other for a moment, as if the world had just turned upside down. Abby imagined Bear Hunter thrusting a tomahawk at Isaac's head, using the scar as a target. Or his agitated warriors threatening with guns and knives. Alarmed, they rushed toward the town square, followed by a few mule skinners.

Abby gasped. Her imagination hadn't been too far off. In the distance she saw Bear Hunter and his men circling Bishop Thomas's house, brandishing tomahawks, whooping and hollering. She turned to look at Scooter. His face had turned as hard as a whetstone, as if the Shoshoni were the Plains Indians that had killed his friend, Tommy.

"I swanny," Scooter said, tucking his chin to his chest. "I had the feeling something might happen." He planted both feet on the frozen turf and clenched his teeth.

Oscar looked as though a rattlesnake were crawling up his leg. He pulled out his revolver and cocked it. And then he aimed it at the direction of the Indians.

"Don't do anything hasty," Abby said. "I'll find out what's going on."

"I'll go with you," Scooter said grimly. "You men stay here. But be ready for anything."

As they left, Abby overheard one of Scooter's mule skinners say, "I'd like to put a hole through one of those Injuns big enough to drive a wagon through."

She turned and hurled a hot glare at the mule skinner, a glare that said hold your peace, a glare that said don't start a war in the settlement. She raced toward a group of settlers standing at a safe distance from the Indians. Winny and Carl were there, along with Isaac, worry and fear etched on all their faces.

Half out of breath, Abby asked, "What's this all about?"

Carl shook his head angrily and said, "It ain't a quilting bee."

Winny said, "The men sacked up twenty-four bushels of wheat for Bear Hunter, but he wants more. The bishop said no, and they argued for a few minutes. The bishop held his ground, and then Bear Hunter started this. He's acting like a spoiled child."

Abby watched as Bear Hunter and his men continued to rage and dance around the bishop's home. She could taste their hostility. Their moves were bold. Their war cries were arrogant, persuasive, uncompromising, guttural, and loud. They gripped their tomahawks so tightly their knuckles turned white. Their weapons made wide, arching sweeps and then short, choppy ones. They were moving constantly, like maggots writhing in a carcass.

Children had emerged from the school with the teacher, peering out with wide, curious eyes. Carl ran toward them and shooed them back inside. Despite the show Bear Hunter was putting on and the tension it created, Abby wished Yahnai was tucked inside the school with the other children.

Finally, when the bishop held up an arm in a gesture of peace, the Indians quit. Abby heard the bishop tell the chief that he would reevaluate the settlement's supply of wheat. If Bear Hunter would come back tomorrow, he could possibly have more. Bear Hunter's smugness fell away just a little. He twitched and shuffled and looked uncomfortable, but he finally nodded. Then he mounted his steel-gray stallion. With a look as hard as woodpecker lips and with a disgusted sneer, he tugged on the lead rope of one of the loaded packhorses and began leading his warriors away from the granary toward the Bear River.

Winny said, "Tomorrow, I hope someone else comes instead of Bear Hunter."

"Does this happen often?" Scooter asked as the Indians disappeared.

"He has a history of being hotheaded," Abby said. "We can tell you about him later. Right now I'd like to think of something more pleasant. Winny, I've invited Scooter for supper. To thank him for his kindnesses. Could we do it at your place?"

Winny's reaction was immediate. She offered a winning, magnificent smile, a smile that said, *I told you so.* The cold eyes that had stared at Bear Hunter turned warm. "Why, yes, you can," Winny said. "Of course."

Just then Isaac ambled toward them. He looked like a man juggling emotions, angry at Bear Hunter but trying to conceal his jealousy over the fact that Scooter had arrived. "What are you doing here? We thought we'd seen the last of you."

"Just passing through, old-timer," Scooter said, extending his hand.

Isaac accepted the handshake, clearly running conclusions through his head and doing his best to look comfortable. He trawled back his memory. "Well, thanks again for helping me. Staying long? I suppose you must hustle back to Salt Lake."

"We can all express our thanks to him tonight at my place," Winny said. "Abby has invited Scooter to dinner."

Isaac wilted a little. "Oh, splendid. I'll look forward to it."

Chapter 10

I SAAC PROVIDED ANOTHER DAMP GUNNY sack full of garden produce. Abby fried the potatoes and onions to a perfect golden brown and boiled carrots, beets, and cabbage until the vegetables were soft but not mushy. Her plum preserves—which she'd been saving for a special occasion—somehow made it to the perfectly set table along with hot bread.

Winny laughed at her. "Who are you trying to impress, Isaac or Scooter?"

"No one."

Winny looked at her as though Abby had just told a fib.

Scooter and Isaac arrived almost simultaneously. She watched for signs of friction. One man old, the other young. One man nearly bald, the other with a full head of golden hair. One with a scar on his forehead, the other with smooth skin. They acknowledged each other but gave muted stares as they took off their hats, coats, and gloves. Isaac danced close to her as if staking his claim.

"Mmm, smells good," Isaac said. "Why, look at that table. Looks like you girls were expecting Brigham Young or Abraham Lincoln instead of us."

"I ain't seen food like this for a long time," Scooter agreed, patting his stomach.

Carl pulled a wooden bench away from the sawbuck table over which the women had placed a yellow tablecloth. He said, "Please sit. It's time to dive in. Thanks to you, Isaac, for providing the food, and to my lovely wife for shuffling our children off to the neighbors. But first, I'll give thanks."

Abby opened one eye briefly during the prayer. Scooter had reverently folded his arms and bowed his head. Isaac had opened one of his eyes too. It was trained on Scooter. Afterward, she leaned over Scooter's shoulder to fill his plate with food and pour a glass of buttermilk. She caught a whiff of his spicy cologne. He had shaved his face clean again, probably the first time since she'd seen him last.

"Thanks again for what you did last November," Isaac said, half graciously.

"Don't mention it," Scooter said. "Happy to do it for y'all."

Scooter's folksy lingo intrigued Abby again. Curiosity ate at her, but she didn't pursue it for now. She knew he wanted to know more about Bear Hunter, so she asked a question. "We're all wondering about Bannack City," she said. "What's it like?"

"It's a primitive place up yonder," Scooter said. "I reckon there are well over four hundred men wintering out."

Isaac made a face as though smelling something rotten. "Ruffians, no doubt."

Scooter forked enormous bites of food into his mouth, chewed politely, and swallowed as though a home-cooked meal were as precious as gold. Every little noise he made sounded like appreciation. "Actually, some of them are the nicest people you'd want to meet. But some of them are the worst. Surprisingly, there are around forty women."

Isaac rolled his eyes. "Probably all ladies of the evening."

Carl rolled his eyes too—at Isaac. "Where are the miners coming from?" he asked.

"Most from the mines in Colorado, like Pike's Peak. After that, just about every other place you could think of: Minnesota, Kentucky, New York, Ohio, Missouri, Oregon, even a few from Utah. By and by, there'll be four or five thousand people there. Bannack City is going to be second to no city north of Salt Lake. Miners have already taken $700,000 worth of gold from the banks and bars along Grasshopper Creek."

Abby pulled a funny face. "Grasshopper Creek? Who came up with that name?"

"The gold was discovered by men who left the Colorado mines after they played out last summer. They saw clouds of grasshoppers along the creek."

Imagery came to Abby's mind. "I don't suppose seagulls flew out of the heavens and showed the miners where to look for gold."

Scooter laughed. "No, but I know all about how seagulls saved the crops of your early pioneers. The quality of gold they're getting is very good, better than California. Not only in the creek. Now they've found ledges of gold-bearing rock a mile below Bannack. Men were running up the steep hills with wooden stakes, marking their claims. I imagine their letters home are full of optimism."

Isaac perked up at the mention of letters. Abby guessed it was because now that he was healthy again, he had a job to do. He had contracted with the Overland Mail Company to establish an express rider relay station in Franklin. The route to Bannack City was scheduled to begin operating in the early spring.

Carl asked Scooter, "Are you tempted to try your hand in mining up there?"

"No," Scooter answered. "I'll stick with freighting. My profits were better than I expected. Got paid in pure gold. Even so, there won't be enough provisions to sustain everyone up there this winter. That's why a few miners left Bannack City and came south to winter out in Salt Lake."

Abby wondered who was guarding the gold stashed in Scooter's lock box.

Scooter asked, "What's gold worth nowadays at the Mormon mint in Salt Lake?"

"How would we know?" Abby said. "We rarely see a gold coin around here."

Carl extended an arm in the air, waving. "I have a gold coin."

The response surprised Abby. "You do?"

Carl rose from the table and opened a chest. "Yes. It's a five-dollar gold piece, minted by the Church the year we settled Franklin, 1860."

Abby's fingers twitched. "Oh, please, let me see it."

She ran her fingers delicately over the etching, eyeing it closely. On one side of the coin she saw a crouching lion etched in the center, with three mountain peaks in the background and a small stretch of water in the foreground. The words *Holiness to the Lord* were etched around the edge, written in characters of the Deseret Alphabet, along with the year. On the reverse side she saw an eagle with outstretched wings. It had a beehive on its breast and an olive branch and arrows in its talons.

"Would y'all let me have a look?" Scooter asked.

As Abby handed it to him, Isaac sat with his arms folded, paying scant attention to all the fuss about gold coins.

"It resembles the regular five-dollar gold piece of the United States," Scooter said, holding it up for scrutiny.

"That it does," Carl said as Scooter handed it back to Abby.

She remarked, "I've never wanted anything in the way of gold in my life, but someday I am going to own one of these." It reminded her of Evan because it was minted the year they helped establish Franklin.

Isaac said nothing. He edged away from the coin, like it was infectious.

After a few more moments, she handed the coin back to Carl, who wiped it, rose from the table, and put it away as Abby ladled more food onto Scooter's plate. As Scooter ate with relish, Winny asked him, "So what's next for you?"

"Skedaddle back to Salt Lake. Winter out there. Buy more goods. Maybe even more wagons. Head back to Bannack City when the roads permit."

"You better get an early start for Salt Lake in the morning," Isaac said. "Bad weather brewing. The passes will be clogged with snow soon."

Scooter ignored the comment.

Carl asked, "No Indian problems this trip, between here and Bannack City?"

"Naw, no tussles at all. They were holed up in their winter camps somewhere. I reckon the Bannacks up yonder are more peaceful than the Shoshoni."

Abby said, "Our Church established a mission up that direction a few years ago."

"Yes, I've heard of Fort Lemhi and that it was abandoned. Miners raised vegetables at the site last summer. I know your church is big on missionary work."

The comment piqued Abby's curiosity. "What about you? Are you a religious man? Were you brought up in a God-fearing home?"

His face clouded with uneasiness. He smiled a little sadly, a little wistfully. "I guess you could say I was raised on prunes and proverbs. But right now, ever since I left home, religion ain't my bowl of soup. I just ain't had time."

Isaac smiled. The traction Abby was getting on this subject seemed to please him. Like a querulous seagull, his eyes glittered. He placed his eyes on Abby as if to say, *Keep going with this*, and then placed his eyes on Scooter, as if expecting him to squirm.

Winny asked, "But you believe in God?"

"Sure. I want to go to heaven, but something tells me I won't be making the final call on that."

"Surely you've formed an opinion of Mormons by now."

"I'm impressed with the construction of your temple. That's quite a feat, hauling those giant stones from the mountain."

Isaac said, "A fellow like you probably has no idea why we build temples."

Scooter looked lost. He shrugged his answer. "I reckon a place to hold worship services on Sundays. But y'all have a long wait from what I've seen. What? Another twenty years?"

Isaac snorted a superior laugh. "When it's done, it'll be closed on Sundays, but open the other days of the week."

"It will? So what do you do in temples?"

Abby let Isaac answer. It was his conversation now. He cast longing and anxious eyes at her. "For one thing, marriages."

"Marriages?" Scooter sounded surprised. "I thought your Endowment House was for that."

"Yes, it is," Isaac said quickly. "But just temporarily. When the temple is completed, all marriages—for time and for all eternity—will be there."

The room went silent for a moment. Abby stared at her food and wondered what both Isaac and Scooter were thinking right now. Across from her, she heard the sound of Carl's fork scraping his plate for another morsel of food.

Winny broke into the awkward silence. "How long do you intend to stay in Franklin?" she asked Scooter.

"My boys are anxious to get back to Salt Lake, but what'll happen when Bear Hunter comes back tomorrow? He's about the angriest lookin' Indian as ever toted an ugly head. We're not leaving till we find out."

Chapter 11

ABBY GRIMACED, KNOWING THAT THE conversation would turn to Bear Hunter sooner or later. She twisted her hands in her lap as she thought of the Indian chief's return tomorrow. She hoped there would be no disturbing surprises.

"Has Bear Hunter always been a problem?" Scooter asked.

"He's a thief," Isaac said matter-of-factly. "He'd take *all* our food if we'd let him and wouldn't feel a bit bad about it."

Abruptly, Abby began to clear dishes. "We have apple pie for dessert."

"I love apple pie," Scooter said. "But tell me more about Bear Hunter."

Abby sighed. Scooter tried to scoop up his last bite of cabbage as she took his plate, and she had to hide a grin when the bite fell down the front of his shirt.

Carl said, "Bear Hunter has been a problem right from the beginning. That first year he established a camp right in the middle of a wild grass field that the settlers intended on using for hay. The bishop down there, a man named Peter Maughan, told Bear Hunter that the settlers had come into the valley to make their homes. They wanted to live peacefully among the Shoshoni and become their friends, but he said the Shoshoni could not camp there."

Isaac added, "Bishop Maughan gave Bear Hunter an ultimatum. His warriors had to be off the land within two hours or else."

"So what did Bear Hunter do?"

"Fortunately," Carl answered, "Bear Hunter's young warriors feared the whites and immediately left. That humiliated Bear Hunter. So he vowed to get rid of the white men by whatever means possible, starting with Bishop Maughan. One morning after breakfast, Bishop Maughan had the impression that he should examine his rifle. He took it from the pegs on the wall. As he did, the door opened, and Bear Hunter burst in brandishing his own rifle. You can imagine his surprise when he saw his enemy waiting for him with a rifle pointed right at his heart. Bear Hunter got out of there, puzzled at how that happened."

Scooter let out a triumphant laugh. "Bully for Bishop Maughan. Judging by what happened today, Bear Hunter hasn't changed much."

Her arms full of plates and dishes, Abby rolled her disappointed eyes at Winny. "Men!" she whispered. "Aren't they impossible when they get off on these subjects?" Winny responded with a sympathetic smile.

"No, he hasn't," Carl answered. "Bear Hunter and his band stole grain left behind when Cache Valley settlers temporarily moved to Brigham City during what we call the Utah War. Three years later, two of my friends were killed while digging irrigation ditches. And just after that, Abby's husband was killed. Not by Bear Hunter personally, but we think his band was behind it."

"And another Shoshoni chieftain felt bad and gave you a boy?" Scooter asked.

Abby's eyes dropped, and her shoulders drooped at the mention of Evan's death. But the memory of Sagwitch arriving with Yahnai was a pleasant one. Both incidents had been etched into Abby's mind forever, even more vividly than the day she was baptized. She remembered how the child had sat on Sagwitch's shoulder like a dove. Only four years old, Yahnai clung to the chief's back like glue. He was scrawny, in bad need of proper nourishment, clothing, and love. He never once looked her in the eye—not from the back of the pony and not when Sagwitch gently lifted him off the paint horse. Yahnai hid behind the chief and stared at the ground. She remembered his campfire smell and the fact that he had no clothing. Just like the chief, he was dressed only in a breechcloth. When Sagwitch rode off, Yahnai gave a forlorn look in the chief's direction and then just stood there staring at his bare feet. It took a long time to melt the distance she felt between her and the boy. But it melted, and now it was almost as if she had given birth to him.

Scooter shook his head sadly. "What happened when the Civil War broke out? Did that help or hurt your relationship with the Indians?"

Carl said, "Early on it made things worse. The Shoshoni, with no soldiers stationed nearby, simply became emboldened. They raided wagon trains, harassed mail carriers and miners, and stole our livestock."

"But the Civil War brought Union soldiers to Salt Lake," Isaac added. "Now that Fort Douglas has been established, things will be different. Colonel Patrick Connor is a tough nut, and I'm glad he is. I'll give you an example. A while back, a young white boy was taken captive by Indians following a raid on a wagon train. Connor forced Bear Hunter to give the boy up."

Abby was slicing her thick apple pie. She tried to imagine how she would feel if Yahnai's adult relatives knocked on her door and forced her to give Yahnai back to them. But there was a difference. The white boy had been kidnapped. Yahnai had been given to her.

"And there's soon to be another example," Isaac said. "You've probably heard that a couple of express riders were killed recently between here and Bannack City."

Scooter nodded. "Yes."

"And you've heard that a miner from Bannack City was killed by the Shoshoni when the group he was traveling with was trying to reach Salt Lake."

Scooter nodded again.

"Connor is vowing revenge." Isaac's tone grew more and more firm. "How and when, we don't know. But I'll be glad when he does it."

Abby set plates of pie in front of the three men. She knew it was a possibility that Connor might retaliate. For Yahnai's sake, she hoped he would at least wait until spring. Right now would be a terrible time for soldiers to march north from Fort Douglas. She hoped Isaac, Scooter, and Carl would gulp down the pie and find something else to talk about.

Scooter took a huge bite. "Mmm. Good. Flaky crust. Sweet apples. Thank y'all."

"You're welcome," Winny said.

Scooter said, "So that brings us to today, with Bear Hunter doing his little war dance for more wheat."

"Yes," Carl said. "He'll be back tomorrow."

"I've already given the bishop my opinion," Isaac said. "Not one more sack."

Abby had tired of all this talk about Bear Hunter. For her, the evening was over. She stood, knitting her fingers and flexing them over her head. She snatched everyone's pie dishes and said, "It's been a long day, and I need to go home."

Scooter immediately rose. He caught her eye, did the same with Winny and Carl, and even Isaac, one at a time, and said politely, "I've enjoyed the evening. Thank you for the dinner, thank you for the delicious apple pie, and thank you for the conversation. I've learned a lot, more than y'all will ever know. Thanks again, ya'll."

His distinct Southern accent caught Abby's curiosity again. There was something about him that was suspicious. "You say you started your business in St. Louis?"

"Yes, ma'am."

"But where were you born and raised?"

There was awkwardness in his face, calculation in his eyes—all of which caused Abby's curiosity to burn even more.

"Why, Missouri, of course."

Abby shook her head. "You can't fool me. Your accent is Southern."

"That's what they speak in Missouri."

Abby shrugged. In her young life, she'd been around all kinds of Southern accents. He didn't sound like a Missourian. The Carolinas, Georgia, or even Virginia, but not Missouri. A mystery. And why he was out West hauling freight at his age, she didn't know.

Chapter 12

ALL DURING THE NIGHT, ISAAC had worried about what decision Bishop Thomas would make about giving Bear Hunter more wheat. Isaac worried to the point he hardly slept. He thought about Scooter too. He'd felt a tinge of jealousy last evening when Abby took him by his hand, as if the mule skinner's confession had touched her somehow. The mule skinner was still a mule skinner. Still a freighter. He hoped that Abby would forget about Scooter after he left later today. He wished Bear Hunter hadn't showed up yesterday. If he hadn't, Scooter would have left the settlement by now, on his way to Salt Lake to wait out the winter. He hoped Bear Hunter would arrive soon, take what extra wheat the bishop might allot, and disappear back to the north—and that Scooter would disappear to the south.

Isaac had bundled himself up against the cold and joined a knot of men around the granary to listen to the bishop's decision. Snow was in the air again. Big feathery flakes drifted around, reluctant to settle. They swirled and hung in the air and rose up again like tiny birds. Children were playing stickball in the town square. Pet dogs, including Abby's dog, Riddle, were chasing along.

"The safest thing to do is give Bear Hunter what he wants," the bishop said, his breath smoking in the frigid air. "I don't think we have any other option. We don't want a war to break out over something so minor."

Most of the men nodded their heads and expressed their support. Not Isaac. The Indians had been given enough wheat. The thought festered deep down within his soul until he couldn't keep it to himself any longer. "Bishop Thomas," he said, "you realize we're now dipping into the wheat we need to sow our crops in the spring."

"Perhaps," the bishop admitted, "but I think it's the best course of action. If we don't, we run the risk of them stealing horses and cattle all the rest of the winter."

Isaac stomped a foot into the frozen turf. "Double the guard. We can't give in."

"No. I've made my decision," the bishop said.

"Until when?" Isaac asked. "Until Bear Hunter shows up in a week or two?"

The bishop shook his head. "No. I'm going to be firm. Nine more sacks. That's it. It'll have to last them the rest of the winter."

Just then something caught Isaac's eye. He turned. Bear Hunter and his men had entered the town square, brittle with cold. The hair on the back of Isaac's neck stood out. Children playing near the school scurried inside.

Isaac saw Abby open her door and step into the square, fully bundled up. He saw Winny come out too, with Carl. Isaac's eyes fell in disappointment when he saw Scooter cresting the horizon of the river bottom, full of curiosity, walking toward the granary. Soon he had joined Abby in her walk toward him, trailing behind the Indians.

Bear Hunter rode the same steel-gray stallion. He had wrapped himself in the same red blanket. He rode straight toward the men gathered at the granary. He didn't dismount. He didn't utter a greeting of any kind. To the bishop's credit, he threw words like stones at Bear Hunter, telling him that nine sacks was the limit. Bear Hunter looked as though he'd been punched in the mouth. He touched his knife but didn't unsheathe it. He fondled the rifle he carried over the withers of his horse. He touched his tomahawk.

But Bishop Thomas was unfazed. "Nine sacks. That's all."

Bear Hunter twisted on his horse and began speaking Shoshoni to his warriors. He spoke with a hiss. He spoke at times in low, guttural tones. He gestured broadly. One of the warriors laughed and then the other. Bear Hunter broke out in a laugh too. Isaac had no idea what they were laughing about, so he asked Abby.

There was worry in Abby's eyes. "They think it's funny that they're taking wheat needed to seed our fields next spring. I don't think they believe the bishop. Other than that"—she shrugged—"I don't know Shoshoni that well."

Just as it appeared Bear Hunter was going to reject Bishop Thomas's offer, he began speaking broken English. Amazingly, Bear Hunter told the bishop that he would accept the nine sacks. Isaac breathed a huge sigh of relief.

"Brother Jacobs, Brother Davis, open up the granary doors," the bishop said.

Bear Hunter backed his horse away from the white men. So did his warriors. They made clicking sounds with their mouths and rode toward the granary.

Isaac made a beeline to the granary. He and Carl opened the door. Its hinges creaked and squealed, and the strong smell of stored wheat leaked out. As Carl grabbed a shovel, Isaac opened a burlap sack. Others followed their lead.

Bear Hunter watched from atop his horse. The gray horse was calm. It lowered its head, shuffled its feet, and waited. Two sacks were filled, and then three. Then four. Settlers secured them onto Bear Hunter's packhorses.

Suddenly, Abby's dog turned to the south and barked.

"What is it, Riddle?" Abby asked. The flat gray sky was spitting tiny flakes of snow. Overhead, noisy seagulls circled, waiting for a taste of spilled wheat.

Winny placed her hands flat against her forehead and squinted. "I can see something moving way out there."

Isaac stopped shoveling. "What? Where?"

Scooter pointed. "Way out there. See?"

Isaac wasn't certain. His eyes weren't as good as they used to be.

"There's definitely something out there," Winny said.

Bear Hunter said nothing. At first he didn't pay any attention. Then slowly, deliberately, he twisted atop his horse. The expression on his face changed. Isaac shielded his eyes with both hands and squinted. Finally he saw what the others were seeing: tiny specs getting larger.

"What do you think, Isaac?" Carl asked.

"I don't know. What do you think?"

"Lot of movement," Carl said.

"Looks like soldiers to me," Scooter said.

The word *soldiers* caused Bear Hunter to jerk on the reins. His horse reared its head back, snorted, and then spun on its heels until it faced south.

Isaac felt the rising tide of curiosity that prevailed in front of the granary.

Everyone stood stock still, as though they were frozen to the turf, hands over their eyes, mouths open with wonder. No more shoveling. No more tying burlap sacks.

"Definitely soldiers," Winny said. "I see horses and men and wagons."

"Could be bad, could be good," Carl said as Riddle continued to bark.

Abby's hands went to her mouth. "Why would soldiers come today?"

"To get control over the Indians around here," Isaac answered bluntly.

Isaac could see tension in the way Scooter was holding himself. The soldiers in the distance, coming closer and closer by the minute, were Union soldiers, bitter enemies of the Confederacy. He half expected Scooter to make a mad dash toward his camp and get ready to light out. But he didn't. He just stood there like everyone else.

One of the settlers looked up at the worried Bear Hunter and said, "Here come the *toquashes*. Maybe you'll all be killed."

Bear Hunter glared at the specks swelling larger and larger, looking more like men, more like horses, more like wagons. His look was deadly, like a wolf ready to attack a yearling elk. "Maybe *toquashes* be killed."

Isaac tried to decipher what the chief said next. Something about he knew that the soldiers were coming but there were not enough of them for him to worry about. If true, Isaac wondered how Bear Hunter got information like that. With that, however, and with incredible haste, the chief jerked at his gray horse and motioned to his companions to leave.

Bishop Thomas held up a hand. "You're three sacks shy of your allotment."

Bear Hunter didn't look back. He kicked at his stallion and tugged at the packhorses. Within minutes he and his warriors looked as small as the approaching soldiers.

Isaac felt Abby's hand on his shoulder. "I'm afraid. Afraid for Yahnai."

"Don't jump to conclusions until we talk to them," Isaac said.

Isaac took note of Scooter again. There were lines of worry on his face and in his body movements. He wondered why the man didn't leave. Then, as he watched Scooter's blue eyes trained on Abby, the odd behavior made sense.

He was staying for her.

Chapter 13

$\mathcal{S}$COOTER TRIED TO HIDE HIS reaction. He took several deep breaths and told himself to relax. Utah Territory was a long way from Virginia and the Civil War. The only way Union soldiers out here would suspect him is if he did something crazy. Like run. Connor's soldiers had been mustered in California. All had to be from Northern states. But he couldn't help asking himself if he had blundered into some kind of trouble.

His name was not David Perkins. His real name was Jesse Kemp.

And he was a deserter from the Confederate army. Not from the Union army, but a deserter nevertheless.

He'd galloped away on the horse his mother brought to him. She'd carried the news that not only had his two brothers been killed in the war but his father as well. She'd demanded that he leave, saying she couldn't bear to have her only other son killed in that abominable war. He'd traveled fast those first hours, those first days, those first weeks. Home Guard units seemed to be everywhere, especially at first, on the lookout for deserters. He'd heard stories of how they shot first and asked questions later. That's because avid defenders of the Confederacy considered desertion one of the greatest crimes a man could commit—second only to treason. They advocated no leniency. Both sides felt that way. Sometimes they even went so far as to exchange information. The papers in St. Louis had been filled with stories of deserters who had been hunted down and executed.

Everywhere he went, he'd avoided soldiers like a plague.

They were there in St. Louis, where he went into the freighting business. They were there when he hired his men and bought wagons and mules. They were all along the trail that led to Salt Lake City. They were there to protect freighters, express riders, gold seekers, and immigrants. It was risky talking with soldiers, but sometimes he had to. Luckily they never questioned him. Never asked where he was from. Never asked if he'd been a soldier. Just figured he was performing a needed service, hauling goods from St. Louis to the West.

Soldiers had been in Salt Lake City, too, at Fort Douglas. He knew all about Colonel Patrick Connor. He hated Union soldiers. They'd killed his father and brothers.

Dreams of the death of his brother Billy haunted him. He had served with Billy in the Battle of Shiloh. Practically every night since Billy's death, his brother's voice would come to him. "Come over here. You can see 'em better." There, over the brow of the knoll, absolutely exposed, he could still see his brother sitting on a boulder, loading and firing as calmly as though there wasn't a Yankee near him. Scooter remembered yelling at him to come back under the cover of the hilltop, but Billy said he could see better there. He refused to leave his vantage-ground. Minutes later Billy was hit and died in Scooter's arms, the victim of a gunshot wound to his chest.

His training as a soldier gave Scooter a natural compunction to fight, but he hoped to stay out of the way of Union soldiers. He wanted no part of a hangman's noose.

Scooter knew he wasn't the only person who felt distressed at the sight of the soldiers as they swarmed the settlement. They were intrusive, acting as if they owned the very ground where the cabins stood, where the corrals stood, and where the meetinghouse stood. Abby was making the connection swiftly. Her normal long-limbed looseness was all wiped away by a feverish tension, and her eyes were strained and red. Shock had traveled throughout her body and to her face. He guessed she was as near to distraught as she was ever going to get. Like him, she was taking a count of the soldiers. There were close to two hundred. Another seventy or so had been left behind in Brigham City because of the bitter cold. The soldiers were not only unsaddling and graining their horses, but they were checking their Colt .44 and Colt dragoon revolvers, their Springfield Model 1861 rifles, their Smith carbines, and occasionally unsheathing and rattling their dragoon sabers just for the fun of it. They were even unharnessing two teams of horses that had pulled two twelve-pound mountain howitzers.

What all this meant was simple. Connor was going to attack the Shoshoni Indian village Scooter had passed yesterday. The winter camp that held Abby's six-year-old boy. It meant war, war between Union soldiers and the Shoshoni nation. It wasn't hard to imagine the cruelty that would be inflicted.

"Oh, Winny! What'll I do?" Abby asked as she buried her face in her hands. "I've got to get Yahnai out of that camp!"

Scooter wondered if that was practical. Bear Hunter would warn the others, but he didn't know Connor's true strength. The chief had muttered something about there not being enough soldiers to worry about. Bear Hunter was wrong. There were more than enough soldiers to wreak havoc on the camp. Scooter was certain that Connor wouldn't allow Abby or anyone else to ride to the camp.

Abby had a problem. A huge one. She knew it, and so did Winny.

She said, "Winny, I'm going to ride to the camp right now and get Yahnai out of there before it's too late."

"Abby, don't be hasty." Winny's tone was low and serious, almost a whisper. "I'm certain these soldiers won't let anyone out of the settlement. Not even you."

Winny's blunt statement had an impact. Scooter watched as Abby stiffened in an all-purpose expression of misery. She was on the verge of collapse, as though she had taken a savage beating. Her breathing was shallow, and her tear-filled eyes were vacant. Winny took her by the hand to comfort her.

Within earshot, two red-faced, frostbitten soldiers made it worse with their upbeat conversation about the impending battle. The first, a man with eyes as cold and mean as if he hated his own mother, said, "I can't wait till we hit that Injun camp."

The other bull-necked soldier asked as he inspected his rifle, "Are these cussed Mormons even worth it?"

"We're not doing it for the Mormons. We get to kill Injuns."

"It'll make the long trip in a blizzard worth it when we riddle 'em with bullets."

"Soon those Injuns will be *pfffft!*"

Scooter had been around these types of soldiers before, men filled with some kind of dumb courage and strength and resilience, ready for battle.

"No wonder Bear Hunter left so quickly," Winny said wistfully.

Abby hung her head. "I shouldn't have let Yahnai go. I was wrong—stupid—to let Sagwitch take him away. I had a feeling I shouldn't, but I ignored it."

No doubt the attack on the Shoshoni camp was imminent. Scooter knew that as soon as Bear Hunter hit the camp, all the Shoshoni would be simmering in a broth of doom and fear. But he didn't know if imminent meant right now, in the morning, or in a day or two after Connor's soldiers and their mounts rested. They'd been on a continual march since Salt Lake City.

It began to snow harder. The flakes swirled around Scooter, blowing over and under his hat, clogging his hair and his eyelashes, and drifting down his neck. Every layer of air pulsed with cold.

Abby paced the frozen turf and glanced in the direction of the settlement's corrals, not far away. Scooter followed her gaze. Several of the settlement's horses were there running in circles, trying to adjust to the influx of the cold and hungry army horses. The animals' ears were perched forward,

Scooter grasped Abby's arm firmly and warned, "I know what you're thinking. Winny's right. Without permission, Connor won't let you leave."

"Then I'll *get* permission," she said defiantly. "I have to, for Yahnai's sake." She thrust herself in front of the nearest soldier and asked, "Where is your colonel?"

The soldier took a long drag on his cigarette and blew out gray smoke. "Having his dinner with our guide, Porter Rockwell, and some other Mormons."

"Porter Rockwell? Where?"

Scooter had heard of Porter Rockwell, a famous Mormon.

The soldier said, "He was invited to one of the cabins. The Jacobs' cabin."

Scooter watched Abby's jaw drop. It wasn't good news for her. Nor was it good news for him.

"Follow me, both of you," Abby said. With those words, she locked her eyes on Isaac's cabin and started a beeline in that direction. Scooter twitched and shuffled and hesitated for a moment. To be out in the square with ordinary soldiers was one thing. Standing face-to-face with Colonel Connor was another. He questioned how deeply he wanted to become involved with all this.

She turned. "Scooter, please. I need your support."

Her voice was full of supplication, as though he had become the most important man in her life. He heaved a ponderous sigh and followed. As far as he was concerned, Abigail Butterfield Browett had the ability to talk a cow out of her calf. But could she talk a power-hungry colonel out of attacking the Shoshoni camp? He had his doubts. Scooter paced himself alongside her, head down, hands in his pockets.

When they reached the cabin, Abby didn't knock. She thrust the door open and stepped inside with clenched fists.

Chapter 14

T WAS OBVIOUS IN A flash to Scooter who each man sitting at Isaac's table was. Porter Rockwell was the man in civilian clothes with a full beard and long dark hair. Colonel Connor wore a blue army uniform. His mutton-chop sideburns seemed to have taken over his whole face. Isaac Jacobs and Bishop Thomas sat opposite Connor and Rockwell. The smell of baked bread and beef stew wafted through the cabin. The bishop's wife was there, taking over the meal since Isaac had no wife; she ladled stew onto plates. The men had been enjoying a meal with bright, happy faces, but now they stared in unison at Abby, waiting for her to prove her intention.

Nobody spoke for a few seconds. The silence was strange. It seemed to carry in it unstated answers spiraling crazily upward and outward.

Porter Rockwell politely stood at the sight of the women. He had a confident bearing but was not a tall man. Following Rockwell's lead, Isaac and the bishop stood also. Isaac's look was one of apology, as though he'd stepped on a raw egg.

Connor remained seated, surly, unwilling to make the kind of social gesture that standing for a woman would represent. Abby gave him a look that would have blinded him if looks were knives. He was not a big man but not small either—average build, not too lean, not too muscular. A man perhaps in his early forties, he looked like he'd been a soldier since birth. Scooter knew enough about the colonel to know that plenty of Irish blood flowed through his veins, filtered by service in the US Army since age nineteen, with action in the Seminole and Mexican Wars. Like many officers Scooter had known during the war, Connor reeked with worldly ambition and a lust for dominance.

Abby didn't wait for a proper introduction. She pointed a stiff, admonishing finger at Connor. "I know why you're here. You plan on attacking the Shoshoni. I have an adopted child in their winter camp. I'm going to saddle my horse and ride out to get him. You're the commanding officer. It's up to you to tell your soldiers not to stop me." She spoke with the rambling fluency typical of the truly anxious.

Her words hung in the air like a heavy layer of smoke.

Scooter lowered his hat. He breathed in and out, telling himself to relax. Connor's eyes were on him for a split second. He had the feeling Connor immediately knew he wasn't one of the settlers but also not a specific target of suspicion. Nothing wrong with being a freighter. The colonel turned his full attention to Abby. He cocked his eyebrows and looked irritated, as though he'd just eaten a plateful of garlic and onions. His gaze swept Isaac Jacobs, Porter Rockwell, Bishop Thomas, and then returned to Abby.

"Who is this woman?" he asked in a booming voice, the voice of an officer questioning a lowly private.

Isaac Jacobs swallowed hard and raised a hand. "Colonel, this is Abigail, my intended. Let me handle this."

"You haven't taught her to knock? You ought to take her out and spank her."

Scooter glared at Connor, bunched his hands into fists, and inched closer to Abby.

Isaac hopped toward Abby, put an arm around her, and tried to pull her toward the door, but she didn't budge. Isaac used a hushed, low-pitched tone, the way a father might speak to a disobedient child. "Dear, could you please just go home? I'll come over in a while and fill you in. I know you're concerned about Yahnai, and so am I. But he'll be fine, and so will all the children in that camp."

Abby shoved Isaac aside. "Isaac, you're delusional if you believe that. When the soldiers start shooting, what makes you think Yahnai will be safe?"

Porter Rockwell calmly sat down. He picked up a table knife and buttered a hot slice of bread. He twisted slightly toward Connor. "A response to the little lady won't hurt anything, Colonel. I think you owe her that." There was authority in Rockwell's voice but no menace, just the kind of easy command born of years of experience.

Connor shrugged his shoulders in resignation. He snatched a napkin, wiped around his mouth, pushed his wooden chair back with a noisy rasp, and stood to face her. He had the air of a hero who had been enjoying the worship of not only his soldiers but settlers as well, all up and down the Utah Territory settlements. But when he turned his full attention on her, his mean little features came into proper perspective. He had a pointed nose, high forehead, long brown hair, and yellow teeth. The tips of his fingers were stained with nicotine. His mouth was set in an impatient scowl.

Isaac tried again to calm the situation. "I apologize for her intrusion. She does have a reputation for the dramatic. Preventing her from speaking her mind is like trying to stop snow from falling out of the sky. But what she says is true. She does have an adopted Indian boy, and he's in that camp."

Connor shook his head. "I don't know why a woman like her would adopt an Indian. But she is *not* leaving the settlement." He smiled a confident smile.

Abby folded her arms and widened her stance. "But I *have* to. And I *will.*"

Connor's smile thinned to a sneer. He sliced a flat hand downward through the air. "The answer is no. I will not permit anyone warning the camp. I don't care if you adopted a whole house full of little savages."

"But Bear Hunter saw you coming. He'll warn everyone anyway."

Connor looked at her for a moment and then let out a prideful bark. "You underestimate me. You know nothing of strategy. There was no way we could leave Camp Douglas in full strength without the Indians knowing. So I dispatched seventy men days earlier than our main group. Bear Hunter will be confident. Overconfident. He thinks our ranks are thin. But, as you know, we have a very large force."

Connor had a basso voice, developed from years of smoking, drinking, and yelling. A confrontational voice. Scooter was surprised that the colonel was so willing to share information about his army. But he knew the colonel's tone, the nuances, and the way he spoke.

It told him things. It told him the man was all business, a soldier's soldier, but hostile to civilians—especially women.

Abby clamped her teeth. Scooter could hear them click and grind. "Go back where you came from," she snapped. "We don't need you."

Connor shook his head emphatically. "Little lady, you know as well as I do that the Shoshoni have murdered miners traveling back and forth from Bannack City. And murdered immigrants on the Oregon and California Trails. We've marched through a constant blizzard to get here. I had to leave some men in Brigham City because of frostbite. We *will* prevail. We brought plenty of supplies and two howitzers. I have warrants for the arrest of all the Shoshoni chiefs."

"Every tribe has a few young renegades. If you must, arrest Bear Hunter. Maybe one or two others. But leave everyone else alone."

Isaac pointed his finger at Abby. "Colonel, she knows all about Indian problems, bless her. Shoshoni Indians killed her husband the first year we were here."

"All the more reason to punish them," Connor said.

"The loss of my husband demonstrates my point," she responded. "Just young renegades. I hold no animosity toward the Shoshoni people. One retaliation just leads to another, and things escalate beyond control. Chief Sagwitch apologized to me. He's the one who brought me a boy to adopt. My son's six years old now and the love of my life. I cannot bear the thought that he might be harmed."

Porter Rockwell looked astounded but steadied himself by continuing with his supper, taking enormous bites of bread and choking them down with big spoonfuls of stew.

Isaac Jacobs hung his head.

Colonel Patrick Connor remained pigheaded. "I have no quarrel with women and children. Our fight will be with the warriors. Your child will be safe."

Scooter thought the colonel's promise totally worthless. Put a bunch of young men trained for aggression and reaction against a camp of Indians that included women and children, and gruesome things would happen.

"I don't believe you," Abby said bluntly.

The colonel snorted in derision. "Missy, there are those—and perhaps you are one of them—who contend that this land is inhabited by a noble people who live peacefully and tread lightly, living in harmony with all of nature, but that is not the case. The depredations of the Shoshoni are well documented. I cannot turn back; I will not turn back. After we finish our job, your settlement and the entire area will be safe. My men didn't ride all this way, sleeping in the snow these past nights, just to turn back. We have a job to do. They're itching to show these Indians a thing or two."

"If your men are itching for a fight," Abby said, "let them fight in that terrible Civil War that's raging back East. President Lincoln needs them more there than here."

Scooter cringed. He wished Abby hadn't brought up the war.

"Missy, my men would be proud to fight for Mr. Lincoln, but fate has already rendered its verdict. I have my orders. People throughout the territory are clamoring for total elimination of the Indians. Now I think it's best that you leave while we menfolk speak of important things, things a pretty little thing like you wouldn't understand."

Abby narrowed her eyes. "So you plan to warm your men in our homes, eat our food, and then attack in a day or two?"

The colonel laughed defiantly. "You know nothing of military strategy. We're moving out at three in the morning. We plan to be there before daylight."

Abby visibly faltered. "Before daylight? You *cannot* do that. You *will not* do that. Go back to Salt Lake!"

Connor lost his smile but not his sense of superiority. "Don't blow your nose in military affairs, missy."

Abby thrust a fist toward the colonel's face. "You need to be stopped. And if you call me *missy* one more time, I will slap that smirk off your face."

Scooter placed a hand over his mouth to stifle a laugh.

"You sure you want to get smart with me?" Connor said in a huff. "You're in a big puddle of muck here, and you don't have the shoes for it. I recommend that you do not test my patience." Connor took a menacing step toward Abby.

To counter it, his gut crunching into knots, Scooter took an equally menacing step, placing himself in front of the colonel.

Abby whirled and walked to the door. She placed her hand on the handle and gave one last look at everyone.

"What are you going to do?" Isaac asked. "You need to pull yourself together."

"The colonel leaves me no choice," she said. "I'm going to get Yahnai."

"I'm warning you," the colonel said. "You stay here."

As Abby jerked the door open, Connor said to Rockwell, "Stop that woman!"

"I'm trying to finish my meal," Rockwell said without a trace of emotion.

Chapter 15

THE CONFRONTATION IN ISAAC'S CABIN broke up in a sudden burst of energy. Abby ran outside. She knew Scooter was following her, trying to keep pace. And behind Scooter, Isaac. And behind Isaac, the colonel. She heard Connor's cursing and heavy footsteps on the frozen turf. She riveted her eyes on the nearest cluster of army horses twitching their tails as they fed on grain and hay. She sprinted to them. She found one that had not been unsaddled. She swung up on it and dug her heels into its side.

But Connor had caught up with her. His eyes had gone wide; he was ready to attack. As the horse jumped at her command, Connor grabbed its bridle. Abby felt the horse spin beneath her. She also felt Connor's arm twisting hers. She pitched off onto the frozen ground, landing hard on her back. Air rushed from her lungs. She fought for breath, but it wouldn't come.

Soldiers rushed to the scene, some with guns drawn. Abby looked up as Colonel Connor gave them a quick command, pointing. "Place a guard over this woman."

No sooner did he get the words out than a figure emerged from behind the gathering soldiers. Connor saw the figure too, entering like a bull into a ring, and braced himself. The two men collided. Scooter's broad shoulder ground into Connor's sternum with crushing force. He drove the colonel onto the frozen turf, landing hard on top of him. Scooter drew his fist back to continue the assault, but soldiers pulled him away.

Now it was Connor who gasped. His chest was convulsing, heaving for air that wasn't there. He slowly rolled over, twitched with spasms, and struggled to get to his knees. After a moment, he rose, and when he could get air, he cursed—cursed her, cursed Scooter, cursed the Shoshoni, and cursed the Mormons. As he cursed, he held a hand over his ribs, as if a few of them were broken.

Abby was still on the ground. When she finally caught her breath, she jumped to her feet, but a soldier held her. She glared at the colonel. "You got what you deserved."

"We'll see about that." Connor directed a cold glare at Scooter.

"Please, Abby," Isaac said. "Calm yourself down."

Scooter lurched at the colonel, his Southern accent more pronounced. "You do not knock women off horses around me. Haven't you been taught to respect women?"

Connor ignored the outburst. "Do you know what the penalty is for striking an officer?"

"I'm not one of your men," Scooter retorted as soldiers took his revolver and his knife. "Do you know what God's penalty is for mistreating a woman?"

Connor pointed his finger at Scooter. "Who are you anyway?"

Scooter returned the stare and said nothing.

"You're not one of the settlers, are you? Arrest him. And the woman too."

"He's just a freighter," Isaac said. "He's not from around here."

Abby thought about Yahnai and screamed with frustration. With bony fists she pounded at the soldier who held her, managing to scratch his face. With all the strength she could muster, she broke free and ran a few more steps. Another soldier ran her down, this one big enough to hunt a grizzly bear with a switch. She whirled to lash out at him, but it was useless. He wrapped his powerful arms around her.

The big soldier asked the colonel, "What shall I do with her?"

She screamed at him. "Let me go!"

Connor's anger boiled like lava. "Take her to her cabin, wherever it is. Lock her up. Stuff rags into her mouth. Tie her with rawhide if you have to."

She fought the big soldier again. He tightened his grip—so hard she couldn't breathe. It was useless. She was trapped.

Connor pointed at Scooter. "Take him too. Lock him up with the woman."

Scooter said nothing. Several soldiers held him captive.

Connor turned to Isaac. "Your woman is a wildcat. If I were you, I wouldn't let her in my house, let alone marry her. You Mormons are odd."

Abby's world began to spin. She had been rendered helpless to save Yahnai.

❄ ❄ ❄

Scooter felt awkward in Abby's cabin. The big soldier's presence was foreboding. Scooter stood by the fireplace with Abby but didn't say anything. Sometimes he paced in a tiny circle. Sometimes he wrung his hands. Sometimes he stared at the soldier. He had no regrets about the way he'd put Connor to the ground. He had deserved it. Carl and Winny had come to the door and reported that an army doctor had examined the colonel. Just bruises, no broken bones. That meant Connor would direct his thoughts and anger against the Indians, not against Scooter. Compared to Bear Hunter, he was a mere pimple on the end of Connor's nose. Connor was looking for Indians, not for Confederate deserters.

He looked through Abby's window. The sun had fallen away from the settlement, and darkness was setting in. The temperature was dropping like a stone. Soldiers had pitched tents in the town square and outside it too. Most soldiers were in their shelters, trying their best to stay warm. Only a few remained outside. Some were smoking. Some were tending horses. A light wind rose. It found invisible cracks in Abby's cabin and made invisible drafts and lonesome sounds—cracking, crackling noises. He could hear the brittle chafing of frozen foliage and hollow clicks from frozen tree limbs. The wind sucked the air out the log structure.

Oscar came to visit. Scooter told him to stand by.

Abby paced too. He knew how alone she must feel. Alone against the US Army, alone against the pending sunrise when troops would attack the Shoshoni camp, perhaps even alone against her people. It seemed to him that her only true friends were Winny and Carl. Not even Isaac.

Abby showed no fear. "Let me out of here," she demanded.

"You know I can't," the soldier answered. He stood in front of the door with his arms folded over a massive chest, giving her a slow shake of his huge head.

There was a rap on the door. The big soldier opened it. Isaac Jacobs stood there in the cold. He had no news in his eyes, just concern. "Are you all right?" he asked Abby.

"No. Talk to Porter Rockwell and get me out of here."

"I've already tried," he said. "The colonel wants you locked up until morning."

Abby closed her eyes and opened them again, like she was erasing this nightmare from her memory.

Isaac eyed Scooter. "If it weren't for the fact that the colonel has a lot on his mind right now, you'd be in serious trouble. You struck an officer of the Union army."

"I know," Scooter said. "I guess I buggered him up good."

Isaac reached out and touched Abby's shoulder. "I'll check on you later. Carl and Winny are home with their children. Said they'd see you in the morning."

Abby said nothing, just nodded as Isaac left and the door closed.

She turned her attention to the corn-fed soldier who had been giving her disapproving looks. He had an air about him. Like he knew he was big. Like he knew he was a sergeant. Like he had earned his rank with some kind of act of valor.

"What now?" she asked.

"Just stay calm," the big soldier said. "You're in trouble. The colonel doesn't like you. If I were you, I'd keep my mouth shut until we're gone."

"Keeping my mouth shut has never been one of my strengths."

"I can believe that."

Scooter lit a candle. The sergeant's meaty red face was stern, fully bearded, his eyes incisive and clear. Staring at Abby. Staring at him.

"What's your name?" she asked.

"Sergeant White."

"I don't trust your colonel. I don't think you do either."

"I'm a soldier. I serve my country."

"Some of the soldiers out there are evil. What will they do in the morning to the women and children?"

Sergeant White shrugged. "I can't speak for every man."

"I have an adopted Indian son in the camp. He's all that matters to me. I desperately need to get him out of there. Let me leave."

"You know I can't do that."

"People will die in the morning. Some of the Indians are my friends."

"And some are bad. We aim to make it safer for whites around here. The colonel has a passion for military justice."

Sergeant White's words fell heavy on Scooter.

Abby said, "Your colonel is as charming as a mouthful of sawdust and water."

"He may lack charm, but he knows a lot about fighting Indians."

"Word from our people in Salt Lake is that Colonel Connor's ambition is to ruin us economically and compel us to give up our beliefs."

"He considers it his duty to encourage Gentiles to settle in Utah Territory and overturn Mormon dominance. He wants to purge the West of Indians so more people will come here."

"Including Indian women and children? Does he want to purge Mormons?"

"He thinks Mormonism is a fool's errand. Me, I'm not so sure."

Abby's tone turned low. "You know it's wrong to kill children. Sneak me out of here and maybe you can face your Maker come Judgment Day."

"Sometimes it's ugly business, doing one's duty. I'll be outside with the others."

The sergeant touched his forefinger to the tip of his hat in a lazy imitation of a salute, but it showed his respect. He took small steps to her door, walking half backward, taking his leave of the gloom inside.

"What now?" Scooter asked, still feeling peculiar.

Abby paced the floor, twisting her hands. "How long do you think it would take to reach the Indian camp by horseback?"

"Half an hour, depending on how much galloping the horse could take."

She nodded at the window. "I have a fast horse out in the corrals."

"It's obvious you're not going anywhere until the soldiers leave. Get some sleep."

"How do you expect me to sleep?"

"I don't know. Do your best."

Her toned turned hushed, almost a whisper. "You shouldn't have stopped here yesterday. Now you're in trouble, big trouble."

She sat at her sawbuck table and fell silent. She placed her hands on the table and twisted them again. Scooter said nothing as he sat across from her. He put his hands on the table. She moved her hand, very slowly. Her fingers moved almost imperceptibly over the rough surface of the table until they were a fraction of an inch from his. Then she lifted and moved until they were directly over his and just a fraction above. It was like there was a layer of warm air between their hands. She brought her hand down, and her fingers lightly touched the backs of his. Then she pushed down. His hand felt warm. He turned it over, and she pressed her palm into his. He squeezed back. They held hands for several minutes.

"Thank you for being here," she said.

Chapter 16

THE LENGTH OF THE NIGHT was a torment for Abby, with nothing to do but drip with anxiety. She was a prisoner. She felt hopeless. All she could think about was Yahnai. Scooter lay on the floor but didn't sleep either. Finally, she heard soldiers harnessing their teams to wagons and saddling horses in the dark. Aggravated, she rapped on the door.

"Sergeant White? Sounds like the wolves are leaving their lair," she said. "It must be three o'clock. So why don't you leave too?"

"Don't you ever sleep?" he asked.

Abby looked out her window. It had quit snowing. A half-moon shining through broken clouds illuminated the busy troops. The wind howled across the square with a low drone.

"Leave me, Sergeant White. All of you."

"I have new orders," White said. "You will be under guard until daylight. By then, the colonel and our army will be at the Shoshoni camp."

The little cabin went quiet, like all the air had been sucked out of it. Bad news and Abby groaned at it. She guessed that Bear Hunter wouldn't run and that he was preparing the Shoshoni people for the battle of their lives. She just hoped that he and Sagwitch had the sense to evacuate Yahnai and all the women and children and elderly. She closed her eyes and tried to envision what it would be like, fleeing the camp. Perhaps like walking across a canyon on a tightrope that was being shaken on both ends. She hoped Yahnai was on the back of someone's horse, hanging on to the rider, headed perhaps west toward the Malad Valley or north toward the headwaters of the Marsh Creek or even east toward Bear Lake.

She asked the sergeant, "Aren't you afraid you'll miss your share of killing?"

"I'll leave just before daybreak and ride fast. I won't miss much."

"God will forgive you for what this army is about to do if you six men break ranks and warn the camp."

"No dice, lady."

"I hope you all freeze to death before you get there," she said.

❈ ❈ ❈

When the first wisps of red fanned out over the eastern sky, Sergeant White and the other soldiers rode away. Abby opened her door as they vanished from the square. It was a relief to hear their horses' hooves thundering off to the north. The image of Yahnai swam in her eyes like a curl of smoke or a flake of down. Whenever she closed her eyes, she could imagine Connor unleashing his firestorm of death. She felt so helpless.

Scooter burst to life, peering out the door. "They're gone. Let's ride."

Abby held a hand over her heart. What had started as a curious social call had turned into a life-and-death situation, something that was none of Scooter's business. Yet he had just volunteered to go with her. She stretched a knitted wool cap over her head and nodded her acceptance.

"Do you have an extra horse?" Scooter asked.

"Yes. There are saddles and tack in the stable near the corrals. Carl will probably be there, along with other of our men. Are you sure you want to do this?"

"I'll be cheering for the Indians," he said.

His statement gave her a lift from the awful situation. She put everything she had for warmth on her body and rushed to the corrals, Scooter keeping pace with her. The square was littered with manure and covered with horse and wagon tracks. Several settlers were already saddling up, talking, their curiosity boiling over. They told her they intended to form a communication line between the battle field and Franklin in case the Indians prevailed.

Abby nodded. She didn't know which would be worse: soldiers killing Indians or Indians killing settlers. It had come to that.

Evan Browett had left her with two horses, a bay mare and a sorrel gelding with a white face. Snip had an erratic disposition but was noted for her speed. Abby cornered the mare and put a rope around her neck. The muscles in Abby's arms bunched as she lifted her saddle onto the mare. Her fingers were precise and quick with the straps and the cinch and the buckles. Scooter saddled the gelding Evan had named Bolly.

"Sister Browett, where are you going?"

Abby whirled to find Isaac behind her, a bridle in his hand. He leaned toward her like he had a point to make. "Where do you think?" she said.

His tone was aghast. "That's no place for a woman."

"And no place for a child either," she shot back. "The soldiers could keep me here, but you can't."

"You'd better stay," Bishop Thomas said. "We'll bring you a report."

Abby shook her head and tightened her cinch. "It's impossible to sit here not knowing what's happening. Maybe I'll find Yahnai before the soldiers do." She put her left foot in the stirrup. The mare huffed through her nose and shifted her feet. Abby gripped the saddle horn with her left hand, bounced twice on her right leg, and swung upon the bay as deftly as any man in the settlement.

Carl handed Scooter the gun and knife the soldiers had confiscated the previous day.

Isaac let his hand glide over the long winter hair of the bay mare's neck. "Your horse will collapse under you if you push her too hard."

Abby pulled on the reins, forcing the mare to back away from Isaac and the bishop. Her bonnet was down over her eyes. She heard the crunch of cold leather behind her as Scooter and Carl swung onto their mounts. She clicked her tongue and kicked her heels. "Let's ride," she said.

The purple color of dawn grew lighter and reddened at its base, spreading upward and outward until half the sky was streaked with light. Abby hardly noticed. She pressed Snip into a steady gallop until the mare tired so badly that she had to slow to a walk. She wished Snip felt the same sense of urgency she did. She also wished Evan were with her. He had spent most of his life on a horse and could ride in any condition short of paralysis. Surely he was watching over her during this perilous hour.

Scooter and Carl were a hundred yards behind her.

The unvarying emptiness of the winter landscape disturbed her, and she was already disturbed enough by the thoughts of what might be happening. The world was deep-frozen. Her cheeks and chin were numb. Her eyes watered. Her lips were too cold and cracked to speak. Even her teeth hurt. Nothing was moving except the wind. It was blowing steadily out of the west, scouring powder into small, stunted drifts and exposing ridges of ice that glittered blue in the dim light.

She was the first to see the two howitzers stuck in a snowdrift and left behind by the soldiers. Lucky for the Indians, the artillery pieces had proved to be as maneuverable as a piece of bread in a bowl of cold mush. She wished Connor were stuck there too, frozen as an icicle, but he wasn't.

She reached a bluff overlooking Bear River. As the sun continued to rise, the blueness diminished, and she tried to assimilate the distant scene before her. The Shoshoni had established their winter camp in a deep ravine on the north side of the river. It stretched out for nearly a mile. She coaxed Snip into a trot and moved closer. She heard rifles and revolvers firing. Dull percussion sounds, robbed of their power and impact by distance and wind and earth. But nevertheless the sure sound of death. She bit back tears. She saw soldiers below, some tending to the wounds of others. Across the river she could see heavy smoke. The battle was nearly over. Where was Yahnai? Scooter and Carl rode near her but said nothing.

Abby's heart pounded in her ears. "We'll have to cross the river."

Scooter nodded. "Be careful though. The river has ice in it."

She dug her heels into the mare again and screamed her son's name. "Yahnai!"

Snip broke into a gallop straight toward the river. Abby leaned forward, expecting the mare to lunge into the black water and cross, but that didn't happen. At the river's edge, Snip skidded to an abrupt stop. The inertia hurled Abby off, and she plunged headfirst into a frozen abyss. The icy water took her breath away, just as it had at the crossing the day she'd met Scooter. Reflex was her only compass. She floundered. She knew she had to reach the other side. Fueled only by adrenaline, barely conscious of her actions, she poked her head to the surface. A force was carrying her downstream. She flailed her arms wildly, swimming. Her elbows and knees stiffened. Her clothing, heavy and burdensome, pulled at her. She lunged at the opposite shore, but her muscles wouldn't obey.

She felt the river towing her away, away from Yahnai. *Dear God, no! I'm the only person who can save my boy!* Her resolve caused her to scream out Yahnai's name again and again. She found she could stand. Suddenly her body was in motion, panic and instinct taking over. She dug her feet into the rocky bottom of the river and clawed her way forward, screaming again, "Yahnai! Yahnai."

Behind her, she heard the sound of two horses plunging through the river. She heard Scooter's voice. "Abby! I'm right behind you!"

Abby whirled. "Help me!"

He stopped the sorrel and reached for her. She reached for him. Her icy hands grasped his warm, strong one. He tugged at her. She knew her soaked clothing made her heavy, maybe twice her normal weight. He shook his foot away from the stirrup. As he pulled, she found a way to get her foot into the stirrup. Water dripped off her. She settled behind Scooter and kicked at the sorrel.

"Let's go! Hurry!"

The sorrel plunged through the water and reached the other side. Bolly pawed at the bank with his front legs and used his hind quarters to propel his body out of the water. She kicked the sorrel in the ribs again. He galloped as if in a race. And it was a race, a race to save Yahnai. The horse sped toward the Indian camp, less than a half mile away. Carl was right behind them. Abby could smell burnt gunpowder. She heard screams. She couldn't see anyone, but she knew it was bad. She trembled, knowing Yahnai was out there in the darkness somewhere.

Even though she'd had nightmares for hours, she wasn't prepared to comprehend the savage destruction of human life. There had been, and still was, a drumbeat of death among Connor's soldiers. They had overrun everything. The camp was hardly more than a crypt for the dying and dead. There were clusters of burning wickiups and teepees, surrounded by bodies, all Indian. More bodies clogged the river.

She wondered how many had been shot right in the river as they attempted to escape.

"Yahnai!"

In the middle of what had been the battlefield, she slid off Scooter's horse. The smell and look of death were everywhere. She shivered in a violent, uncontrollable spasm. She closed her eyes for a few seconds, keeping a hand over her mouth to protect her from the stench. Injured women were being raped. She looked away, ashamed that white soldiers were responsible. She felt the urge to find a club and use it against the soldiers. Her desire to protect the women was overrun only by the desire to find her son. Something pushed her onward, to believe he was still alive.

"Yahnai!" There was no answer. "Scooter, do something to help those women!"

Scooter found a discarded tomahawk and threatened a soldier until he stopped his attack against one of the women. Abby pressed forward.

The soldiers had begun a systematic walk through the camp, using their bayonets to determine if an Indian was dead or alive. Abby saw a soldier walking through the battlefield with erect shoulders, revolver drawn in one hand, ax in the other, looking for survivors. His legs moved stiffly, as if in pain. The wind was cold, the blowing mist snapping away his frozen breath. Dogs were everywhere, licking at the dead. Abby staggered back in horror, the image of all this searing itself into her memory forever.

"Yahnai!"

Abby felt the tightening grip of someone behind her.

"This is too much," Scooter said. "Even for me. I've got to get you out of here."

Abby ripped herself free. Her face was a frozen slab. She was breathing hard, freezing air burning down her windpipe and searing her lungs. "No, you're not! Yahnai? Yahnai? Where are you?"

"Stay with the horse. Let me find him for you," Scooter said.

"No! I'll find him. Leave me alone."

A soldier gave Abby an icy stare. He held his revolver like a child would hold a toy. "Look around you, lady. This is the end of the Shoshoni."

"Go away," Carl growled.

She tried to ignore what the soldier had said. She felt the same horror as mothers under King Herod, mothers whose babies had been slaughtered without mercy. She begged God for mercy and grasped the thought that both John the Baptist and Jesus had escaped that great massacre. Surely God could spare Yahnai.

"Yahnai!"

Was there not at least one soldier whose volatile sense of guilt would spark a strong, courageous desire to stop what they were doing? Where was Sergeant White? Alas, soldiers returned curious stares at her and continued their wanton carnage.

Then she saw it, the body of a child that could be Yahnai. It was a boy about the same size and age, but no blue sweater or sheepskin coat visible. She felt that her head would burst. In the faint hope she'd find signs of life, Abby knelt by the boy and turned him over. A moment passed before her mind cleared and she confirmed that it was not Yahnai.

She let out a cry of relief mingled with sorrow for the loss of the little one.

Next to the boy, an old man lay dying. With each breath he let out a throaty moan. His wounds had bloody bubbles on them. Abby collapsed to her hands and knees and vomited. After a few minutes she crawled away and began to wail. Terrible sounds came out of her; tears coursed down her cheeks, freezing in immutable layers. There were tears of confusion, tears of horror, and tears of fury.

Scooter squatted next to her. He put his elbows on his knees and slowly clasped his hands together. And then he gently touched her, placing a hand on her shoulder. "I've got to get you across the river, away from all this."

"But where is Yahnai? Where is he?" she sobbed.

Scooter shrugged helplessly.

Not far away, a few survivors huddled together like terrified sheep.

Carl reasoned with her in a voice that rattled with shocked tension. "Abby, it's a good sign we haven't found him. It means he's alive."

"The soldiers said a few escaped," said Scooter. "Maybe he was one of them."

"But he's so young, so defenseless," Abby said.

"He's young and strong," Scooter said. "Keep your chin up."

Abby couldn't do it. Despite the fact that Scooter and Carl were doing all they could to calm and comfort her, she let go of all hope. She wanted nothing more than to ride one of the wandering horses over the nearest cliff. In a world of such darkness, it would be a mercy.

Chapter 17

SCOOTER COULD BARELY FATHOM WHAT Abby had endured. It was imperative to get her across the river. She was not only in shock, frozen, and sick, but she'd begun to go into a stupor of sorts. Her eyes were twin pools of terror and tragedy, brought on by what she'd seen. She'd seen chaos, and she'd seen horror. She was soaked from head to toe. Ice was forming on her clothing. The cold battered Scooter, too, froze and tormented him. His ears burned, and his nose and chin prickled and itched. He knew it was worse for her. He remembered how she hated the sight of blood. She'd seen enough of it here to cure her fear of it.

He felt low, lower than he'd ever been in his life, almost ashamed to be human. He'd seen the killing that soldiers inflicted on each other at the Battle of Bull Run and at Shiloh—where thousands upon thousands died—but nothing that matched this outright cruelty and savagery. At those battles, no children died. Women were not raped. Abby's grieving reminded him of his mother's grieving over the loss of her husband and two sons. He prayed Abby would be spared such poignant sorrow. There remained the possibility that Yahnai was alive. Perhaps he *did* escape. There was reason for hope. They had searched but had not found him.

How the gruesome battle unfolded and why the soldiers had been allowed to kill children after Connor's promise was pregnant with mysteries. Scooter aimed to find out. He wished he had his Richmond rifle, a Confederate copy of the Springfield Model 1861 rifle he'd used in the war. He pictured raising it to the ready position, nestling the stock high against his right shoulder, and aiming it at one of the Union soldiers he'd seen violating Indian women.

It was time to leave this frozen scene only hell could rival.

The *pop-pop-pop* of shooting had almost stopped. Soldiers were rounding up Indian horses and looking for articles of value, like buffalo skins, firearms, tomahawks, knives, arrows, and beaded items. They were smashing clay pots full of roots and dried fish. Torching anything in the way of shelter. Sacks of flour and wheat by the score were being carted across the river—whose churning waters ran red with blood. A few wounded Indian women had been left to fend for themselves.

He insisted that Abby leave. He mounted the sorrel and pulled Abby up behind him. She felt almost lifeless. He could feel her shiver. He shivered too. No more did she shout Yahnai's name. He felt her body against his back, her head against his shoulders. He put the sorrel into a brisk walk. The horse snorted often, as a horse will do when it smells blood, and shied away from the bodies. When they came to the river again, the sorrel paused, sniffed at the water, and plunged in without any trouble, leaving the gruesome battlefield behind.

Scooter could understand soldiers killing warriors, but killing children was senseless. He wondered who had killed the boy Abby found. He began to think that he should have been as vocal as Abby last evening when she quarreled with the colonel. If he could have persuaded at least the Mormons to swing to her side, perhaps the colonel would have at least gone out of his way to prevent his men from harming women and children. Tears came to his eyes as he thought about it.

In the distance Scooter saw a fire, and he headed for it. Soldiers may not have gotten a full night of sleep, but they were functioning, caught up in the excitement of their victory. Some were dragging lodge poles across the river, poles that had been used to support teepees, to use for the fire. Others were erecting a makeshift shelter. Soldiers were now using axes to chop and split wood as if it were a routine day in camp. None looked tired or stressed, which Scooter found impressive, given the weather and the forced march.

When they reached the fire surrounded by several soldiers, Abby surprised him by sliding off the back of the sorrel. He thought it would be hours before she showed any life. Before Scooter could stop her, she reached down and grasped a chopped-off end of a pole, about the length of a man's arm. She gripped it tightly in her right hand and headed for the nearest soldier, screaming at the top of her lungs. The soldier saw her coming but couldn't believe it. He looked blank. He angled away from her, but he wasn't quick enough.

"Murderer! Murderer!"

Abby focused on him, driving off her back foot. She swung the club in a fast blur, whipping it in the air, aiming at his head. It struck him perfectly, just above the ear. Scooter heard the crack. The soldier felt the full impact. He let out a howl. Momentarily he went loop-legged, struggling to regain his balance. He finally collapsed to the frozen turf, holding his skull. The other soldiers jumped back, shocked at what they'd seen.

Scooter jumped off the sorrel, but by then Abby was attacking another soldier, one that held an ax. She twisted at the waist, building torque, and hurling her club at the retreating figure. She caught him in the right forearm with another swing. The sound was different. No crack, just a dull thud. The soldier dropped the ax and jerked back with a scream. He staggered backward on stiff legs, crying that his arm was broken.

The first soldier was still on the ground, scrabbling around on his back like a turtle, trying to get up again, probably ashamed he'd been felled by a woman. He botched snow angels in the ground, his head snapping right and left, groaning.

Abby chased yet another soldier, swinging her club, using sweeping, scything actions, her breath smoking in the frigid air. The soldier danced away, casting a helpless glance at Scooter. Where Abby got her stamina after all she'd been through, Scooter didn't know. She was a force of her own.

"Murderer! You're all murderers!"

Scooter closed in on her. "Abby! Don't do that! Give me the club."

A dozen or so soldiers closed in on her too. She held them off, still swinging.

One said, "You *are* a wildcat, just like the colonel said."

"You can't club us all to death, lady," said another. "Put it down."

"Murderers!" she screamed as the wary soldiers circled.

Scooter stepped into the circle. His eyes met theirs. He gave them a look that said, *You die, or I die, right now.* They stared back, confused. "Don't touch her," he said.

"Get their revolvers, Scooter," she said. "How would they like to be shot in the face, like they did to those women?"

Undeterred, Scooter took the club from her. With all the venom he could muster, he spoke to the soldiers. "Move out of our way."

Abby hadn't cooled off yet. "All these men will burn in hell. They're murderers!"

Scooter pinned Abby's arms. She didn't want to be pinned. He lifted her, flailing and screaming, off the ground and carried her to the fire.

What she had done amazed him, given her condition. She was not only half frozen but had lost everything in her stomach. Her color was still off; she was pale as the snow that covered the ground.

"You take our fire," said one skittish soldier as he followed other dispersing soldiers. "We'll build another. There are blankets by the fire. Take those too."

Scooter guessed that Abby's outburst had done more to raise her body temperature than the fire would. She was shaking. Whether still in anger or if the cold had gotten to her again, he didn't know. She sank to the ground, letting the heat reach her. He wrapped a wool blanket around her.

He saw Bishop Thomas and Isaac Jacobs walking toward them, hugging themselves against the cold. Abby didn't acknowledge them. Scooter spent ten minutes telling them what had happened—how Abby had been pitched off in the river and scoured the battlefield, searching for Yahnai. They asked questions. He answered them. Yahnai had not been found. There remained the slim possibility that he had escaped.

Isaac shook his head sadly. Concern filled his eyes. He placed his hand on her head. With the other, he reached into his pocket. He spoke softly. "Sister Browett, dear, I'm sorry for what you've been through. Are you hungry? I have some corn dodgers."

Abby shook her head and wiped tears from her eyes. "How can you think of food at a time like this?"

Isaac dropped his head. He stood there a moment and then stepped back as two soldiers approached the fire. The larger man was Sergeant White. He looked unhappy, like a man with bad news to bear. The other soldier was skinny, even in his winter clothes, and had big eyes that bulged a little in his thin face. He stood behind his sergeant as if expecting Abby to erupt again.

White said to Scooter, "Some of our men say Mrs. Browett has gone plumb crazy. You need to take her back to the settlement. She's made a lot of men nervous. They don't want to be around her."

Abby struggled to her feet stiffly, in slow motion. She made a gesture with her hand like she was pushing the sergeant's observation aside. As if she could feel the mass hatred of all Connor's soldiers for any human covered with copper-colored skin. As if the soldiers were carrying out an assassination rather than a mere police or military action. She had a hard time forming words, but she did. "Better crazy than a murderer."

Sergeant White backed off, and so Abby knelt again by the fire.

"Where is your colonel?" Scooter asked.

White said, "Back and forth, tending to the wounded, interviewing soldiers."

"What about Sagwitch?" the bishop asked.

White hunched his shoulders. "We've found the bodies of Bear Hunter, Sanpitch, and Lehi. We think we got Sagwitch, but we don't know for certain."

"How many warriors got away?" Carl asked.

"Not many. It'll take days to find out, maybe weeks."

"Anything we can do?" the bishop asked.

"That's why I'm here," the sergeant said. "The colonel has instructed Rockwell to hire settlers to bring sleighs and wagons here to haul our dead and wounded back to Franklin. Rockwell wants to know if any of you men would help. The army will pay forty-two dollars per sleigh."

"I have freight wagons at the settlement," Scooter said.

Abby erupted again. "Don't you *dare* do it, Scooter."

"I guess my wagons are not for hire," Scooter said to the sergeant, lowering his voice. "But we'd like to have your version of what happened here."

"I don't want to listen to it," Abby said.

"I've already heard all I want to hear," the bishop told Scooter. "I'll stay with Sister Browett while you step away. Isaac can help me build the fire up."

With Sergeant White, Scooter stepped out of earshot and spent several minutes getting details of how the battle unfolded. White told the whole story, holding nothing back, starting from when the Indian camp came into view at the first twinges of daylight, the attack, the fighting, the death and injury of several soldiers, the Indians running out of ammunition, and the final victory.

"You didn't say anything about killing women and children," he said when Sergeant White finished his story. "We got here as the battle was winding down. After we crossed the river, we saw soldiers raping women and using axes to finish off the wounded and to kill children, even babies. Did you see any of that?"

Sergeant White looked down and shuffled his feet. "There were a lot of things you *didn't* see, like how their women fought just as savagely as warriors and some of the older children too."

"I'm certain the women and children had to fight for their lives, but I hope to God you did not take part in the raping of women or killing innocent children."

The sergeant shook his head. "No, I didn't take part in it. I'm sorry it happened. Just between you and me, the colonel lost control. We were lucky the Indians ran out of ammunition. We would have suffered a lot more casualties."

Scooter wondered how much Sergeant White's story would vary from the official report Connor would later make, or even from other soldiers' accounts. He suspected that every soldier's perspective would be different. Scooter had his own conclusions. The Shoshoni warriors were handicapped because of the large number of women, children, and aged adults that needed protection. They were fighting with outdated rifles along with traditional weapons such as bows and arrows and tomahawks. And they ran out of ammunition, whereas the soldiers had an almost unending supply. Scooter concluded that Colonel Connor's ruse had worked. It was obvious that Bear Hunter thought Connor's strength was far less than it was. Had Bear Hunter known the truth, he might have scattered the camp before the soldiers arrived. Scooter speculated that there were still a few shocked and devastated Indians hiding in the willows and that a few had escaped to the north. Unless Yahnai's body was in the river, maybe he was with them.

Scooter had his own challenge. He had to get Abby back to Franklin. Right now she was kneeling by the fire in a stupor, with her Mormon bishop watching over her. She was wrapped in blankets, her teeth were chattering, and her color was off.

Scooter trudged back to Abby, amazed at what he had gotten himself into.

This was all madness.

Chapter 18

WHEN THEY RETURNED TO THE settlement, Winny was there. They went inside Abby's cabin, where Winny had a fire going. The two women hugged and cried. Scooter waited it out. He knew how they felt. As Winny asked questions, Abby sputtered answers. Scooter helped when he could. Winny's eyes were full of sympathy and concern. Abby's eyes were full of hate for the soldiers. The events had aged her another twenty years. Scooter built the fire up, then went back outside and watched Connor's soldiers trickle into the settlement. When Winny came out, she said that Abby wanted to rest forever under a pile of quilts with the fire banked up.

"Do you think she'll sleep?" he asked.

"I hope so," she said. "She refuses to give up. She thinks Yahnai got away."

"It's a good sign that we didn't find him," Scooter said.

Winny left to be with her children. Scooter hovered all afternoon in front of Abby's cabin, talking to Oscar. He had no intention of letting any soldiers near her.

The wounded came on a fleet of eighteen sleighs provided by the settlers. Scooter missed out on any profits he could have made by hiring out his wagons. It would have made matters worse for Abby. She'd be angry enough when she found out that Isaac and the bishop hired their sleighs out, but it was the Christian thing to do. Soldiers were human beings, God's children, same as the settlers. Same as the Indians.

He watched as soldiers were transported into the settler's log meetinghouse. Those with the worst wounds were tended to in homes. The wounds varied in degree. Some were minor—soldiers shot in the arms. Some were worse—shot in the gut, shot in the chest. A few were expected to die. Several already had.

He wondered if Abby would burst out of her cabin and give Connor and the soldiers another tongue lashing. But for now, her door didn't open.

The main body of soldiers returned on military wagons and on horseback, leading Indian ponies they had captured. Even many of those soldiers suffered from frozen feet, so bad they couldn't walk. The joys of being a soldier.

Bishop Thomas sent a few settlers to the battleground to continue the search for Yahnai and to see what they could do for the few surviving Indians. He also ordered a warm fire built and new straw to cover the meetinghouse dirt floor.

The cold finally got to Scooter, crowding him, battering him, tormenting him. He went inside the meetinghouse to warm up. The door was stiff from the cold, but it was warm inside. The fireplace held a crackling fire. Settlers were congratulating soldiers on their victory. God's intervention, some said. The Indians hadn't accepted white man's ways. Less time would have to be spent guarding livestock.

Scooter watched the soldiers with suspicious eyes. He worried about repercussions. After all, he'd flattened the colonel, something not easily forgotten. He only spoke when spoken to. He didn't want anyone to question his accent. He slowly realized no one seemed to be concerned about it. There were other things to be concerned about—ministering to the wounded, feeding the soldiers, and giving them proper rest. Nevertheless, whenever he mingled with the soldiers, Scooter kept a few of his own men around him. Fascinated by what had happened right under their noses, his mule skinners seemed in no particular hurry to return to Salt Lake City.

Connor, he found out, was in Isaac Jacobs's cabin warming up. Scooter was struck by the upbeat spirit of the soldiers. Few complained about the cold or about their frostbitten faces, hands, and feet. Rather, the buzz of talk focused on their triumph and the gory details of the battle. Some seventy teepees and wickiups had been destroyed and their occupants killed. Three soldiers bragged of finding and killing Bear Hunter. Of how they whipped, kicked, tortured, and shot him.

Others told of shooting at an Indian that might have been Sagwitch. The Indian escaped on horseback with a warrior clinging behind him. Well-aimed rifle shots killed the warrior but not the other rider. The other rider might have been hit in the hand. If it were Sagwitch, Scooter wondered where he was now and what he was doing.

Connor made his entrance along with Porter Rockwell, Isaac Jacobs, and Bishop Thomas. Although thoroughly warmed, Connor still gave a theatrical shiver as he stepped into the meetinghouse. Wrapped in exuberance, high-spirited, and loud, he walked among his soldiers. He patted them on the back. He told settlers that the battle had been a complete military success. He added that he still hoped to capture Sagwitch and arrest Shoshoni band leaders such as Pocatello and Washakie, whose people were not in the camp. He suspected them to be in the Malad Valley. Further, he warned the settlers that once the Indians had licked their wounds, they would seek revenge.

Scooter wondered what Sagwitch's attitude would be. After all, the Franklin settlers were nursing and feeding soldiers.

"Believe me," Connor repeated, "I'll eventually wipe out all the Shoshoni."

No sooner had Colonel Connor gotten those words out than the door to the meetinghouse opened. The light revealed the figure of a broken young woman. A gust of warm air seemed to escape, as if the log building were heaving a weary sigh at its uniformed visitors and all the talk of death.

As Abby walked through the door, her sallow eyes searched for one man. Soldiers and settlers alike scurried aside as if Moses were parting the Red Sea. Scooter wondered if she were going to give Connor another tongue lashing. Sergeant White rushed to protect his leader.

The colonel stepped behind Sergeant White. It made a comical sight, Connor trying to make himself scarce. He made a small sound in his throat, the kind of thing Scooter had heard before, when jokes turned out not to be jokes or when dire situations turned from bad to worse.

"Not you again," Connor said. "Tell her to save her sermons. I don't need them."

"You didn't listen very well last time," Rockwell said. "You assured her nothing would happen to the women and children. You've lost credibility in that regard. She may have lost her adopted Indian boy out there. She may have been on the front row when tongues were handed out, but let her speak her peace. You owe it to her."

Connor looked cold as a dead snake. He heaved a big sigh and braced himself.

"You can speak now, Sister Browett," Rockwell said. "But I'd advise you to refrain from scratching the colonel's eyes out. You already broke one soldier's arm and gave another a bad headache, so don't make a move toward him, or I will haul you back to your cabin myself."

Colonel took out his fixings and rolled a cigarette, perhaps to calm himself.

"Would you mind not lighting that?" the bishop asked.

Connor ignored the bishop, lit the cigarette, and blew gray smoke in Abby's direction. He could not hide the wicked expression of his cunning eyes.

Connor fired his first salvo. "So, missy, you have a weak stomach for war?"

Abby's reaction surprised Scooter. There was no salvo of her own. Her face was sad, not angry. Her voice was low, not high. "You lied to me," she began simply.

Connor took another drag on his cigarette and stood rigid as a fence post. "Don't hold your breath, but I've lied before."

Abby maintained control, pressing on with a sad voice. "I hear you've counted two hundred or so dead. There's got to be nearly twice that. Don't women and children count for anything? You think Indians are only potential humans or part human? Is it easier to not know the names of the dead when you do your body count? So much for the glory of the army. My son's name is Yahnai. Y-A-H-N-A-I. Where is he?"

The soldiers stared at the ground and shifted their weight from one foot to the other.

"I was raised in Massachusetts to admire plucky soldiers, but you have disgraced your uniform. You represent Lincoln's army. Don't you have a responsibility to act with some deference to common decency? You should be building a public trust. Not wrecking it. You've broken what little faith we had in the army. What did your soldiers do, have a contest to see who could kill the most babies? Rape the most women? You act as though killing is a sport, not a sin. You feel no guilt? No personal responsibility? What you did is a total betrayal to humanity. Yet you seem to embrace it."

Connor finally spoke, defending his actions. "Consider what we've done to the Shoshoni merely as a gesture of kindness, enabling God to command their souls to heaven more expeditiously. It seems only right."

Scooter expected Abby to erupt, but she didn't. She let Connor shame himself with his comments.

The colonel went on in an irritated huff. "It may interest you to know what we found in the Shoshoni lodges. Evidence that your beloved Indians are guilty of killing and robbing immigrants: jewelry, meerschaum pipes, even hand-sewn women's and children's clothing made by whites. So who has been killing women and children? *The Indians.* We will continue to do what we have to do to solve the Indian problem in all areas of my jurisdiction."

Abby looked away. "I don't know if God will ever forgive you."

The colonel waved her off with a curt gesture of dismissal. "Time for you to go home. I want to wash up and have something to eat."

Abby said, "You can wash off dirt, but you'll never be able to wash off the blood that's on your hands."

Porter Rockwell stepped in front of Abby. "You've made your point, Sister Browett. I'm going to ask the bishop take you back to your cabin. The soldiers will be here tonight and leave tomorrow. Then you'll be rid of them."

Bishop Thomas touched Scooter's arm. "Help me, will you?"

Scooter felt the uneasy stares of everyone in the building. He took a gentle grip on Abby's arm and led her to the door. He agreed with everything Abby had said. There was no excuse for these Union soldiers to kill women and children. Indians were members of the human family. Just like him. And just like his father and two brothers. As Scooter reached Abby's cabin, her knees buckled. She staggered a step, and he caught her and held her tight. Her tears soaked his shirt.

Chapter 19

ABBY DIDN'T SLEEP A WINK that night, not a minute, not a second. She tossed and turned, her eyes and brain jammed with ghastly images and fevered hallucinations. Scenes of the battle swam into sight, as real as if they were hovering just above her ceiling. She saw soldiers ravaging women and throwing babies into the air like they were rag dolls. She saw herself turning the young boy over, the boy who could have been Yahnai. The dead look on his face haunted her. She saw Connor's wicked smile and endless evil. She saw him slipping like a ghost from one end of the battlefield to the next, showing concern and sympathy for his wounded and killed soldiers but none of that for the Shoshoni.

She gave up just before dawn. She was going to go for a walk, but she was afraid she'd be seen. Soldiers were camped in the square. She was offended just by looking out her single window. It was dark, but she could make out the image of the tents. She thought she was hungry, so she found some bread. But in the end, she couldn't eat. She just picked at the bread, tired and dispirited.

Self-pity was an impulse Abby seldom tolerated, but now, as tears welled up from deep within her soul, she knew she had no choice but to let them come. She cried for the women and children who had died on the battlefield. She cried for Yahnai. She cried for the loneliness that filled her heart. And she cried for the future, which suddenly felt so uncertain.

❊ ❊ ❊

Scooter called on Abby the next morning. She had a look in her green eyes that frightened him. He really didn't know what the look meant. But one thing was evident: her mind was somewhere else—on Yahnai, on the battle, and on Connor. But certainly not on him.

The army was pulling out. Scooter concluded he just as well leave too. He had a responsibility to get his men and wagons back to Salt Lake City. With Connor's army ahead of him, he would have an easier time making it through the snow-clogged roads and mountain passes. Winny, Carl, and Isaac, plus all the other tight-knit settlers, could care for Abby. He knew Abby would continue to mourn over Yahnai, whether actually dead or just missing. And she would continue to be haunted by what she'd seen on the battlefield.

He was having a rough time of it too. The scenes came vividly to him in dreams while he slept in a tent with his men. For once, he didn't dream about Billy at the Battle of Shiloh, or about Tommy with his scalp taken off. The Bear River dream had been worse. When he returned to Salt Lake, he would have to find ways to take his mind off those dreams—and off Abby. Rebuilding harnesses, sharpening knives, weaving horsehair lariats, taking care of his livestock, investing his earnings in more livestock and wagons—he could stay busy.

Scooter found Abby still in her cabin when it was time to say good-bye. There was a kind of hopeless, crushed languor in the air. Bereavement showed in the way her shoulders slumped and in her gestures. She ran her fingers through her unwashed hair and then clamped her palms on her ears and twisted side to side, as far as her neck would turn. He wasn't sure if she was easing stiffness in her neck or trying to rid herself of inner turmoil. He stepped inside the door and took off his hat. She didn't look up.

"I'm fixin' to leave," he said.

Her head was down, and her face was pale and filmed with sadness. Her eyes were blank. In the soft light of the flames from her fireplace, her simple and vulnerable beauty was emphasized to the point of heartbreak.

"I know," she whispered. She twisted and looked at Evan Browett's picture and then twisted back again. Everything was quiet, like an observance.

Scooter paused, wishing they could part under more favorable circumstances. Yahnai's bunk was covered with his things, making it a shrine of sorts. There was a drawing of a team of horses pulling a plow.

A paper where he'd practiced his ABCs. A pair of summer moccasins he'd worn. A mason jar filled with sprigs of autumn leaves and sagebrush. They spoke of loss and bewilderment. Abby seemed to be soaking these things up as if the items would help bring the boy back.

"You made some good points with Colonel Connor."

She made a defeated face and asked, "But what good did it do?"

"It did a lot of good. It may make Connor a better man in the future. And it had an impact on me. This whole experience, capped off by what you said, makes me have a different attitude toward Indians."

"Well, I guess that's something," she said.

"Yes, it is," he said.

There were a few moments of silence. He looked at her, noting how her beauty had changed. It was still there but sad and empty. He wondered what feelings she had for him and what feelings she truly had for Isaac Jacobs. If she never healed from this tragedy, would she make a good wife for anyone at all?

He had a question he had to ask. "Will you be Mrs. Isaac Jacobs by spring?"

She shrugged. "I'm determined to look for Yahnai until there is no hope. I'll stay in Franklin at least through summer and fall. Then perhaps I'll go back to my parents in Salt Lake. Without Yahnai, I have no reason to marry Isaac and stay here."

"So you don't love him?"

She didn't answer. He took it that she only loved Yahnai at this point. And that love was causing her pain, too much pain to think about anything else.

"I might pass this way again in the spring."

Her look was still vacant.

"I haven't said my prayers for quite a while, but I'll pray that your boy made it out alive and that someday you'll find him. Time heals almost everything."

"I find that hard to believe."

"What do you mean?"

"That a Missourian would say a prayer."

The statement shocked Scooter. Was she now directing her venom toward him? He knew enough about the Mormons and their experiences in Missouri: Their being perceived as an economic, social, and religious threat. The opposition and persecution that followed. Armed mobs plundering Mormon homes and settlements. The state of war that developed. The government siding with the mob element. An extermination order and expulsion. The hard feelings that developed. Feelings now manifested by Abby. Scooter didn't want to be guilty of the association. He wasn't a Missourian, and perhaps now was the time to clear up the misunderstanding. But at what risk? He had never told anyone about his true past, not even a trusted associate like Oscar. He wondered if confiding with her would help her healing. He decided to take a chance. "I'm not from Missouri."

Her visage turned colder. "Seems that telling lies is quite fashionable. Connor lied to me. Turns out you have lied to me as well."

"I said that I was from Missouri, I suppose, because I started my business there."

She rolled her eyes and looked away.

Scooter realized he had some making up to do. "I'm from Virginia."

"That doesn't necessarily make you a prayerful man."

"I was raised in a God-fearing, Christian family. My parents taught me how to pray. We read the Bible as a family often."

She said nothing.

"Do you believe me?"

"I have no way of knowing for certain. Besides, I guess at this point it's not important where you are from."

Scooter felt compelled to reveal more. "I felt uncomfortable around the soldiers."

"Join the crowd."

"If I go on, you must promise to keep a secret."

"Are you about to tell me another lie?"

"Promise me. Will you keep what I'm about to tell you a secret?"

"If I must." Her eyebrows lifted.

"You must, or I won't continue. You must promise to tell no one what I'm about to tell you. It is extremely important. In many ways, my life depends on the secret I am about to divulge."

She gave him a strange look. "Tell me, then."

Scooter drew a deep breath and then let it out slowly. He began spooling out his background. "I was raised on a large plantation in Virginia, just outside of Richmond. When the war broke out, my father, being an influential man, was persuaded to join the Confederate army. General Lee made him an officer right off. Of course, that meant that I joined. So did my two brothers." His confession hung in the air for a moment.

She stared at him as though he'd just confessed to shooting Abraham Lincoln.

He blurted out the worst. "So that means I'm a deserter, a deserter from the Confederate army. I left my post—not because of homesickness, not because I was afraid to die or because of unsanitary camp conditions, lack of proper clothing, or lack of pay. Or because my mother was starving and needed my protection."

Abby's mouth was open wide in disbelief.

He paused, wondering if he were doing the right thing. Living a life of secrecy defined who he was. He owed the whole of his life to that secrecy right now—his liberty, his status, his freighting business, everything. The war and his leaving his post, becoming a deserter, had initially turned his life upside down. Now he treasured his anonymity. He liked his secrecy. It felt warm and comfortable and reassuring. He guarded it.

He wanted to reach out and touch Abby. But he didn't. He reached deep down and continued. "I'm sure you've heard of the Battles of Bull Run and Shiloh."

She returned a slight nod.

Scooter felt his eyes turn misty. He clasped his hands together. "Those battles took my father and my two brothers."

Abby's jaw dropped.

He continued, "It devastated my mother, as you might imagine. She couldn't stand the thought of losing her last remaining son. She showed up one day at my post. She told me to run, to go out West until the war was over. I didn't want to do it, didn't want to be known as a coward, not then, not in later life. But she begged and pleaded. I had to honor my mother. So I left. She gave me a horse and a passel of Union money, more than enough to go into the freighting business with no debt. So here I am."

He hung his head and looked away. "And as you might expect, my name isn't really David Perkins."

"It's not?" she asked with a bewildered look.

"No. I've gone by the nickname Scooter all my life. So that part is real. But my name is Jesse Kemp."

"Jesse Kemp?" Abby looked as if she wanted to know more details, so he went on.

He'd traveled from Virginia to St. Louis as though everyone were looking for him. Eight hundred miles of lurking in the shadows, camping alone, traveling at night. But he'd changed in St. Louis. He'd had to. He went into the freighting business. Ever since St. Louis, he had been friendly and gregarious on the surface, without ever saying much about himself. He told no one his real name. He found that going by his childhood nickname worked just fine. If someone pressed, he used his alias, David Perkins—both names borrowed from fellow soldiers who'd been his friends.

Being a deserter, being careful, became a defining feature of his life. It made him what he was now. He had never stolen anything. He had never cheated anybody. He wasn't married. He was as anonymous as he could possibly be and still be in business. From St. Louis to Salt Lake City, another thirteen hundred miles, he had gradually learned to relax just a little. Strangers, even soldiers, believed he was David Perkins, a freighter.

"So that's it?" she asked when he stopped.

"That's it," he answered, knowing that there was one other thing in his past. But it was something not to be shared at this point. No use in disclosing the fact that he had nearly been engaged to a young lady in Virginia. A girl named Millie, a girl from whom he still received letters, which he kept in his lockbox under his wagon seat along with letters from his mother. A girl who expected him to return and marry her.

"Well, thank you, then. I guess that clears up the matter about your accent."

"Yes. I'm sorry for the deception."

"I forgive you. But I can't forgive Colonel Connors."

"I understand your feelings."

"I hope so," she said.

"It's time for me to go. My men are waiting. We have to follow the army. Otherwise we risk getting bogged down in the snowdrifts."

"I understand."

"Good-bye, then."

"Good-bye," Abby said.

He stepped out into the cold and closed the door. He walked away. No handshake, no kiss, no touch. Scooter buttoned his coat and jammed his hat down over his ears. He felt strangely relieved that he'd shared the secrets of his past. He felt he could trust Abby to keep her promise not to tell anyone. He hoped so.

The weather hadn't changed. The cold still went right through a man's body. Scooter walked across the square to tell Carl and Winny good-bye. They were huddled in their small cabin with their daughter and baby.

"I came to tell you I'm leaving," he said. "Thanks for your hospitality, but I've got to get my men and my outfit back to Salt Lake."

Carl shook his hand. "We're the ones who owe you. You've done a lot for Abby."

Winny gave Scooter a warm, friendly hug and then said, "Yes. Thank you. Abby will remember you forever."

"I just said good-bye to her." He wished Abby would have given him a hug, like Winny just did. But she hadn't, and it left a hollow feeling in his heart.

"How is she?"

"Her pulse must be as slow as a bear in winter. I'm worried about her."

"We'll watch her."

"I hope they find her boy," he said.

Winny wiped a tear from her eye. "We do too. We're ashamed of the way the soldiers acted."

Scooter said, "The world is a strange place at times. I don't like people who place little value in the lives of some humans. There's no honor in what Connor did to the women and children."

There was a moment of silence.

The baby cried. Winny cradled the boy in her arms and rocked him. Carl put a husky arm around Winny and pulled her in. Scooter got the impression that they would eventually heal from the terror and calamity that would become known as the Battle of the Bear River. But perhaps not Abby.

"Well," Carl said, "thank you again. I wish I could have done more. I wish we could have ridden ahead of the soldiers. I should have ridden out with you and Abby when we first saw the soldiers. I hesitated. It was the wrong thing to do."

Winny said, "Don't punish yourself. No one knew when Connor was going to attack for certain."

Scooter shook his head sadly. "From a military standpoint, Connor did the right thing. He pushed on. He attacked immediately. I look back at it, and he was right. I should have recognized it quicker. I should have taken Abby to the camp when we saw troops out in the distance. We could have beaten the soldiers there easily. Warned everyone."

Winny asked, "Will you be back this way again?"

"Yes. In the spring."

"Be sure to call on us. And Abby."

Scooter was glad Winny felt this way. "I will. You folks take good care of her."

"Yes. We will."

Chapter 20

ERRIBLE FEELINGS OF GUILT PLAGUED Abby in the days that followed. The thought came to her that she had killed Yahnai the day she accepted him from Sagwitch. The minute he came into her life he was dead! It was all her fault.

She couldn't see it then, but she could see it now. It was always going to end this way. The ugly clash of soldiers against the Shoshoni was inevitable, brought on from the first moment white people discovered this part of the West. Lewis and Clark were to blame, and so were immigrants and gold seekers and perhaps even her own people. And most certainly soldiers. She felt like an idiot for not seeing all this more clearly.

She wanted to be left alone in her misery and depression. For a few days, she thought about what Scooter had told her, baring the secrets of his life. But as time passed, she thought less and less of it. Thoughts of Yahnai dominated her thinking. She barely tolerated visits from Isaac, and when she did, they were hollow. She didn't have the heart to forcibly reject his peacemaking gifts or his attempts at comforting her. She began to wonder if he had tolerated Yahnai just so he could be with her. It was an odd feeling to have, but it was there. She could remember how Scooter defended her so valiantly and how Isaac acted more as a coward all through the events, starting the moment the soldiers arrived in Franklin.

Three settlers returned to the battlefield looking for survivors. They found no trace of a boy in a blue sweater. They told the bishop they drove their sleigh as far as the river and rode their horses across. The first thing they saw was an old Indian walking around aimlessly, arms folded, head bowed in grief, lamenting the dead. He wouldn't speak to them and disappeared to the north. They counted nearly four hundred dead, nearly two-thirds of them women and children, but still no Yahnai. They found two women alive, whose thigh bones had been broken by bullets. They also found three young children, two boys and a girl, all about three years of age. All three were willing to go with the settlers. So the men took the children to the sleigh and brought them back to the settlement, hoping that families would adopt them.

Isaac reported all this news to Abby personally. It improved her spirits to hear that Yahnai could not be found. The story of the old man going off to the north intrigued her. She wondered if that's where other survivors went, including Yahnai. Days later, reports trickled into the settlement about Sagwitch. He had not been killed. He had escaped on a horse but had been shot through the hand. He was angry at the soldiers and the Mormons too. Right now he was reportedly camped at the head of Marsh Creek. Abby wondered if Yahnai could be there with him. Isaac told her that launching a search right now was out of the question. Sagwitch and all surviving Shoshoni warriors were bent on revenge. This left Abby nursing a fear that even if she found Yahnai, the Shoshoni wouldn't let her have him again.

As the weeks passed, she grew more and more depressed. Once a voracious reader, she quit, not even opening the pages of her scriptures or of old newspapers from Salt Lake that floated around the settlement. Visits from Winny, the bishop, and even Isaac didn't do much for her. Sometimes, in the middle of a visit, she would drop into a fevered daze and begin talking to Yahnai as if he were in the room. She knew it wore Isaac and Winny out, trying to explain her behavior to others. No one could understand the depths of her grief.

One day, Bishop Thomas tenderly reminded her that she needed to get back to saying her prayers, reading her scriptures, and turning her problems over to the Savior. "Grab your bootstraps and pull yourself out of this," he told her. "Withdrawing from life won't work. You're sinking your own boat the way you're acting."

One night, when no one was looking, she strolled all alone in the town square when the skies were clear and all the stars were out. It occurred to her that perhaps Yahnai was out there somewhere, under the same stars, the same sky. The stars looked so close together. As a young girl, she had enjoyed good balance and could cross creeks by stepping on stones and rocks. If only she could be in the sky and use the stars as stepping-stones. In no time she could find Yahnai. If she followed the stars north and looked down on earth, she could find him. If he were watching the stars, as she was, wouldn't he know that she was thinking of him? The more she thought about all these things, the lonelier she felt. Of course, the stars couldn't help. They were stars, not mirrors. They couldn't show Yahnai how much she missed him, nor could they show exactly where he was.

Another night she had a dream that Sagwitch brought Yahnai back. Sagwitch rode his pinto, with Yahnai behind him. Yahnai jumped off, and she swept him into her arms. When she awoke in the dark and realized it was but a dream, tears poured down her cheeks, and her body wracked with sobs. It had seemed so real, even the feel of Yahnai in her arms, his happy dark eyes and big smile. Hours later she tried to go back to sleep so the dream would return, but she couldn't. The rest of the night she lay awake, remembering the sweetness of the dream.

Another night she saw Sagwitch riding across the prairie on horseback, clad only in a breechcloth, with Connor's head on a stick over his shoulder. Sagwitch was whooping and hollering toward his camp on the Marsh Creek with his fellow Shoshoni warriors cheering for him.

Yet another time she dreamed that Sagwitch was dancing in pain, holding both sides of his head. When he removed his hands, he had no ears, bleeding where they had been. Someone had cut them off because he had not listened to her pleas not to take Yahnai to the winter camp. She wondered if she could ever forgive Sagwitch and if she'd ever see him again, and if she did, if he would have his ears.

Abby told no one, not even Winny, about these nightmares and others she'd had since the battle. The other thing she kept from Winny was her thoughts about Scooter. She never dreamed about him, for it seemed there was only room in her dreams for the terrible battle and Yahnai. But on the average day, Scooter occupied Abby's thoughts as much as Yahnai did—all day, no matter what tasks she had before her. She had been careful to never so much as utter his name aloud. She knew that if she did, a terrible amount of gossip would ensue. While she could withstand the ordinary gossip that made the rounds of the settlement, her feelings for the stranger she'd met only twice were a little too tender to admit.

Scooter had changed the prejudices she'd had of freighters. She now knew there were good teamsters, just as there were good Mormons and bad Mormons or good Indians and bad Indians. Scooter was a good person. He'd stood up to the soldiers for her. Isaac had not. Scooter had been there with her at the battle, every step of the way. Isaac had not. Scooter had stood beside her when she gave Connor a tongue lashing. Isaac had stood next to Connor, looking embarrassed.

She speculated where Scooter was right now. Was he already on his way to Bannack City and passed by without calling on her? Had he taken the Malad Valley route? Had all this business of soldiers scared him off? Had she scared him off, the way she had berated the colonel? Had Scooter found a girl in Salt Lake and married? Every time she heard the roll of wagons outside the village square, she ran out to look. But there were no freight wagons headed to Bannack City. It was too early in the year.

Warmer days arrived, and the valley finally atoned for all its climatic misdeeds of winter. The ground in the village square thawed; green grass began to peek through along the Muddy River bottoms and the benches. Outside the square, farm work began with teams of horses and mules pulling plows that turned over the soil. Seagulls sang their happiness.

There was still no word about Yahnai, but Abby felt herself come out of her trances occasionally. She would rise up early in the morning and take walks. One day Isaac walked alongside her and hemmed and hawed until he was able to actually speak. They talked about what had happened to them, from the tragedy at the crossing and being rescued by Scooter to the terrible battle at the Bear River. Isaac seemed to dwell on Scooter, as if Scooter was in competition for her hand. But he wasn't. All she could think about was Yahnai. She couldn't remember all the questions Isaac asked about Scooter, and she couldn't remember her answers. Isaac finally got around to mentioning the Endowment House, timidly at first. When Abby didn't respond, his words became bolder and his plans more clearly expressed. He'd treat her kindly. He'd care for her till his dying day. Marriage. A week in Salt Lake City. Time alone, away from Abby's memories. They'd come back to Franklin refreshed and ready to start anew. She stopped suddenly and then retreated to her cabin without a word.

She looked out the window. Isaac stood motionless, his chin on his chest.

Chapter 21

ONE DAY ABBY HEARD FOOTSTEPS in front of her home followed by a knock on her door. When she opened it, Winny stood there in a sprinkle of rain, practically out of breath.

"Abby! There's news of Yahnai!"

Abby jerked the door the rest of the way open and put her hands to her face, expecting the worst. And then the thought flashed across her mind that if it were going to be bad news, really bad news, the bearer of the tidings would be Bishop Thomas, not Winny. There was no bad news written on Winny's face. She looked happy and excited.

"He's alive, Abby! He's alive!"

Abby's spirit soared. The pit of her stomach tingled. Yahnai alive! For a few moments, she couldn't speak. She wiped at tears with both hands. "How do you know?"

Winny talked in excited tones with a vivid, happy expression. "Word came this morning from minutemen in Millville. Sagwitch and his men had stolen some of their horses in retaliation of the attack. So Carl and several of our minutemen rode out to help get the horses back. When they rode up one of the canyons, they saw movement among the aspens. They captured several Indians, including Sagwitch. While he was held prisoner, Sagwitch told them to give you a message that Yahnai was alive. He claimed that the day of the battle, two warriors of Bear Hunter's band took Yahnai north with them as they escaped. They had been angry that Sagwitch had given Yahnai to a white woman. After camping temporarily at the head of Marsh Creek, the warriors took Yahnai farther north and gave him to members of one of the Bannack Indian bands."

Abby bit her lip and shifted her weight back and forth as she digested this story. Horrific nightmares of the battle swept into her mind again, slowly, like bubbles surfacing from the darkness of the settlement's deep well.

"How far north exactly?" Abby asked. "All the way to Bannack City?"

"Sagwitch didn't know exactly. Just north. As soon as Carl and the other men tend to their horses, they'll come over and give you more details."

Abby held the sides of her head as she paced back and forth, trying to think. How many different bands of Bannacks were there? How many different chiefs? Where did they camp in the spring, and where did they roam in the summer? How friendly were they to the whites? She pictured herself in Bannack City, asking questions of both Indians and whites, trying to find Yahnai.

"What are you going to do?" Winny asked.

"This is what I've prayed for," she answered. "Now that I know he's alive, I'm going to find him. I've got to head out, the sooner the better."

Winny shook her head. "But, Abby, you can't go alone. It's too dangerous. Someone has to go with you."

Abby ignored her friend. All of a sudden, time was precious, ticking away, like a deadline approaching. What if Yahnai were sick? What if he were with people who didn't properly care for him?

"I can't see anyone agreeing to go with me right now," Abby said. "Not even Isaac. All the men are about to start their spring farm work. They'll want me to wait a few weeks." She thought about Isaac. Not only would he be busy with his farm but also with his new express station, providing horses for the riders that came through.

"If Yahnai's living with other Indians, he's probably fine," Winny said.

"I can't wait, Winny. I've driven myself half crazy all winter wondering what happened to him. I can't stand it any longer. I've got to go, or my head will burst."

"What about Scooter? He'll be by any day."

Strangely, Abby felt her pulse leap at the mere mention of his name, but she shook her head. "I doubt I'll ever see him again."

"Why do you say that?"

"He's got better things to do than help a Mormon girl he barely knows find an Indian boy. Think about it. He was caught in the middle of something that was none of his affair. He just happened to be here when the soldiers arrived. When I couldn't find Yahnai, I didn't give him the time of day. He saw me at my worst. Scooter probably thinks I'm crazy. Sometimes *I* think I'm crazy. I can't get Yahnai out of my mind. I'm good for nothing until I get him back."

Winny digested this information calmly. "I disagree. I think he'll call on you."

Abby shook her head again. "Even if he did come by, do you know how long it takes his wagons to cover the distance between Franklin and Bannack City? Two hundred and eighty miles. I'd go crazy traveling that slowly."

"But freighters will get there, Indians or no Indians. Abby, you can't do this alone. The men won't let you leave."

It occurred to Abby that she would just have to trick the settlement. She would strike out north and make everyone think she went the other direction. That way she could be far away before anyone, even Isaac, knew the truth.

"I'll sneak away," she said. "You have to make me a promise."

"What kind of promise?"

Abby thought of the promise she had made to Scooter not to reveal his secrets. Now she was asking Winny to make a similar promise. "That if one morning I'm gone, don't tell anyone where I went. Make them think I went to the Salt Lake Valley to see my parents."

Winny gave her a grim look. "Abby, you can't be serious."

"Winny, make me that promise."

"Abby . . ."

Abby spoke her words slowly and carefully, wagging her finger. "Promise me, Winny. Make me that promise."

Winny dropped her eyes. "I don't feel good about it, but I promise."

Chapter 22

THE NEXT DAY, ABBY STEPPED out of her cabin and stared at the corrals that held her two horses, contemplating her plan. It had been raining again, but the sun had burst out of the dark clouds for a moment. It shimmered off the sod roofs of the cabins, the grass in the square, and the corrals. As she stood there, she suddenly became aware of noises. A string of freight wagons was heading north, past the settlement. Their wheels were sinking into the soft, muddy road. Muleskinners were making their whips sing.

Freighters!

Feeling gooseflesh, she ran out to the road. But all she saw were rough-looking men who stared back at her, walking with gigantic freight wagons. Abby exhaled in disappointment. No Scooter. No Oscar. The sun went behind a dark cloud, and a gentle shower began again. She stood there for a while, letting the rain drizzle off her bonnet.

She wondered what to do. She pondered her options one by one. She could follow Winny's advice and wait for Scooter. But what if he didn't come at all? What if he had already headed out for Bannack City but took the safer Malad Valley route? By horseback, she could catch up to the teamsters who just passed and take her chances. Among them, perhaps, were a few good men, like Scooter, who could help her. A group on their way to Bannack City consisted of dangerous men. There were not only miners who'd seen the gold fields of Pike's Peak and California played out, and deserters from the Civil War, but also prison escapees, thieves, outlaws, Mexicans, and gamblers.

But she had to take a chance.

Settlers in Franklin were not very high on her list right now either. They had greeted the soldiers with open arms that dreadful day in January. They cheered for them during the battle. They brought wounded soldiers back from the battlefield and tended to their wounds. They regarded Colonel Connor a hero of sorts, despite his anti-Mormon views. Connor was a criminal in her eyes. They would want her to wait. Isaac would want her to wait, as if the planting season were more valuable than a boy's life.

She couldn't wait.

Another option would be to strike out alone using Snip as a saddle horse and Bolly as a packhorse. If she hitched them to a wagon, she ran the risk of another wreck at some creek crossing. She could take more supplies on a wagon, but she didn't need much—just a bedroll, a change or two of clothes, and food. Either way, she could tag along behind freighters here and there for safety, if she felt the need to, and then make better time when the trail seemed to justify it.

She wondered if the freighters and miners she would inevitably encounter would bother her much. What if they tried to molest her? There were ways to counter that. For one thing, she could dress like a man and make herself unattractive. Evan hadn't left much in the way of clothing, but she still had his things. Another would be to play with their minds. Did Bannack City have a sheriff? What if she told the freighters and miners that her husband was already in Bannack City and had been hired as the sheriff? And that she was on her way to join him? That would give them something to think about.

She smiled, liking the plan to go on horseback. Sometimes, she thought, if you wanted to know for certain if the stove was hot, the only way to find out was to touch it.

She would leave, and no one would stop her.

Chapter 23

THAT EVENING ABBY WENT OUTSIDE. She saw low black clouds boiling out of the southwest like smoke off grease. The day had been a mixture of intermittent showers. It had rained so much the dirt roof over her cabin had begun to leak. The world around Franklin would continue to turn to water—perfect for her getaway. Quickly but calmly she made her final preparations. She wrapped her bedroll in oil cloth, tied leather strings around it, and then stuffed it, her food, clothing, and Book of Mormon into her pack. Finally she found her yellow slicker.

She had one pair of scissors. By the dim light of one candle she used them to cut her blonde hair short enough that she could pass as a man wearing Evan's clothing and hat. She threw her hair into the fireplace and burned it, not wishing to leave evidence of an unannounced departure.

Head down, she walked to the corrals. Rain poured off her hat brim in streams right in front of her face, forming a little waterfall, which made it hard to see. Lightning streaked across the horizon like the tongues of snakes, and then in an instant, it was even closer, with strikes as thick as poles and earsplitting cracks. She had trouble cornering Snip. All the horses in the corral had been spooked by the bright lightning and the claps of thunder. Fortunately none of them squealed. Snip made deep, vibrating snorts, demonstrating her alarm. She bolted from one end of the corral to the other. Abby gradually cornered her and calmed her down. She managed to bridle and saddle the animal. She tied on the saddlebags and caught Bolly. Abby threw a pack saddle on him. Inside the packs, she stuffed the belongings and food she would need for her trip. She snubbed the gelding with a short rope. Followed by her dog, she led the horses away from the square, enduring the steady, cold rain. After she swung into the wet saddle, she turned south until she hit the road and then turned north. She was certain that Isaac and the others—if her tracks could still be seen by morning—would think she went south.

She felt funny about leaving but not funny enough to turn back. This was something she had to do—find Yahnai. It began to rain even harder, in bucketfuls. The cold rain gave her a chill. But she kicked Snip's ribs, and the mare responded with alert, pointed ears and began a steady walk, sloshing along the muddy road.

Abby hated to admit how scared she was, even with Riddle tagging along. It surprised her that she was a good deal more afraid than she thought she'd be. She began to wonder how foolish it was to ride alone. She was easy pickings for lawless miners, outlaws, and renegade bands of Indians looking to avenge what Connor had done.

She crossed her fingers, hoping for good luck.

She knew the road would take her to the Bear River, the site of the battle, but it had to be crossed sometime, and it had to be at the ford. Otherwise the river would be too deep, and her horses might have to swim. She hoped Snip would cross this time.

She wondered what she would feel like, peering at the scene of the terrible carnage. It gave her an eerie feeling as she neared the bluff at daybreak, just when the rain let up. She crested the bluff and stopped. There in the distance, dizzyingly, she could see the ravine where the battle took place. For a moment she forgot to breathe. Before her was the river that had run red with blood not long ago. She could almost smell the stench of death again. She took in great gasps of air to keep herself from sobbing. Again she wondered what the condition of the bodies might be, what wolves and coyotes had done to the carcasses, and if any surviving Shoshonis had done anything to care for the dead. With the first wisps of dawn filtering light through the eastern sky, it was almost as if a trumpet were sending clarion calls for the dead to arise. She paused, hoping something like that would happen, but it didn't.

When she arrived at the river crossing, the rain had diminished, but dark clouds hung oppressively low in the heavens. Except for the river, there was absolute stillness and silence everywhere. More than at any other time since she left the settlement, she felt vulnerable. The swollen river frightened her. It frightened Snip as well. Abby kicked with both feet at her flanks. But Snip balked, snorted her suspicion, and threw her ears back. Abby tightened her grip on the reins and tried turning Snip to the left and then right, but Snip balked again. Nothing worked. The mare's snorts were getting deeper and longer and sharper.

"Snip, you've got to get across," she said. "I can't make it to Bannack City without you. Please, I beg of you."

She kicked the mare, turned a full circle, but Snip would not step into the water.

"Riddle," she said, "bite Snip's heels and help me out here."

Why the horse wouldn't cross was in itself a riddle, as much as when the brown-and-white dog showed up at the settlement one night. It was a riddle where the dog came from, but he turned out to be a good cow dog. Now Abby hoped Riddle would turn out to be a good horse dog and somehow get Snip and the sorrel across the river.

Riddle looked up at her, confused.

Abby dismounted. She held the reins in one hand and knelt down. With the other hand, she touched the stream. "See, Snip? It's just water. It's good to drink. There's nothing that will hurt you. Forget about last time. I don't blame you for not wanting to cross. It was terrible over there in the battle. Today is different. Come on; get me across."

She remounted, backed up, and tried again. Kicked the mare in the ribs. Clicked her tongue against her teeth. Kicked again, harder. Snip threw her head and snorted. She laid her ears back on her head. She would not step into the river.

Suddenly, Snip's ears alertly perched forward. She whinnied, the sort of whinny that comes as a warning to humans or other horses of pending danger. Riddle turned south and barked.

Abby whirled and focused on the faint image of three riders approaching from the southwest, threading their way through the trees. They were riding bareback. Indians. Two options came to her mind: One, run for it, back to Franklin. Two, take a chance the three men would turn out to be friendly. Snip was not good at crossing rivers, but she was a good runner. Abby threw the reins over Snip's head. She reached for the saddle horn and swung up. The Indians were closer. No doubt they had seen her. She decided running was a lousy idea, but so was staying. As she felt her heart thump, she fidgeted and took such a tight grip on her saddle horn that her knuckles turned white.

Riddle's barks turned to low growls.

A veil of mystery surrounded the Indians as they approached. Were they friendly or seeking revenge? They didn't put their horses into a gallop, a factor in Abby's decision to stay put. They were riding right at her, close enough now that she could hear their horses plodding through the sloppy ground. She looked like a man, a threat to them. She thought about taking Evan's hat off. Be a woman, a woman subject to captivity. Become a captive wife to one of them. Unbearable to think about. But so was death. Yahnai needed her. She didn't know what to expect. She felt her mood sinking lower and lower. Her pulse thundered, and her fingers tingled.

The Indians were armed with bows, arrows, and tomahawks. They continued at a steady pace, as if taunting the lone traveler they had trapped on the south side of the river. Two rode pintos—one a dark brown with only a few blotches of white, the other either a black horse with white blotches or white with black blotches. From this distance Abby couldn't tell. The third horse was dark brown, a chestnut color, with a white star on its forehead. The whinny of one of their horses broke the silence. Snip answered with another whinny of her own, adding to Abby's tenseness.

The three Indians rode right up to her. One of the pintos was a stallion. The sight and smell of the stallion caused Snip to squeal. The stallion squealed back. Abby squeezed the reins and pulled on them, trying to calm her mare. The Indians came closer. They were not young warriors, but they were not old either. Perhaps they had wives and children somewhere. Perhaps their wives and children were dead, victims of the soldiers. Maybe they were men full of revenge.

What they did next surprised and electrified her. They dismounted. They made a sign. She dismounted. They smelled like wood smoke. Their deerskin leggings were stained, and their dark-brown eyes were full of mischief. One man was little larger than the other two, a little taller. He began speaking to her in sign language. Abby had familiarized herself somewhat in sign language, but with her heart pounding so hard, she struggled to understand what they were trying to say.

The tall Indian pointed to her felt hat. He wanted it off. Mustering every bit of courage she could find, she removed it, exposing her head and the uneven haircut she had given herself. She knew they could sense her uneasiness, but the hair seemed to astound them, and they smiled as though they recognized her. Had they seen her before? She didn't recognize them. Not one of them.

"Yahnai?" the tall Indian asked with a smug smile.

Swallowing her apprehension, Abby exhaled deeply. He knew who she was—the white woman who had been given an Indian child by Chief Sagwitch. "Yahnai, yes," she said, nodding.

The three men briefly conversed in Shoshoni, bobbing their heads.

Abby took Snip's reins, tugged on her mare, and walked toward the water. She made signs that she wanted to cross. Snip snorted once again. Abby pointed at Snip and made a negative sign.

The Indians wanted to know why she needed to cross the river. She just pointed, shrugged her shoulders, and gave them her most helpless look. With a packhorse, she reasoned, some of her intent was obvious. She was traveling north.

The tall Indian seemed to understand. He laughed as the horses nickered and squealed back and forth. He mounted but gestured for Abby to remain where she was. His companions also mounted. The tall Indian took the reins from her. He nudged his horse into the river. Another man thumped Snip on the rump with a leather strap. Snip didn't snort or balk. She just plunged into the river. Abby's packhorse followed. The tall Indian kept going; so did Abby's horses. The depth of the water was well over the horses' bellies, but in a few minutes, the three Indians had crossed the Bear River. So had Abby's two horses. Abby was relieved. They had forced Snip to cross.

Her relief was only momentary. Her horses were on the north side of the river with the Shoshoni warriors. She was on the south side of the river. A body of water separated her from her horses and all her belongings. Her heart raced as she realized her stupidity.

"What do I do now?" she asked Riddle. Riddle didn't know.

She focused on the warriors. They were laughing together, pointing at her. Abby felt a knot tighten in her stomach. The Indians had cleverly stolen her horses and her packs. She felt herself go tense with resentment. She turned and looked toward the settlement. She wondered how long it would take to walk back and what she would say to Isaac and the others.

Behind her, she heard a splash. The tall Indian was crossing again, pulling Snip behind him. Slowly he came toward her. She tried to relax. She tried to breathe normally. Both horses reached the bank of the river where she stood. They pulled themselves out of the river, right to her side, dripping water. The tall Indian motioned for her to mount. With bewilderment, Abby froze for a few seconds. The man said something in Shoshoni and motioned again. Abby mounted.

The Indian held Snip's wet leather reins and tugged on them. Abby kicked at Snip's ribs. The mare responded. Snip followed the Indian's horse into the water. Soon Snip had taken her across the Bear River. Snip stopped when the lead horse stopped. There, the three Indians had a good laugh. They tipped their heads back and laughed at one another. They laughed at her, pointing. Snip was calm—just stood there dripping, exhaling, relaxing, making soft sighing noises. Bolly nickered at Snip. Snip nickered back. They were together.

Abby managed an awkward smile. The men smiled back.

Abby said, "*Aishenda'ga.*"

The tall Indian nodded an appreciation that she knew how to say thank you in their language.

Abby smiled her awkward little smile again. She sat on her horse on the north side of the river—but still in the company of three Shoshoni warriors.

The tall Indian mumbled something inaudible. He riveted his eyes on her packhorse and pointed a dark, bony finger.

Abby interpreted this as meaning the Indians were hungry. They wanted to be repaid for their hospitality. She hesitated for a few seconds and then dismounted. She opened one of her packs. The tall man gave her a stiff nod. He moved her aside and peeked inside. He amused himself for a few minutes going through her belongings, his black eyebrows arching in satisfaction and his eyes twinkling. He pointed to her saddlebags, where she had stored some of her food. The Indian looked there too. Abruptly and without comment, he pulled out her Book of Mormon and handed it to her. Then he unlashed her saddlebags. He did it quickly and deliberately. He removed them from her saddle and threw them over his horse. He laughed heartily, patting his flat belly. His companions made gestures of approval. He remounted, still holding the lead rope from her sorrel in his brown hand. He tugged on it and rode a few paces away.

He said, "*Koihkwa.*" As he said it, he gestured at her. His eyes were no longer friendly. They were dark. No laughing, no smiling. He pointed north. He pointed at the wagon tracks that led north to Snake River country and Bannack City.

Abby stared back in confusion and disbelief. She held her book in her hand, which started to shake. As she let all the air out of her lungs, a realization hit her. They had helped her across the river, an act she appreciated. But the three Shoshoni warriors were stealing her packhorse. Not only the horse but her bedroll and all the food she had. All of it. She understood clearly what the tall Indian had said.

Go away.

Abby felt her face turn red in anger. She knew she had no choice. With an ominous sigh, she swung into her saddle. Her yellow slicker made a swishing sound. She stuffed her book under her belt, holding it tight against her stomach. She looked at the three Indians again and at her packhorse. She gave the Indians a longing look. They stared back. No compassion in their eyes. No compassion about how she would make it all the way to Bannack City without food, without her bedroll and extra clothing. She locked her eyes on the tall Indian and gave him her angriest look. "I need that food. Why are you taking it from me?"

He gestured again, his expression dark. Pointed north. "*Koihkwa.*"

It began to rain again. Lightning cracked, followed by a roll of thunder.

She had no idea how to say it in Shoshoni, so she said it in English, pointing her finger at them and lowering her voice. "You are thieves. You help me across, and then you steal from me. You have taken advantage of a woman. You ought to be ashamed."

"*Koihkwa.*" His voice had lowered, and his eyes were a little darker.

She shouted at them. "I'm going. With or without food, I'm going to Bannack City. I'm going to find my son. I would normally thank you for getting my horse across the river. And I suppose I ought to thank you for not taking both horses. And for leaving me with a head of hair and my slicker. So you *koihkwa* too. Good-bye."

She felt better. She had shouted the words in the most indignant tone she could muster. With the same tone she had used when she poured her wrath out against Colonel Patrick Connor. She watched for a reaction. There was none. Not one of the Shoshoni men showed any emotion. It had been wrong to trust them. It would be a long time until anyone would earn her trust again. Indians or whites—it didn't matter.

Her anxious feeling came back. She felt as alone as she would have on a deserted island in the middle of the world's largest ocean. She thought about going back. She wondered if Snip would cross the river. She looked south toward the settlement and decided against it. She turned Snip's head and started up the muddy road, followed by her dog. Snip wanted to follow Bolly and the Indians, but Abby prevailed and coaxed her mare away from them, following the trail north. Her legs felt as heavy as if somebody had put lead in her boots. She wondered if that feeling would be with her all the way to Bannack City.

"Here we go, Riddle. We might starve to death, but we're alive now."

She glanced behind her. The Indians were headed west in the rainy, hazy pall, toward the Malad Valley. She'd always had a low tolerance for stupidity. Now she had been stupid. But she felt Yahnai pulling on her. It was as though his voice echoed from the north, beseeching her.

She had no choice but to ride toward Bannack City.

Chapter 24

*I*T RAINED HARD FOR AN hour or so, and then it quit. The sun broke out in patches, lighting the grass, sagebrush, and hundreds of puddles along the trail. She looked all around, but there wasn't a soul in sight. She could feel vast, silent emptiness all around. It hissed at her. She was alone and by no means sure of herself. It scared her. She began to realize she had done a foolish thing. She didn't regret leaving, but neither had she calculated on losing her packhorse and supplies. She wondered if those warriors were members of Bear Hunter's or Sagwitch's bands or if they belonged to Pocatello or Washakie. She wondered if she'd have dreams about them in the next few nights, dreams in which they either scalped her or took her captive.

Unconsciously, she reached under Evan's felt hat and touched her hair. It was still there. She hoped she didn't run into more Indians. Some of them might do worse than just take her horse.

She wondered, too, how hungry she would get until she caught up with freighters. She hadn't eaten since her evening meal, and her stomach was growling. She hadn't taken a drink from the river, but she had her canteen. She looked ahead and to the left and to the right. There were rolling hills covered with sagebrush and aspen groves and distant, snow-covered mountains with stands of pine on both sides of her.

She put her mare into a lope. Snip didn't like crossing water, but she could eat up the miles. With such a horse under her, Abby felt a little less vulnerable. Snip likely could outrun most Indian ponies. This aspect of her mare pleased Abby. She had never cared for docile horses. She wondered if that's why she never really loved Isaac. He was too docile. Scooter was more like Snip, young and athletic.

Snip followed a road filled with deep wagon wheel ruts. She came to a creek crossing and slowed Snip to a walk. She didn't want to be pitched off. She didn't know if the little bit of training the thieving Shoshoni warriors had given Snip was temporary or permanent. As she descended toward the creek, she encountered swarms of mosquitoes. They attacked her and her mare. They settled on her so quickly that she wiped them off like stains. Snip kept flinching as if inhaling hundreds of them with every breath. When they finally came to the water, Abby was anxious to get away from the mosquitoes. Snip began snorting again, but Abby didn't know if it was because of the creek, the mosquitoes, or both. Abby clicked her tongue against her teeth and kicked the mare's sides. The creek wasn't wide. Snip didn't lay her ears back. She perched them forward and crossed without a problem. Abby breathed a sigh of relief. Snip grunted as they pulled up the hill, out of the creek basin.

Abby was still slapping mosquitoes when she saw the freighters that had passed the settlement yesterday. For an instant she felt the same apprehension as when she saw the three Shoshoni warriors. The men ahead of her could be descent, God-fearing men. Or they could be evil men, traveling with no thought of God. Or a few of both. She hoped and prayed there would be a least one good man among them.

But there they were. And she needed them.

As Abby closed the distance, she wondered if she should just follow them until they stopped or if she should ride alongside the wagon in the rear and begin a conversation with one of them. In a light drizzle, she urged Snip up the brow of a hill so that she could see all the wagon tandems. There were several, each pulled by a long string of mules. The canvas covering the wagons was wet. Mud caked the wheels. She estimated there were around two dozen men in the group. She knew she couldn't trust them totally, but she had to have something to eat. She estimated that the freighters would stop within two or three hours for the evening. She licked her lips, wondering what would be in their Dutch ovens tonight.

While she was paused on the ridge, an express rider galloped by, his horse well lathered. The horse undoubtedly came from the station in Franklin, operated by Isaac. As she watched the rider, she wished she could travel that fast. She'd be able to arrive in Bannack City in just a couple of days.

The drizzle dried up, and the sun came out again. She took off her slicker and tied it behind her where the saddlebags had been.

She returned to the trail, choosing to follow at a distance to keep her safe from Indians, if there were any. The wagons approached a creek crossing with light soil on each bank, causing the first wagon to sink up to the axle trees. Fighting mosquitoes, the men unhitched mules from another wagon. The additional mules were enough to get the wagon out. The freighters cut sagebrush and willow boughs and laid them down, which helped support the other heavy wagons for the crossing. While she watched, she rehearsed what she would say to the freighters when they stopped.

Finally, when the freighters began forming their wagons into a tight semicircle, Abby knew the men were stopping for the evening. She had no choice but to be decisive and confident. As she headed for the middle of the circle, she wondered how long it would take the freighters to recognize her as a woman. Snip whinnied at the mules, just as she had done at the horses the three Indians had ridden. A few of the mule skinners spotted her. Two or three stopped what they were doing. They stared at her. One pointed and then another. She heard one of them warn the others, "Rider comin' in!"

She sat up in the saddle and took a deep breath. The mule skinners who had noticed her didn't do anything unusual. They regarded her with normal body language. Just a lone rider. A man on a horse. Not an Indian. Maybe a miner headed north. Some of the freighters were unhitching mules. Some were gathering firewood. Two or three were saddling horses, maybe for a quick hunting trip. Three or four mule skinners watched her come in and didn't take their eyes off her. Abby rode toward them.

One mule skinner seemed to stand out. He looked familiar. He had a greasy red beard, a walrus mustache, and matted red hair. He wore an atrocious hat and a long buffalo coat. As she rode near him, his eyes widened and his jaw dropped. "Why, that there ain't a man," the redhead said to the others.

Soon several mule skinners were staring at her. Abby swallowed hard.

"It's a woman," the redhead said, reaching for Snip's bridle.

Waves of anxiety hit Abby. She recognized the redhead. She'd seen him before, last November at the crossing. He'd threatened to shoot Isaac's horses. Scooter had pulled him to the ground. But if this was Cad, where was Scooter?

Riddle growled.

Cad had locked his eyes on her and tilted his head to an odd angle, as if wondering where he'd seen her before. "Why, you're a woman or my name ain't Cadmus Arbuckle. Don't let that dog bite me."

Abby tried to hide the quivering of her hands and hoped Cad wouldn't recognize her. Thankfully, after their confrontation, Scooter had made certain that Cad stayed far away. But his presence brought tantalizing questions to her mind. Her eyes did a quick scan, but she didn't see Scooter or Oscar. Did this mean that Cad had left Scooter's employment and had taken up with another group?

Abby's thoughts were interrupted when a second mule skinner spoke, this one with light skin, a brown beard, and brown hair. "Why, Cad, it *is* a woman! My, my. What's a purdy thing like you doin' out here all alone?"

A third man took off his hat, letting a shock of coarse and greasy black hair pop out. "Lady, you are plumb weak north of your ears if you're ridin' alone in this country."

Abby bit her lip, trying to decide how to react. These men looked like they might do more than rob her if the mood struck them. They waited for her to respond.

"Yes, I am a woman, and I'm alone, except for my dog."

The men looked as though they'd been knocked off balance.

More mule skinners laid their eyes on her. The one with black hair said, "She didn't wear her best appearin' out clothes, but lookee that face."

Another said, "Why, she's got skin creamy as cow's milk."

"Creamy, yeah," said another with a fighter's nose, "but she's as nervous as a dog dreamin' of catchin' a rabbit. Look at 'er shake."

By now nearly every mule skinner had gathered to stare at her. She had no control over her shakes or the beet-red color of her face. These men were a rough set. Clothing stained with mud, sweat, food grease, and tobacco-juice spatters. They didn't quite know where to put their eyes.

Cad couldn't contain himself. "Are you as useful as you are ornamental? Slide off and cool yer saddle."

Abby's stomach knotted, and the men laughed lustily, some with strange, jerky laughs. She knew what Cad inferred. She returned a cold stare, her foot loose in the stirrup, ready to dismount when she felt safe or ride away if she didn't.

"No answer?" Cad said. He let out a stud-horse whistle and glared at her with a bucketful of insolence. "I'm used to women with the come-hither nickering of an eager mare. I don't see your bedroll. I'll make room in my tent tonight for you."

Another man with a thin wisp of mustache at each corner of his mouth said, "Cad, you've got no more chance with this blonde than a rooster at a mass meeting of coyotes."

Cad took aim at an ant hill and spat a stream of tobacco juice. The spittle caused the ants to scurry. "She's mine," he said. "I saw her first."

Abby flinched. She pulled her hat down over her face and looked away. She slowly realized she was clutching her reins so tightly her fingers were going numb.

The mule skinner with the fighter's nose objected. "You're dumber than a road lizard if you think we're not gonna share her."

Abby felt like a circus animal in a cage. She was about to kick Snip in the ribs and try to break the grip Cad had on the bridle when a broad man in a blue shirt approached. "Who are you?" the man asked. His voice was deep and rich—and friendly.

Abby could barely speak. "I'm Sally. And who are you?"

Cad said, "That's Hagen, biggest toad in the puddle."

"Hagen Farrar," the man said. "What are you doing out here all alone?"

"On my way to Bannack City, same as you," she answered.

"Why, yer a workin' lady." Cad grinned. "And you stopped here to shake your hoops at us lonely mule skinners."

"You don't know that, Cad," Hagen said. "Can't you see the way she's dressed?"

Cad took off his hat and slicked his hair back. "You plant a tater, you get a tater."

"I'll handle this," Hagen said with a wave of a hand. He turned back to her with a skeptical look. "You haven't explained why you're all alone."

Abby told herself to relax. She took a deep breath, forced a balmy smile, and looked down on the men from her perch atop Snip. She decided now was the time to spin the story she'd made up. She hoped Cad wouldn't recognize her face or her voice.

Hagen looked impatient.

"My husband is sheriff in Bannack City. We're originally from Massachusetts. My husband was in law enforcement in Boston and later in St. Louis, so he figured the people in Bannack City could use him. By now, I guess, he's got a claim that he can work as well. He could have sent me money for my stage fare, but I didn't want to wait."

"Well, that makes sense." Hagen nodded. "Bannack City needs law and order. They say it'll double in size every few weeks this year. And you can see why. You can pull up a sagebrush and shake a dollar's worth of dust from its roots. They're ordering everything from window panes, printing presses, furniture, equipment for sawmills and brewing beer, clothing, guns, and pianos—you name it."

Abby had heard this line before, from Scooter.

"But how'd your husband get out of Boston without being made a soldier to fight in the war?" he asked.

Abby thought a moment and spun more of her fib. "We left Boston just before the war broke out. He was a deputy in St. Louis for a while, and then we came west. I stayed in Salt Lake City while he tripped to Bannack City."

"I still can't imagine you traveling without so much as a saddlebag."

"Oh, I had a packhorse until this morning," she said, finding humor in telling the truth. "Indians found me. They took my pack-horse and my supplies."

"Funny they didn't take you too," Hagen said with a look of disbelief. "Some Indians shine for a white woman wife, same as some whites shine for a squaw."

"I shine for a blonde on a bay mare," Cad said.

"Button it, Cad," Hagen said. He turned back to her and asked, "Were they local Shoshoni?"

"Yes," she said. "I know I'm lucky to be alive."

Hagen tilted his hat to one side, his skepticism evident. "It's hard to believe they took your packhorse and not your mare. Are you sure you're tellin' the truth?"

"Maybe it's because I'm a woman. Maybe it's because they felt sorry for me. But I swear I'm telling the truth."

Another mule skinner spoke. "Yer not one of them plow-chasin' Mormons?"

"I told you, I'm from Massachusetts."

"Good," Cad said. "Then you won't mind it if we tell you that we stopped at every Mormon settlement and got us a collection of Gold Bibles and hymn books. We use 'em to start fires." He laughed a laugh that matched his rough look.

Abby cringed at the thought.

Hagen changed the subject. "We'd be happy to share our food."

"She looks hungrier than a woodpecker with a headache," said a young mule skinner with blond hair, hair that was even lighter than Abby's. "I say we feed her."

Abby's stomach growled. She didn't know what the mule skinners were going to eat for supper, but she was ready for anything from boiled rattlesnake to fried muskrat.

Hagen spoke to a man who was obviously the camp cook. "Masher, get the boys to rustle up some firewood. What's for supper?"

Masher, an older, wrinkle-faced man, stepped forward. "More beans, I reckon, 'less the men wanna get their scatter guns out and bring in a mess of rabbits."

"Best cook as ever throwed dishwater under a chuckwagon," Hagen said to Abby.

"Get the distilled refreshments out; let's celebrate," Cad said. "Let's get drunker than a peach-orchard sow. Whoopee!"

Hagen shook his head as the men laughed. "Don't pay any attention to Cad. At times like this, he's as worthless as a pail full of hot spit."

Abby looked away.

"All right, boys," Hagen said. "Let's get a fire going and feed the little lady. Masher, get yer beans in the pot. Dinsdale, tether her horse."

Abby felt she could trust Hagen. She dismounted and pulled off the saddle. She arched her back from the cramp she'd gotten from riding so long. She pressed the heels of her hands into the small of her back to relieve the pressure. Snip immediately enjoyed a good roll, grunting and scratching her sweaty back. The young blond mule skinner took Snip and tethered her.

The skies darkened again as Hagen's men scattered and went to work. With Riddle right on her heel, she followed Hagen wherever he went, saying next to nothing.

Mosquitoes annoyed everyone terribly as Masher got out his Dutch ovens and his beans. While some of the men took care of the stock, others built extra fires, gathered dry manure, and kept the camp enveloped in smoke as much as possible. Some of the mules quit grazing and stood in the camp smoke to free themselves of mosquitoes.

The campfire grew lighter and the skies darker as the earth lurched away from the sun. Masher's ovens soon emitted a savory essence, and the boys of the outfit took to the food like a bear in a honey tree. Abby dove in too, showing only traces of Eastern etiquette, trying to satisfy her famished condition. The mule skinners' rude behavior and crude remarks continued. Whenever she caught one of the men looking at her, she met the look with a cold stare. Cold stares did not bother Cad. She felt his eyes on her all during the evening meal. He watched her constantly, consuming distilled refreshments by the fire, as if she belonged to him. Thankfully, he hadn't recognized her.

Hagen seemed concerned over her plight. "You're in a pickle. You're welcome to throw in with us. I can get you to Bannack City to join up with your husband."

"Thank you. I might do that," she said.

For a few minutes, the men began talking about the Bear River battle. It had been big news all up and down the Bannack trail. It was amazing to Abby how their perception of the battle varied with the facts. She listened, trying to block out the horrific memories of the things she'd seen.

Dinsdale changed the subject abruptly and suggested that the men cut cards for her. Cad took a prolonged swig of whiskey and laughed. "I'd fight the whole boodle of ya before I'd cut cards with ya, Dinsdale. Yer crazy as a loon if ya think I'd trust ya."

"Leave her alone," said Hagen.

"She ain't no school marm, boss man," Cad said.

"Don't make me wrathy, Cad," Hagen said. "Back off. She's had a bad day, losin' her packhorse to those Injuns. Besides, she's got a dog, and he looks like a mean one."

She smiled at Hagen in appreciation. Cad took another swig and started humming some tune that Abby didn't recognize. Hagen handed his plate to Masher and walked to one of the wagons. He returned with a pile of wool blankets.

"These are yours," Hagen said. "There's more if you need 'em. Wagons are full of them. You can bed down under one of the wagons. All our tents are filled with men. Put your slicker under the bottom blanket. I'll dig a little ditch around the wagon behind you to divert the rainwater, just in case. Let me know if any of the men bother you."

He touched his holstered six-shooter. "Just scream, and I'll blow his guts out."

Cad kept humming his tunes and casting lusty glances at her. She thanked Hagen and spread the blankets next to the fire for now, staying near Hagen. Verbally, so the men could hear, she told Riddle she wished Sagwitch would jump out of the trees and feed Cad to the coyotes and wolves. There were coyotes yapping out there somewhere.

Her conversations with Riddle kept Cad away, but he continued his morbid fascination for her. One of the men got his dice out, and soon they were playing, but that didn't stop the stares. Laughter came easy for them, as easy as tipping their bottles. She wondered if Cad or any of the other men could imagine what it was like to be terrified.

Chapter 25

DARK CLOUDS FORMED AGAIN, AND it began to rain. Lightning started hitting the ground as Abby dove for shelter under the wagon. It rained torrents. The men got totally soaked before they put things away and went into their tents. In ten minutes there was a little river running down the middle of the trail that led to Bannack City. The rain increased until it seemed it wouldn't be possible for water to fall any faster. Hagen's little ditch worked, however. Water ran around the wagon, not under it. She made the blankets into a kind of bed with her slicker beneath them. It quit raining just as quickly as it had begun. The men returned, saving the fire. She lay awake for a long time, apprehensive, but the mule skinners made no move to disturb her.

She wished Scooter was with her.

She had almost drifted off when she heard sounds she didn't understand at first—sliding, scraping, slithering noises, repeating rhythmically. Her skin began to crawl. Someone was beneath the wagon, inching toward her. When Riddle growled, Abby jolted upright in the pitch blackness, banging her head against the wagon's frame.

"I'll shoot the dern dawg if you don't quiet 'im," a voice said.

She heard the clicking of a six-shooter.

"Quiet, Riddle," she said, rubbing her head and trying to process what was happening. She rubbed her eyes and tried to focus on the man, but there wasn't enough light to know which of Hagen's men it might be for certain. But the odds were it was Cad, and that's where she placed her suspicion.

"I just came fer some company," the voice said. "Just cooperate, and it won't take long. My intentions are good. I'm whatcha call a *real* nice man. I believe that cha catch more flies with honey than with vinegar. So just relax. I'm a fixin' to marry ya."

Abby recognized the voice. It *was* Cad.

She found the notion that she was about to be attacked by such a reprehensible man almost impossible to believe. She breathed in, breathed out, and then laced a response with all the venom she could muster. "I don't want you. Go away."

"That don't make no matter 'cause I want ya, and I want ya real bad," he said. "I have a knife too. I'm determined, and I *will* have you."

Abby was about to risk losing both her life and Riddle's by setting him on Cad and screaming as loud as she could, but Cad said something that set her back.

"Ya haven't fooled me. I figured out who ya are. You're Abby, from Franklin settlement. I've wanted ya from the day I first saw ya. I'm sorry fer the way I treated ya that day. You *will* be mine. I promise not to hurt ya." He inched closer, nearly face-to-face.

The smell of his hot whiskey breath hung fetid in her nostrils. She could also smell his smoky clothing, his greasy beard, and his manure-covered boots. His weapon touched the fabric of Evan's clothing. She felt the hardness and the coldness of the metal through her shirt.

She inched away. He answered with matching pressure on the gun. The metal was pressing hard into the softness of her flesh. Her skin was yielding into a deep crater. It hurt. Her shakes worsened. She was starting to gag. She couldn't remember when she last took a breath.

"What cha doin' out here alone—really?" he asked.

She said nothing.

"It has somethin' ta do with yer Indian boy, doesn't it? I know'd ya couldn't find 'im after the battle. That was a terrible thing weren't it, that battle? So yer out lookin' fer that Injun child? I kin help ya. All you have to do is cooperate, and I'll be yer best friend. I'll help ya find 'im. I promise."

Cad's words solidified Abby's suspicion that she was dealing with a madman. She gathered herself and asked a question, hoping it would somehow change his mind. "You don't work for Scooter anymore?"

"Scooter? He owns this outfit too. Expanded when we got back. He knows ya don't have any interest in him. But I know that old feller in yer settlement isn't the one fer you. I'm here. I'm yer man now. That's enough talk. Quit piddlin' around. Let's git down to business. In a few minutes, we'll be married, nice and proper."

Abby had formed the conclusion that Cadmus Arbuckle was more than just a little bit crazy. *He was a whole lot crazy.* His perspective of marriage was different than any she'd ever thought about. In frantic desperation, she focused every bit of her mental energy on how to get out of this predicament. The pressure of the gun digging into her flesh went away. She guessed that right now both his hands were busy tugging at his trousers. She assumed he had laid his six-shooter on the ground. She rose to her knees, crouched on her haunches, and waited.

The man's form inched closer. She waited no more. She touched her dog. "Sic 'im, Riddle!"

When the dog attacked, Cad screamed, and so did Abby, shrill and loud, loud enough to drive off coyotes and owls, hoping to awaken the other men. It was so dark that Abby couldn't see the damage Riddle was inflicting on Cad, but she knew it must be terrible by the way the man cursed and let out terrified squeals. Frantically, she began groping in the dark, hoping to find Cad's weapons.

Her fingers touched his knife.

She took a tight grip on the dagger. From her kneeling position, she gathered momentum and lunged toward Cad, who was losing the battle with Riddle. She landed against his chest. Her force punched some of the air out of him. He gasped. She scythed her right arm with all the force she could muster. She knew when the knife hit flesh. She felt his body go slack. She could feel him grasping at his left shoulder. He screeched like a stuck pig. He screeched again when she twisted it. She knew blood was coming out of his shoulder, and it make her woozy. She was glad she couldn't see, for she knew she might have fainted. She could feel the blood on her right hand, hot and sticky. She pulled the knife out as swiftly as it went it. He was shrieking desperately.

She pounded him with her fists. She could tell when her blows landed on his face. His bones were hard. She gouged at his eyes, his nose, and his mouth. She felt teeth. She didn't care if she knocked every rotten tooth out of his mouth. The litheness was going out of Cad's body. He was giving up.

Riddle had hold of an arm or hand, trying to drag Cad away from her. There was a lot of noise. Riddle growling, Cad screeching, and her screaming. Abby became aware of men running toward the wagon. She heard a lot of voices, including Hagen's.

"Help me!" she screamed.

"She's done kilt me with my own knife!" Cad bawled. "Get this dawg off me!" He added a long line of curse words.

"Down, Riddle," she said. "Down, boy."

Someone had lit a lantern. By its light, she saw Cad being jerked to his feet. His manic eyes were big as saucers. He gazed at the emptiness beneath the wagon where he had been with her, like he was unable to understand what had just happened. Riddle stood poised, ready to attack again on command.

"If the dog ain't kilt you, I will," Hagen said, "you black-hearted, dumb, slug-in-a-ditch scalawag."

Abby crawled out from under the wagon. Her heart felt like it was loose in her chest. She stood up, sick and cramped and unsteady. One of the men caught her elbow. She wiped her hands on Evan's trousers, trying to get rid of Cad's blood.

More lanterns were lit. The light showed Hagen pressing Cad's body against the wagon with one hand at Cad's throat, the other hand pressed a six-shooter against his chest.

"I didn't do nothin'," Cad said. "And now I'm bleedin' all over."

"Does nothin' really amount to nothin' when yer belt is gone and we found you under the wagon?" Hagen said. "I'm gonna feed what's left of you to the wolves."

Abby hoped he would.

Hagen turned to her. "I hate to ask what happened. You okay?"

Abby felt to urge to cry, but she held back her tears and edged closer to the lanterns, hoping Hagen would note that she was fully dressed. She said nothing to Cad. She stared into the night as if she could make him vanish by not looking at him. "Yes, thankfully. You got here just in time."

More mule skinners arrived at the scene.

"What happened?"

Another answered, "Cad slipped his hobbles. Attacked the girl."

"She set the dawg on me and knifed me. All I wanted was conversation," Cad said between his pitiful moans.

"You better look at him," Abby told Hagen. "I did get him with his knife, but I don't know exactly where. He had a gun too. It's still under the wagon."

By the light of a lantern, one of the men found Cad's revolver.

"My shoulder," Cad moaned. "She stuck me in the shoulder."

"Put that lantern on Cad," Hagen said. He ripped off Cad's shirt. "You're bleedin', all right, but she missed anything vital. You'll live."

"That dawg got me too," Cad said. "One of my hands is all chewed up—and one of my ears. Is it still attached, or have I lost it?"

Hagen said, "I don't care about your ear. I hope the dog ate it. You'll feel worse by morning because I'm gonna chain you to one of the wagons away from the woman."

"I'd druther not be left outside," Cad pleaded. "It's clabberin' to rain again, and I'm bleedin' and feelin' puny. Put me in my tent with the boys."

Hagen's voice turned icy. He permitted no argument. "No. Come morning, we might hang you." To his men he added, "Pour some cheap spirits on his wounds and put leg irons on him. And two of you watch him until daybreak."

"Yes, boss," one of them said.

Cad stopped talking. He just whimpered.

"I'm sorry for this," Hagen told her. "Cad is a coward. Cowards are bullies. Bullies are cowards. Are you sure you're not harmed?"

In truth, Abby felt demoralized and knew she'd feel that way for a long time. "I'm fine," she fibbed, "but I can't quit shaking."

"Get her some clean blankets out of the wagon," Hagen told his men, and one scurried away to comply.

"I have a question," Abby said, steeling herself in case the answer came back negative. "Do you know of a teamster named Scooter—David Perkins?"

"Why, I sure do," Hagen said. "Why do you ask?"

"I met him during his first trip to Bannack City, at Franklin settlement."

"Do you mean . . . ?"

Abby hung her head. "I'm sorry, but I fibbed. My name is Abigail Butterfield Browett. I'm trying to get to Bannack City because I hear that's where my son is. He's my adopted son, an Indian boy. He disappeared after the battle at the Bear River."

Hagen held up a hand. "Say no more. I know who you are. I know all about you. I work for Scooter. He owns every wagon and mule you see here."

Abby's mouth fell open. "Then where is he?"

"He's one day behind us as the mules roll, with his other outfit."

Abby peered into the darkness, south, toward Franklin. The revelation hit her hard. Had she been patient enough to wait one more day, Scooter would have passed right by her.

Cad's pitiful moans reminded her of reality. He screamed again when alcohol was poured into his wounds. She didn't care. He was rotten to the core.

"I'd like to find Scooter," she told Hagen.

"And I'll bet he'd like to find you," he replied.

"But why is Cad with you and not with Scooter?"

"Scooter all but fired Cad when they returned to Salt Lake," he said. "Men are hard to come by. But now I'll do it for him, if Cad lives long enough."

"If it weren't the middle of the night, I'd leave now," Abby said.

"You sleep in my tent," he said. "The six of us in there will sleep under the wagons the rest of the night—what's left of it. In the morning I'll escort you back down the trail until we find Scooter."

"I'd be forever grateful," she said, still shaking.

As Hagen and the others vacated the tent, Abby found her way to the creek in the dark. Her feet felt heavy, as if she were wading in wet sand. Best she could, she washed Cad's blood off her hands. The water made her shiver. She returned to the tent and laid out the clean blankets inside it. The tent smelled. It was a musty brew of sweat, tobacco, and other odors given off by men night after night in close quarters. She peeled off Evan's trousers and shirt, wondering how much blood would show on them in the morning. She threw them into a tangle in the corner and shivered again. She realized how wrong she had been to strike out on her own. She also knew that there was only one person she could totally trust, and it wasn't Scooter. It was the Lord. Before she laid her tired, shaking body down to try to sleep, she fell to her knees, praying more fervently than she'd ever prayed before. She thanked God that He had spared her and that she was going to be delivered into Scooter's hands.

A feeling of peace came over her. She knew everything would be okay.

Chapter 26

MORNING CAME BEFORE ABBY WAS ready for it. The terror had exhausted her. Her mouth tasted tired and stale. She had slept little, except for the latter part of the night, after her prayer. She could hear men talking by the campfire. After she dressed and said another prayer, she smoothed out her mud-caked, bloody clothing as much as possible and emerged from Hagen's tent, anxious to find Scooter.

"There you are," Hagen said, standing at the sight of her. "I hope you're feelin' tolerable this morning after what happened last night."

Abby said nothing. She just squinted into a bright sun. It was peeking through the clouds. It put her into a better spirit, though sleep was still in her eyes.

"You look like you just wiggled out of a flour sack. The beans and bacon are still warm, and there's plenty left. The coffee's hot. Fetch you a cup, and I'll pour."

She had little interest in beans and bacon, and certainly not coffee. It wasn't food that would bring life into her this morning; it was finding Scooter. And getting Cad out of her mind. The mule skinners were scattered, some having coffee over the campfire, others tending to their duties, such as harnessing the mules.

She asked, "Where's my horse? I'd like to get started."

"First we need to deal with Cad," he said. "I'll have the boys bring him here. If you want, we'll hang him. Or shoot him. Or send him down the road in just his underwear and hope the Indians get him. Your choice."

Abby heard the rattling of chains. Cad's legs were bound. As two mule skinners dragged Cad toward her, she saw the pain in his eyes and the way his body slumped as he moved. He dragged himself along slowly and apprehensively, as though he dreaded facing her again. As though Hagen might actually string him up by the neck. Behind Cad, another mule skinner had a long rope in his hand. He had already started with a hangman's knot. He had folded one end of his rope into thirds and was slowly winding the end of his rope around the third part. It was starting to look like a hangman's noose. He made sure Cad could see it. When Cad did, the mule skinner smiled at him and made a little nod at the tallest tree in the camp, a tree that had a branch strong enough to hold a man at the end of a rope. He smiled as though Cad's hanging would be the highlight of his day. Little beads of sweat had formed on Cad's forehead.

Riddle growled at him, and Cad flinched. He didn't look very good. Abby nearly fainted as her eyes scanned him. One ear was a bloody mess, torn and hanging. His hand was bloody and torn too. There were crusty brown patches of blood showing through his shirt, especially near the shoulder where she'd stabbed him. He had two black eyes the size and color of rotting pears, and there were swellings on his cheeks the size of hen's eggs, and a split lip—loose teeth, too, judging by the way he was pursing his mouth and moving his tongue as if he were counting how many were left.

"If you're worried about the knife wound, don't be," Hagen said to Abby. "It quit bleeding, but he's sore and will be for a long time. The dog made quite a meal of his ear. From the sounds of it, your dog would like to taste the other ear."

Cad tried to speak. She thought he said something about keeping her and the dog away from him. It was painful just watching him. The sight of him, with his mangled ear and dried blood, made her feel queasy.

"So what'll it be, little lady?" Hagen asked. "Shall we hang him or what?"

Cad finally spoke. The effort of getting words out seemed to exhaust him. He used his good hand to wipe dribble off his chin. Speaking brought out all the tendons in his neck. He licked his lips and then issued a warning, "Leave . . . me . . . alone. You . . . don't want me . . . for an . . . enemy. None . . . none of you."

She closed her eyes. It wasn't up to her. Hagen was treating her as if she were judge and jury. She wasn't a judge, just a victim.

Hagen waited for her response.

"I just don't want to see him again," she said. "Never. Just put him on his horse and send him away."

Unbelief came into Cad's eyes. And total shock. He said nothing while he appeared to digest her words, as if he didn't believe what he'd heard. Hagen shook his head. There was disbelief in his eyes too, as though he were disappointed.

"You heard the little lady," Hagen said to his men with a shrug. "Take him away."

Cad said nothing more, not even thank you. He just waved with a wrist action, vaguely, a dismissive little gesture. Slowly, he let a little smile come over his face. And then the mule skinners led him away, his chains rattling.

Hagen said, "I reckon Scooter to be behind us ten or twelve miles, maybe fifteen. Eat some food, and we'll ride out together."

The cook handed her a plate filled with beans and bacon.

Abby quickly took a few bites and then set her plate on the ground where Riddle finished licking up what was left. Behind her, somewhere in the distance, she could hear the mule skinners removing the chains from Cad's legs. She tried to get him out of her mind. She tried to think about Scooter and how long it would take to find him. She tried to think of the comfort she would feel when she collapsed in his arms.

❀ ❀ ❀

For the first mile, Abby raced south as fast as Snip would gallop. Hagen and Riddle had a hard time keeping up. The speed of the horse reminded her of the morning she'd sped toward the Shoshoni winter camp. She gripped the reins tightly and mashed Evan's hat down on her head every few minutes. She thought about how lucky she was to be alive and unharmed and about to reunite with Scooter. She realized now how vulnerable she was when she traveled alone—and how stupid. Without protection, she was vulnerable to Indians like the ones who took her packhorse, vulnerable to undesirables like Cad, not to mention wolves, mountain lions, rattlesnakes, swollen rivers, and skies that spilled rain on her.

She wondered what would happen to Cad, his wounds trying to scab over, riding alone. Where would he go? What would happen to him? She didn't care.

Within a couple of miles, Snip tired and slowed to a gentle lope, a trot, and then a fast-paced walk. She had lathered up and smelled of sweat.

"Scooter will be surprised to see you out here like this," Hagen said when he caught up with her.

"I know," she answered with a nod.

In a way, she hoped Scooter hadn't reached the river yet. She'd like to bathe in it, to wash the mud and blood off her and run a comb through her hair—if she had one. And to wash the memory of Cad away. But as she thought about it, she didn't know if she wanted to bathe in a river that just a few months ago had bodies floating in it. The countryside was still wet, glistening and as green as Massachusetts, Iowa, or anywhere else she'd ever been. She wondered if Scooter had stopped at the settlement, inquiring about her, and what his reaction had been to the answer.

When she led Hagen and Riddle up a ridge to get a better look at the trail leading south, the freight wagons coming along the muddy, winding road were barely visible.

"That's them," Hagen said, pointing.

"Thank the Lord," Abby said. She kicked at Snip's ribs. "Can you see that golden hair, Riddle? You can bite all the other men, but don't bite the one with golden hair."

Chapter 27

SHE APPROACHED SCOOTER'S WAGON IN a full gallop. She leaned forward and waved her hat. She saw the mule skinners point at her. She saw the one with golden hair. He pointed too. She waved again as she closed in, a hundred yards and then fifty. She saw Scooter's eyes, big as saucers. She saw his lips move.

"Abby! Is that you?"

Abby pulled hard on the reins. Snip slid to a halt on all fours. The mare nickered with a raised head, a soft *rat-ta-tat-tat* sound, as if saying she was glad the hurry-up trip was over, as if saying hello to Scooter.

"Why, Abby, that is you! What are you doing way out here? With Hagen? What's with the hat? And those clothes?"

Abby said nothing. She couldn't. She tried, but her mouth wouldn't form words. Tears leaks from her eyes. She had no control over her emotions. With flashes of Cad's attack going through her mind, she slid off her mare, put her hands to her face, and began to cry. Just a little at first and then with uncontrolled sobs.

Scooter jumped off the wagon. She felt his arms around her.

"Abby, what's wrong?"

She couldn't answer. She laid her head on his shoulder and cried.

"What's wrong with her, Hagen?"

Between her sobs, she heard Hagen's answer. He spoke in low, controlled tones, wrestling with his own strong emotions. He told Scooter how she had arrived in camp, the story she'd told them, and how he had invited her to stay overnight. "She caught up with us just before dark last night. I gave her some blankets, and she tried sleeping under one of the wagons. Cad attacked her during the night. But the little lady and her dog got the best of him. The dog bit Cad's ear off, and she stuck Cad in the shoulder with his own knife."

Scooter leaned back and tried to get eye-to-eye contact with her. She saw him through blurry eyes. Scooter said, "I can't believe it. I should have sent Cad to the willows in Salt Lake when I had a chance. I'm sorry."

Abby didn't respond. She just clung to him and wept.

"I can guess what you were doing out here all alone," he said. "I stopped by your settlement. Winny said you went to Salt Lake to see your parents. I was disappointed I hadn't seen you on the road. She also told me about your men capturing Sagwitch and learning more about your boy's whereabouts. He's somewhere up north, isn't he? And that's why you're out here."

She nodded and laid her head on his shoulder again.

Scooter patted her back gently and asked Hagen, "Where's Cad now?"

"I told the little lady she had a choice. We could either hang him or shoot him or send him down the road. She chose the latter. I dunno why. I told the boys to treat his wounds again, give him his horse, and send him away. And never come back."

"Which way did he go?"

"Dunno. I didn't think he'd come south and risk runnin' into you."

Scooter said, "No telling where he'll end up unless the devil lets loose of his soul. I hope he doesn't end up in gold country. If he does, he'll pay for triflin' with Abby."

Hagen shrugged. "My guess is he'll try to make it to Fort Benton and then head on down the Missouri River and back to St. Louis. But maybe Bannack City. Hard to say."

Scooter freed his right hand and shook hands with Hagen. "Thanks. You'd better get back to your wagons."

Hagen mounted his horse. "Sure enough, boss. I 'spect I'll see you again at the crossing of the Snake. Hope Abby'll be okay."

"She's cried enough tears to fill up the Bear River."

She could feel Scooter's fingers biting deeply into her shoulders. His warmth was comforting. She could hear Hagen ride away, and she hoped he knew how much she appreciated his help. She could thank him more later, at the crossing of the Snake.

"I suppose there's a story behind the way you're dressed," Scooter said.

Abby nodded, lacing her fingers with his. Finally, although her throat was dry, she was able to speak. "Yes, there is. I don't suppose you brought a bathtub on this trip. I'm so dirty I feel like a groundhog. I've got a lot to tell you."

Scooter chuckled and took a tight grip on her hand. "Let me help you up on the wagon seat. I'll see that the boys take care of your horse, and then we'll be off again."

Her reunion with Scooter had drawn a crowd. Every curious mule skinner had gathered around them. She felt uncomfortable, but at least none of them were Cad.

Abby nodded, drinking in the comfort of his nearness.

"Up you go," Scooter said.

❋ ❋ ❋

Scooter looked at Abby and gave her a smile. She looked like a weight had been taken off her shoulders, like she was no longer alone against the world. The last time he saw her, she had no color. Today she'd felt cold and frail when he embraced her, but now, at least, there was color in her cheeks. She'd been through another terrifying experience. The terrible battle at the Bear River had been more than one woman should experience in a lifetime. Now she'd had another. He took the reins off Abby's exhausted mare and went to the rear of the wagon. The mare followed willingly, as though she remembered him. He handed the mare off to Oscar. Scooter made certain he was beyond earshot of Abby.

"Get a lead rope and let Abby's mare tag along behind."

"Yes, boss."

"And remember what I told you. Not a word."

Oscar nodded.

"I don't want her to find out I'm a Mormon."

"Yes, boss. I remember."

"I'll tell her when the time is right. If things work out between us."

"Yes, boss. I understand. You don't have to worry about me."

Scooter had finally told Oscar the truth about his past as they wintered out in Salt Lake City. That he had been born and raised in Virginia. That he'd fought in the Civil War. That he was a deserter. Scooter had joined the Church, something that he shared with none of his men except Oscar. Now there were two people west of the Mississippi who knew of his past. But only Oscar knew of his conversion to the Church. That was something he aimed to keep from Abby—for now.

❈ ❈ ❈

The sun felt good to Abby. She sat on the hard wooden wagon seat and warmed herself. When Scooter returned, he hopped up next to her with a cheerful smile. She felt a protection that only he could give right now. She wondered if anything ever knocked him off his stride, like she had been knocked off hers.

He said, "Just relax. I'll help chirk ya up best I can. You've had a rough go of it."

She said nothing, just breathed a big sigh of relief.

She heard whips popping and felt the wagon being jerked forward by Scooter's long string of mules. The wagon groaned under its heavy burden of freight. Riddle followed, looking up at her often, tongue out. Abby relished Scooter's closeness. Her hips touched his as he leaned into her. She didn't talk just yet. She didn't feel like it. Talk would come later. They had more than three months to catch up on. But she needed a short while to adjust to his presence, to gather her thoughts. She could feel the wooden seat, well worn by miles, under the fingertips of her right hand. She could hear the give and take of the bulky springs. She could hear the worn iron tires crushing stones and gravel and dirt clods. These tires and wheels had traveled the road from St. Louis to Salt Lake, from Salt Lake to Bannack City and back again, and now the road to Bannack City again.

"Talk when you feel like it," he said. "I know you've been through a lot."

She knew he was anxious to hear her story. She smiled and said nothing.

"Sorry again about Cad. Trying to manage a bunch of mule skinners is like trying to herd a bunch of cats. He's been a handful ever since St. Louis. I should've fired him long ago." He paused. When she still didn't speak, he continued. "When you're ready to talk, I'll be all ears. I'd like to know how you got here. I not only saw Winny and Carl, but I saw Isaac Jacobs too. He misses you."

He paused again. Nothing was said for several minutes.

Abby took a few deep breaths. She calmed herself and placed her hand over her heart to help her thaw. She knew the conversation between her and Scooter would last all day. Everything she had to tell him would come out in bits and pieces. After a few more minutes, she laid caution aside and began telling Scooter everything. She knew she was slightly incoherent because of Cad's attack, but she told him her story without guile, piecing her months-long narrative together. She began with how depressed she had felt from the time he left the settlement right after the battle and loss of Yahnai. She told him of the weeks and months of despair. About finally getting the news from Sagwitch about Yahnai. She described how stormy it was the night she sneaked away, how the three Indians stole her packhorse, and then overtaking Hagen's wagons. She told him all the facts, all her assumptions, all her conclusions about finding Yahnai.

She stopped there, wondering how to describe Cad's attack.

He said very little, though he patted her hand from time to time. Once in a while, he would say, arching his eyebrows, "My goodness," or "You've had quite a time of it."

She choked up when she described Cad's attack during the pitch blackness of the night and how she fought him off with Riddle's help. Scooter kept shaking his head, grimacing, doubling one fist and then the other, and giving her looks full of concern.

"I wouldn't blame Hagen if he had hung him," Scooter said hotly. "I can't tolerate such crass behavior."

Abby thought back about her decision to let Cad go. She knew Hagen would have hung him from the nearest tree if she had just given the word. Sometimes that was the best way to deal with a hard individual: hang him and save another woman from a violent attack and rape. The law of Moses imposed the death penalty for rape, but she hoped Cad would just disappear. She'd had enough violence and death. She was glad when Scooter began talking about the trip, what they'd see along the way—the ferry crossing at the Snake River and

Bannack City itself. He did this with his hat tipped back, looking friendly and confident. After a while he handed her the lines and told her to drive, which sort of frightened her. She'd driven teams of horses but never a long string of mules. But the mules mostly drove themselves, just following the road while the mule skinners cracked their whips. It helped take her mind off Cad and all her trials.

About midday, the men ate lunch while the animals rested for a short time. Everyone devoured bacon sandwiches prepared that morning by the cook. When they were rolling again, the lack of sleep caught up with her. She felt ready to collapse with exhaustion. She dozed for the better part of the afternoon, her head bobbing, leaning on Scooter for support, waking when the wagons descended into a creek crossing and the mosquitoes bothered her or when she felt she was going to lose her balance on the wagon seat.

When she perked up again, their conversation continued. Scooter began talking about Yahnai, where exactly the Shoshoni may have taken him, who he might be living with, and how he was faring. "I agree that he's likely near Bannack City," he said. "I think we'll find him."

Despite Scooter's concern and confidence, she knew that no one—not even he—could possibly feel the urgency she felt. She was up against high stakes, a race against time, for the life of Yahnai. What if his life were in danger? What if he wasn't being cared for properly? What if he were about to be moved again?

She said, "I hope you're right. With all my heart. It's pulling on me. I need to find him. The sooner, the better. I almost feel like getting on my horse and striking out again alone. I'm just being honest. I can't help my feelings."

He turned to her with the most serious expression she'd seen. "Look, Abby, as you've already found out, this is no place for a woman to be traveling alone. Just sit tight; have some patience. I'll get you there."

Abby had to admit that patience was best, despite the pull she felt. With Scooter, she felt focused and energized. "How long will it take?"

"Less than two weeks," he answered. "An express rider can get there in less than two days, but these mules plug along pretty slow. As little as ten miles to fifteen miles a day over rough terrain, sometimes almost double that on good roads. Your boy will be fine for a few more days. Just keep saying your prayers."

"I will. I hope you will too. Did you learn to pray as a child?"

"Yes. Of course. My mother taught me."

"I suppose you miss her terribly." After he nodded, she said, "My mother taught me to pray too. Even before our family joined the Church."

"That so?"

"I was very young when my parents joined, only four. We lived in Massachusetts. In Chelmsford, not far from Boston. Many new members of the Church went to Illinois. A place called Nauvoo, on the Mississippi, but by the time my parents wanted to join up with the main body of the Church, the Mormons were leaving Nauvoo because of persecution. I was baptized at age eight, out on the plains, while our family was on its way to the Salt Lake Valley."

Scooter gave her a funny look. "We talking about religion now?"

Abby paused. She didn't know how to answer. Yes, she was always willing to talk about religion. It was her favorite subject. She knew the gospel pretty well for her age. She'd studied the Bible and Book of Mormon and Doctrine and Covenants and Pearl of Great Price. She'd read books written by Church leaders. She'd heard the preaching of Church leaders. But she didn't want to drive Scooter away with endless babbling about her religion. She didn't want to sound as though she was going to force Mormonism on him. She wondered if she had set a proper example. In some ways, yes. She'd shown appreciation by preparing doughnuts for him and his men that first night. But what about the way she verbally attacked Colonel Connor? Had she gone too far? Too angry, too rude, too condemning?

In response to his question, she answered, "Only if you want to."

He smiled. "We've got a lot of time to pass in the next few days. It'll help take your mind off Cad—and off that terrible battle you had to witness last winter."

Abby had often wondered what it would feel like to be a missionary. She had her Book of Mormon tucked into her belt, so she pulled it out and started there, telling Scooter all about the early years of the Prophet Joseph Smith, his personal visit by God and Jesus

Christ, the angel Moroni's visit, and the coming forth of the Book of Mormon. He digested all the information calmly, surprisingly, almost like a sponge, with a sly smile on his face, asking questions only occasionally.

It was more than an hour later when she began comparing the doctrine of other churches to that of her own: He had been baptized as an infant. She had been baptized at age eight. She explained that it was doctrinally meaningless to be baptized as an infant and that the belief that little children who died without baptism would not be saved was wrong, very wrong.

"So let me get this straight," he interrupted. "You think all little kids who have died without baptism automatically go to heaven?"

"Every one of them. That includes all those little children the soldiers killed that day at the Bear River."

"If that doctrine is true, heaven would be crowded," Scooter said. "Since the beginning of man's history, millions of babies have died without baptism. Heaven will be crowded—I like the thought."

Abby nodded grimly. "Hell will be crowded too. With men like Colonel Connor. You can't tell me it would be fair for innocent little babies to be stuck in hell forever with men like Colonel Patrick Connor."

When Scooter put a hand to his mouth and gave a feeble little cough she knew she had won the argument. She folded her arms and sat back on the wagon bench. For a while there was silence.

Finally, he asked, "Was Evan from Chelmsford too?"

"No," she answered. "A small town in Gloucestershire, England. He was two years older than I. Some of his relatives joined the Church and came to America. His parents never joined, and neither did he, but he wanted to come to America and immigrated in 1857 to Utah Territory to live with relatives in a place called Kaysville."

He nodded. "We went through Kaysville on our way here."

"We met in Salt Lake City sort of by chance. We fancied each other and began to court. We were married by my parent's bishop."

"But not in the Endowment House?"

Abby laughed. "No. You have to be a member in good standing to enter the Endowment House. Evan wasn't a member. Remember? We talked about that when you visited a few months ago."

Scooter nodded. "Did that bother you, that he wasn't a member?"

"Oh yes. And it bothered my parents. But I knew he would join the Church one day. He was a good man."

"But . . ."

Abby hung her head. "Unfortunately, he died before he joined."

"And along came Isaac."

Abby sighed. Inevitably, their conversation had to include Isaac. Isaac still held a special place in her heart but less of a place since she'd lost Yahnai. Truthfully, Scooter occupied much of that space now, but she didn't know exactly what to think of it. At one time she had concluded that she may as well marry Isaac. But now? She didn't know. "Yes. He treated me nicely. Yahnai too. He took care of us. He's a good man and a good member of our Church."

"After we find your boy, what are your plans?"

"Go back to Franklin. Evan is buried there."

"So you still plan on marrying Isaac?"

"I didn't say that. I'll just have to see."

He gave her an intense gaze. "But you'd like to marry again, wouldn't you?"

"Yes. But I have some unfinished business right now."

"I know," he replied. He tipped his hat back and pointed ahead. "I see a creek crossing up ahead. It'll be a good place to make tonight's camp. I have a surprise for you, a gift. I'll give it to you later."

"A gift? For me?"

"Yes. Something special."

Abby's imagination ran wild. What kind of gift would a teamster give a young widow?

Chapter 28

ABBY FOUND HERSELF IN THE same location as the previous night. Scooter hadn't asked if it might bother her to be camped along the same stream where Cad had attacked her. He just stopped because it was time, the end of another long day on the trail, the sun sinking low.

She stepped off the wagon and put her feet on the ground. Stiff from sitting, she stretched, steadying herself with one hand on the wagon. She saw the exact location where she had been under one of Hagen's wagon, where Cad found her. She saw where Hagen had pitched his tent, where she had slept after the attack. She saw a little circle of rocks where the campfire had been built. She saw the ashes from the fire. She saw Hagen's fresh wagon tracks, leaving the camp, headed north. In her mind, she could still see Cad and all the injuries she and the dog had inflicted on him.

While the mules brayed for a drink, Scooter told his men to carefully examine the groves of trees and willows and brush that lined the creek, looking for Indians.

"If I see a single feather, I'll shoot at it," Oscar said. Head down, knees bent, he crept toward the creek with the hammer of his Springfield cocked back in firing position. Oscar hadn't witnessed the aftermath of the terrible battle at the Bear River, but he acted as if he had. He moved with caution and with apprehension.

Scooter said to Abby, "The men have been spooked all during the trip."

Abby nodded. She knew surviving Shoshoni, especially young men, were seeking ways to extract revenge in any possible way. All white people were vulnerable.

Oscar gave a sign. All clear. The mules settled down. Their shuffling hooves stopped moving, and she heard lazy huffs of breath from them. The moment an animal was unharnessed, it would trot for the creek, where it would wade to cool its overheated flesh and drink until it was content. Soon all the animals were grazing along a hillside. A few men saddled ponies and rode out to see if they could find a deer or elk to shoot at, or even a sage grouse or coyote. Abby's mouth watered as she watched the camp cook pull out frying pans and Dutch ovens, throw a slab of back bacon on the tailgate of the cook wagon, and begin baking big pones of bread.

Abby watched all this with keen anticipation of what her gift from Scooter might be. Her thoughts ran the gamut from clothing to books to something to help furnish her sparse cabin.

She found a tin cup and went to the creek where water dashed over the rocks. Now that she had found Scooter and the security he gave her, the twilight seemed to soften everything—the trees, the brush, the skyline. Everything seemed to mellow into the shadowy indistinctiveness of a dreamland. As she ate her dinner, spasms of curiosity kept erupting within her. The mule skinners rested by the fire, drinking coffee with loud sipping noises and swatting mosquitoes.

Finally, Scooter rose to his feet. "Come with me," he said.

They walked to the privacy of space between two wagons. He reached into the back of his wagon and pulled out a tent. He smiled almost apologetically.

Abby's eyes fell in disappointment. "A tent? That's my gift?"

Scooter laughed a good laugh. "Yes, it's a gift. I'm also going to give you a dress or two to wear on the trip. But none of that is your special gift."

"Then what?"

Still chuckling, he reached into his wagon lock box and produced a small package wrapped in red paper. When he placed it in her hand, their hands touched. She looked into his eyes and then back at the gift. With precision, she unwrapped the little package, revealing a little black container, the kind jewelers used. She opened the container and saw the gift sitting in a nest of cotton—a five-dollar gold piece. Satisfaction pursed her mouth. "Oh, Scooter! Is it the one minted in 1860?"

He nodded.

Abby held the coin in the air, letting the evening sun reflect off it. Once again, she let her fingers softly run over the coin's inscriptions, savoring every touch of the beehive, the lion, and the wording.

"Oh, thank you! How can I repay you? I can't believe this. Now I owe you for helping me out of the creek, for being with me during that awful battle, and for this."

Scooter leaned against a wagon wheel. He was smiling ear to ear.

Abby tried to ascertain Scooter's motives for giving her the coin. Was he trying to impress her, to perhaps lure her away from Isaac? Or did he merely feel sorry for her because she had lost a husband and then a son? She didn't know which way the wind was blowing in that regard, but it was intriguing to think about.

Abby held the half-eagle to the sky again, peering at its details. "Thank you again, Scooter. I will treasure this forever."

She closed her eyes and hung her head as feelings of guilt swept over her for the way she acted when Scooter said good-bye last winter, right after that terrible battle. But she reckoned she had an excuse, being in such a fit of depression over losing Yahnai. She remembered him sharing his secrets with her. He was a true Southern boy, a Confederate soldier who'd lost nearly everything—his father, two brothers, and in a way, his home. He was alone. His mother was alone. She wondered how he could ever get past all this. His troubles were excessive, piled high and heavy, like the freight he had taken to Bannack City. Higher and heavier perhaps than the grief she'd felt over the loss of Evan. He'd lost three loved ones. She'd lost one. She'd been depressed for months. Scooter had apparently worked through his depression, if he'd had any. He was fully engaged, running a new business, decisive and confident. But she felt sorry for him. Her heart ached for him.

And now this.

A wonderful gift. A gold coin.

Chapter 29

AT DAWN, ABBY AWOKE TO the night herder's song and the silly braying of mules. She knew where she was. The tent smelled of new canvas, different than Hagen's; it didn't reek with the smell of sweat and tobacco. She felt sluggish. Yesterday had taken the starch out of her. She peeked out of her tent, which was wet with dewy moisture. The sun was trying to peek through the clouds. The mules looked sluggish too, some motionless, some grazing. There was a faint breeze, and the smell of wood smoke laced the air. She heard men talking around the campfire. All this—and the thought of being with Scooter—drew her out of her sluggishness and put her in a high mood. She thought about him, the way he moved, his guileless smile, his occasional engaging stares. She'd folded and placed Evan's old, stained clothing in a corner of the tent—who knew when she might need them again—and shrugged on one of the new dresses Scooter had given her, the same blue as Yahnai's sweater. She brushed her hair back, wishing she had a mirror.

She heard Scooter's voice and moved quickly to open the tent flap. His men were currying the mules, rubbing them between the ears, checking their feet, getting ready to harness and hook them to the wagons. He was watching them.

"There you are," he said when he saw her. "Did you sleep well?"

"I got through the night."

"You make that dress look just perfect."

She felt her face redden. "Thank you. What can I do to help?"

Scooter thought a few moments. "You could help me harness a mule or two, if you really want to. Just the two of us."

Abby handed him the coin and the box it came in. "Put this back in your wagon lockbox for safety, will you? I'll get my boots on and be right out."

In a few minutes, Abby found herself standing next to Scooter. He had a set of harnesses, complete with collars and hames. He approached one of the mules.

"I've helped harness a few horses in my day," Abby said, trying to impress him. "I helped my father. I helped Evan."

"Same thing," Scooter said, pointing at his animals. "The mules need to be harnessed properly so they won't injure themselves trying to pull our heavy wagons." He closed in on the dark-brown mule. "It's a good idea to talk to the mules as you work with them. Whoa, Snuffy. You know me, don't you? Here I am with your harness. The boys cleaned it up for me. This here is Abby. She's going to help me."

Abby held her hand out and approached the mule. It smelled no different than a horse. The mule sniffed her and stood still.

Scooter said, "Don't worry about him biting you. He likes you. Get on his nigh side. . . . That's right. You've got a nice touch. Press him up toward the wagon. I'll help."

Abby now stood side-by-side with Scooter, so close they touched shoulders. He handed her the collar and said, "Rub his neck a little until he gets acquainted with you. You're doing fine. Put this up and around his neck."

She did as he directed and moved to the next step without his help, noticing how he hovered and worried over her. She buckled the hip strap and secured it in place. Snuffy stood still as an angel.

Scooter pointed. "Now carry the hip strap assembly over your right shoulder and get it positioned just right."

She gave him a knowing smile. "And grip the hame in my hand. Then position the hame over the withers, right where the withers meet the collar."

"You're doing fine," he said.

"And now I put the right trace and hip strap assembly on the back of the mule so that the harness is centered."

"You really do know what you're doing." He sounded impressed.

"Glad to earn my keep," she said and then turned to the mule. "Easy, Snuffy. I'm going to Bannack City with you. Lots of green grass for you along the way. When we get there, there'll be a surprise for you. We'll find Yahnai. After we find him, I'll rub your neck for a long time, just to show how I appreciate you." She wondered if Scooter would feel the same appreciation if she were to rub his neck as well. She gave him a longing glance.

Scooter approached her with a whip in his hand. "Next, you can learn to use this."

Abby's face clouded with uneasiness. She'd hated it when she saw Isaac using his whip at the crossing. But she hesitated for a moment. The whip mule skinners used was different, much longer.

Scooter said, "Take this whip and throw it out in front of you like you were trying to reach the leaders. I'll show you." Deftly, he made the long whip crack.

"I don't know if I can do that," Abby said.

"Nonsense," Scooter said. With a spring in his step and a commanding air of self-confidence, he placed his body behind hers. His chest touched her back as he reached around her, placing the whip in her right hand, and extending his hand over hers.

"I don't know . . . ," she said.

"Get the right grip," he said, pressing closer. His nearness made her senses spin. "Place your thumb in line with the handle. Where your thumb points, that's where the whip will travel."

"Don't you have a short whip, one for beginners?"

He chuckled as if there wasn't a mule skinner in the world that used a short whip. "The next thing is to cock the whip, letting out the full length behind you, like this." Scooter pulled back on her arm with a jerk, and the whip followed. "Now bring the whip forward, and remember to point your thumb."

She brought the whip forward, but with two hands holding it, the motion was too relaxed, and there was no pop when the whip extended.

"That's almost it," he said. "Try again."

"Do you try to hit the mules?" she asked.

"No. We don't want to break their skin. Too much chance of infection. An injured mule is no good to us. We just want them to *think* we might crack their skins."

Abby thought about Cad. She'd done more than just crack his skin. She'd invaded his flesh with a knife. She turned her thoughts back to Scooter. She felt better, and her whole body relaxed. More acutely now, she felt Scooter's presence behind her again. His muscular body gave her a sense of protection.

"Show me again," she said. Abby stepped away and watched him re-cock the whip and send it out in front of him, the gusto for his talent evident. When the whip popped, it echoed. He did it several times. No longer did she view the man as just a mule skinner, even though that's what he did. He looked powerful and handsome, and her eyes froze on his long, lean form. A thought came to her. Did he suspect how she was looking him over, assessing him?

"You'll get the hang of it before long," he said. He coiled the whip and hung it on his wagon. He stood face-to-face with her, close enough to touch. "Let's eat our bacon and beans and strike out."

He offered her his arm. She took it, and they strolled toward the cook's wagon. She had to admit that he and this particular group of mule skinners were much different than Cadmus Arbuckle. Scooter was not only handsome but hardworking and a leader of men who knew how to get things done.

She wondered where all this would lead.

Chapter 30

THE TRIP NORTH MEANT ABBY was spending hours every day with Scooter, usually seated next to him on the freight wagon, rocking and swaying, or walking alongside. The views were amazing, similar to those surrounding Cache Valley—wide, expansive valleys; sagebrush foothills dotted with bright green groves of aspen; and snow-covered, forested mountains on each side. The winding road crossed creeks every few miles, arching up on the benches occasionally, never straight for very long. It was the same road trappers had followed in prior years. And before that, Indians. She became adept at popping the whip above the heads of the mules. She could pop it almost as well as Scooter. Now when they sat together on the seat of the wagon, they sat so close she could feel the heat of his body. At times he would put an arm around her.

When they badgered each other over religious topics and as she watched him command his men, she found him intelligent and sensitive and Christian in the way he treated people. She knew she was falling in love, just as she had fallen in love with Evan. But it was another cruel twist of fate that Scooter was not a member of the Church, just as Evan had not been. But Isaac couldn't measure up to Scooter, nor could any other man.

She knew Scooter was falling in love with her too, though he never said anything. She knew it by his actions—especially his protective behavior. One morning she stepped off the wagon and almost bumped into one of Scooter's men who'd been walking by, an extremely shy mule skinner. Her sudden appearance embarrassed him so much that he gave her one appalled look and turned and went off, practically at a trot, putting a safe distance between them, as though Scooter had warned him about getting too close to her. He was a heavy man, and the sight of him trying to run made her laugh out loud, something she hadn't done in a while. He didn't turn back and look at her again until he was safely at his own wagon, and then he turned fearfully, as if he expected to be shot for having stood next to her.

Another mule skinner with spiky black hair that stuck out in all directions skinned whatever game was shot. He used a skinning knife a foot long that he carried in a scabbard under one shoulder. He grinned at her constantly, exposing his black teeth. He had an insolent manner and spat tobacco juice constantly while he talked. Scooter told him not to chew and spit around her, and when he forgot one day, Scooter shoved him against a wagon and told him to behave.

Despite the special relationship growing between her and Scooter, she spent a lot of her time thinking about Yahnai. At every opportunity she sought to confirm that Yahnai was in or near Bannack City. She talked to express riders and other travelers, but no one could verify that her boy was actually there.

One evening Oscar and some of the men rode their ponies out of camp looking for game in the hope of having fresh meat for supper. However, they returned early and unexpectedly. They rode right to the cook wagon and told Scooter that four Indians were approaching from the east on horseback. The way they kept looking back made Abby apprehensive.

"They're trailing a packhorse loaded with skins," Oscar reported.

"Let 'em come in," Scooter said. "They probably want to trade."

Abby could see the Indians. Occasionally she could see a flash of the sun reflect off their rifles. Abby wondered if the Indians were Bannacks and if they would know anything about Yahnai. As they approached, they continued to make peace overtures in sign language. The Indians soon made it known they wanted to trade buckskins for caps and powder. Each Indian had a large knife strapped to him and carried his rifle lightly across the withers of his horse. They had long, tangled black hair and wore nothing on their heads, not even a feather. Their leather leggings were greasy, and they wore dark moccasins. The trading was brisk. The Indians used adequate but broken English. Abby wondered if the Indians would use the caps and powder against the settlers in Franklin, an act of revenge for helping the soldiers.

"I want to ask them about Yahnai," Abby told Scooter.

"Let 'em trade first," he said. "They're apt to ignore you till then."

After a short while, Abby had picked out the leader of the band by his actions. The Indian had a large head, squarish and heavy. When the trading had concluded, she quickly made him understand that she was looking for a young boy, an adopted boy, that had been taken north by the Shoshoni—specifically Bear Hunter's men. "His name is Yahnai," she said, speaking slow and combining her speech with sign language. "Have you seen him? He's six years old and about this tall," she added, gesturing.

The square-headed Bannack nodded his head up and down.

A cry of joy broke from Abby's lips at the news, and she grasped Scooter's arm. "Did you see that? He knows about Yahnai!" She asked the man if he'd actually seen Yahnai, but it disappointed her when he said no, that he'd only heard about the child and that he'd been given to a Bannack family near Bannack City.

In the days that followed, Abby thought about the family that was caring for Yahnai, if they were kind and gentle and if they showed Yahnai any love. She wondered if they would willingly give him up. She had Scooter's gift, the five-dollar gold piece. She might need it to buy Yahnai's freedom.

❊ ❊ ❊

Late one day, Scooter's wagons reached a summit. From the top, Abby could see the broad expanse of a plain through which ran the Snake River, but she couldn't see Bannack City. The river ran like a thread of silver, curving and winding its way west, where hundreds and hundreds of Oregon immigrants were headed. Three buttes rose from the level plain of the valley to the west, like immense ant hills. Abby could see them through a hazy veil.

Once she crossed the Snake River, she'd be nearly halfway to Bannack City, halfway to Yahnai.

Chapter 31

WHAT ABBY SAW WHEN SHE arrived at the Snake River ferry site was worth the paint of an artist. The river was a broad, slow body of water running northeast to southwest. Indian teepees, white men's tents, and circles of wagons dotted the riverbanks. On each side of the river, a thick rope cable had been secured to large cottonwood trees. The ferry's wooden platform and an empty freight wagon moved upstream. Slowly, the ferry and the wagon made it across the Snake River, propelled by the force of the current going over and beneath an underwater oar board. Bored miners and freighters waiting their turn to cross cast their lines out into the green waters of the river hoping to catch a monster trout for dinner. Great blue herons wadded in the marshes, aiming their long, sharp beaks at unsuspecting fish. Pelicans, geese, ducks, coots, and white swans floated on the slow-moving waters. Overhead, soaring bald eagles and hawks scoured the landscape for a meal. An assortment of wildflowers of every color dotted the banks of the river and the hillside.

Scooter told her that Indians had been using this crossing for years. Five young braves from the Flathead Valley crossed here a few years ago on their way to St. Louis to find the "blackrobes," Catholic priests, so they could learn the white man's religion. So it was called Flathead Crossing. The river was wider and shallower here.

Abby saw Hagen's circle of wagons about the same time Scooter did. Scooter detected her alarm quickly, placing an arm around her. "We'll make camp right next to Hagen. Don't worry about Cad. He won't be here. If he happens to show his face again, I'll personally dunk him in the river and hold him under until he's blue in the face. And then I'll let Hagen hang him."

Abby was still having recurring nightmares about Cad every night, just as she'd had recurring nightmares about the battle of Bear River. "I'm fine," she reassured him. "I know he won't be around here."

Nevertheless, she clung to Scooter as their wagon drew closer to Hagen's circle. She heard geese honking, mules braying, men bartering, and the loud but cheerful profanity of the mule skinners. She shielded her eyes from a warm, white sun and asked, "Who runs the ferry?"

"Two of your Mormon friends."

She lowered her brows, confused. "I don't know anyone up here."

The ferry was coming back toward them, carrying a stagecoach bound for Salt Lake City. Scooter chuckled. "It's owned by the Bernard brothers of Utah Territory. Smart fellers, those brothers. Brigham Young won't let your people dig in the ground for gold, but the Bernard boys get forty dollars for every wagon, mostly paid in gold dust. They'll make more money this summer than most of the Bannack City miners. It's all legal. They got their permit from the territorial government and brought the equipment up from Salt Lake. The ferry operates like that from morning's first light until dark."

Abby noted that the contents of the wagons sat waiting to be ferried. More outfits waited for their turn as well as a collection of people traveling by horseback, buggy, or small wagon. Even more amazing was the sight of a herd of cattle being forced into the river by a dozen or so nearly naked young Bannacks.

"Why not put them on the ferry?" she asked.

"It's cheaper to pay Indians to swim bulls and mules across rather than pay to have them loaded on the ferry boat. Faster too."

To get the animals started, the Indians—with dazzling determination—shouted and threw sticks and stones at them. A few of the bawling, more experienced cattle jumped in and began to swim. It amused Abby to watch the Indians, who took to the water as fearlessly as a dog. They swam just behind the stock, sometimes catching hold of their tails and sometimes splashing water on the sides of their faces to keep the animals in the right direction. Without losing a single animal, they guided them to safety on the opposite side.

Hagen almost fell over himself with one apology after another when he saw Abby. Even the roughneck men with him apologized for the way Cad had acted that night. She accepted the apologies but didn't want to dwell on the subject. So when she saw the ferry approaching with an express rider on it, she told Scooter that she wanted to ask the rider if he happened to know anything about Yahnai. It was more of an excuse to get away from all the mule skinners and the talk about Cad because she knew it wasn't likely that the rider, a mere boy no older than eighteen, would know anything.

Scooter walked with her to the ferry landing. "You ought to post a letter to Winny. I know she's worried sick about you. And it wouldn't hurt to post one to your parents in Salt Lake too."

Abby nodded and began composing a letter in her head as Scooter added, "I have writing paper in my wagon lockbox. I'll cover the cost."

Chapter 32

As Abby wrote her letter, Scooter had the urge to pen a letter to his mother in Virginia, but he'd sent one just before he left Salt Lake. He received several letters from her during the winter. They were in his lockbox. There were letters, too, from Millie, his Southern belle, who lived just over the hill from his family's plantation. A girl he had courted for several months before he enlisted in the Confederate army. A girl who wrote to him regularly on monogrammed stationery.

By now, Scooter had pushed Millie out of his mind. That's because he was in love with Abigail Butterfield Browett. His infatuation—and later—love for her had come in stages. The cues were there: her personality, her mysterious allure, and her smell. It had started with the glances he stole that first day when they met at the creek crossing. That evening when she treated him and his men to doughnuts. His respect for her when she stood up to Colonel Connor. Her devotion to Yahnai. The disappointment he'd felt when he stopped at the settlement several days ago only to find that she wasn't there. The excitement at seeing her with Hagen. The sorrow he felt for her over Cad's attack. Traveling with her these several days. Sitting next to her. Teaching her how to pop a whip.

She was some woman.

If he proposed to Abby, what would she say? Would she choose him over Isaac Jacobs? One thing was for certain. It was still too early to press the issue. Perhaps the time to propose would be just before they reached Bannack City, and at the same time, he'd tell her that he'd joined her Church.

He'd begun his investigation into Mormonism when he returned to Salt Lake after the battle. In his dealings with them, practically every Mormon talked to him about their Church and offered him a copy of the Book of Mormon. Finally one day he accepted one. After he read it, he wanted to talk more about it. He knew if he became a Mormon he'd do so under awkward circumstances. He was a Confederate deserter. He'd been using an alias since he left Virginia. None of his men knew who he really was. He wanted to talk personally to someone high up in the Mormon Church. He first tried Brigham Young but found him to be a very busy man—governor of Utah Territory, President of the Church, supervisor of the temple's construction.

He had tried other Church leaders. Eventually, he was able to talk to a man named Wilford Woodruff, one of the Twelve Apostles.

He found Elder Woodruff to be the most powerful and engaging man he'd ever met. When Woodruff bore testimony of the truthfulness of the Book of Mormon and the restored gospel of Jesus Christ, he knew it was true beyond any doubt. He knew he had to confess his background to Elder Woodruff. The Apostle's eyes became wet when he told him about the death of his father and two brothers in the Civil War battles. When Scooter told him about Abby and that she had married a young man by the name of Evan Browett, Elder Woodruff told him all about Evan's uncle, Daniel Browett. Daniel and his wife had been lay preachers in the United Brethren organization in England. Woodruff baptized around six hundred members of the group within just a few months. Daniel served in the Mormon Battalion and was at the American River in California under the employ of Captain Sutter when gold was discovered. But he died in California, a victim of an Indian attack—similar to what happened to Evan Browett. Wilford Woodruff baptized Scooter under the name of Jesse Kemp but gave him permission to use his alias until after the war.

Scooter occasionally found himself comparing Millie and Abby. Millie was the prettiest of three Southern belle sisters, all beautiful as magnolia blossoms. She had wheat-colored hair, rosy cheeks, large hazel eyes, and a voice dripping in charm. She was cultured as a strand of pearls, dainty, trim, flirtatious, mannerly, and always delectably attired. When he called on her, she usually appeared in polished plaid cotton, bell-shaped sleeves, and a full hoop skirt. And she had always held a white lace hankie in her hand. Millie was well read and could write prose, do arithmetic, play the piano, dance, paint pictures, and speak the French language proficiently.

Abby was just as beautiful, however, if you didn't count the way she had been dressed the first time he'd seen her at the creek—in that plain, threadbare green dress, or the way she'd been dressed when he'd seen her a few days ago, in Evan Browett's shirt, trousers, and hat. Before she cut it, her hair fell in long, sleek yellow strands that made her green eyes and all her features look sharp. There were differences. Abby lived in a meager log hut, not a majestic mansion on a plantation. She had no slaves to help with her work. She was not well educated. She spoke a little Shoshoni but no French. She had parents in Salt Lake City that he'd never met. She had already been married once. She had an adopted Indian boy.

Abigail Butterfield Browett had her faults; that was certain. She was unpredictable, highly opinionated, prone to mood swings, sharp anger, depression, and fear. From her tent at night, he'd heard her restless groans, her tossing and turning, as she dreamed over and over again of the terrible battle at the Bear River.

But like he'd done with Millie, Scooter had pushed Abby's faults into the back recesses of his mind. He was in love with her.

Chapter 33

ABBY WAS AMAZED THAT IT took more than a dozen crossings to get all of Scooter's wagons and cargo across. As they continued their snail's pace toward Bannack City, they traveled with Hagen, making a long procession of wagons.

The big talk at the crossing had been the news of another gold discovery a few miles northeast of Bannack City, a place known as Alder Gulch. Prospectors made the discovery in May and kept it a secret for weeks. But the news was out, doubling the attraction of gold in that part of the territory. There were now two boomtowns. Scooter told her that the discovery made his cargo worth perhaps double over what he'd thought—good for future business. He hoped to make three or four more trips before next winter.

There had also been a lot of talk about the war. President Lincoln had sent two representatives all the way out here to ensure that future gold shipments eventually made it into the treasury to help fund the war against the South. Scooter talked about it briefly with her, but he didn't seem to be too upset about it. After all, this part of the country was deemed to be in Yankee hands.

One afternoon he gave her his opinion of the war. He contended that the war between the North and the South was not simply over slavery, but rather it was a tariff war—a war over the love of money, a fiscal quarrel. She didn't argue. The rages of the Civil War were a long way from Utah and Idaho Territories. She couldn't see how it would affect Bannack City much. She preferred talking about the doctrines of the Church, and they did that often.

But as Scooter's mules plodded north, Abby began to lose patience. Sometimes the earth seemed to spin fast, and sometimes it seemed to spin slowly. This trip to Bannack City was slow, too slow. She couldn't take her mind off Yahnai as they traveled and camped at Market Lake and then Camas Creek. She wondered what Winny and everyone thought of her letter. Now everyone in Franklin knew where she was. She hoped Isaac wouldn't be foolish enough to come after her. Hopefully he was too busy with his farm work and running his relay station. She'd had the impression that express riders were all young, but that afternoon she'd seen an older man galloping north in a hurry, obviously an express rider.

That evening they camped at Beaver Canyon, not far from Bannack City. One of the men killed an antelope, and they roasted it on the fire. To help make it an exceptional night, the cook made a spice cake. Scooter picked wildflowers and gave them to her, asking her to wear the yellow dress again.

After the meal, they walked together at sundown, their hands intertwined. She felt another confirmation that she had fallen in love. "Thank you again for taking care of me," she said. "For rescuing me out of the creek, for being with me during that terrible battle, and for letting me travel with you."

"Having you with me has made the trip special," he answered.

She squeezed his hand. "You've proved to be a good student of religion."

"And you've been a good teacher."

"You'd make a good Mormon," she said, taking a bold step. "I've been saying my prayers about you. That you will join my Church."

"And if I did?"

"It would be the right thing to do. It would bring you an internal peace."

"Do you have that—an internal peace?"

"Just about," she answered. "I believe in those things we've talked about—the Resurrection, eternal life. To know where your father and brothers are right now—that's what gives me that special peace inside. But it'll be better as soon as I find Yahnai."

"What are you going to do after you find him? Go back and marry old man Jacobs?"

She chuckled a little. "I don't know. Should I?"

"If that's what you want."

"I don't know for sure."

He turned to face her, peering at her intently. "What about us?"

She returned his gaze as her heartbeat increased. "Yes. What about us?"

He placed one hand on her shoulder. With the other, he touched her chin. "You look so beautiful in that dress." And then he kissed her gently.

Abby savored the kiss, her first from Scooter. It sent an involuntary chill through her, and so did his touch. His hands remained on her shoulders. He drew back, looked at her, touched her chin, and then kissed her again.

Slowly, she opened her eyes, and her voice cracked. "Is it the dress?"

"No," he said with a gratified grin. "It's the woman."

She felt her face color.

"I hope I didn't offend you."

She shook her head. "No. Why should it?"

"I've wanted to kiss you for a long time. I just couldn't convince myself that it was right."

"Because . . . ?

"Because of your feelings toward Isaac."

"We can fix all that," she said. "I could change my mind about Isaac."

"You could?" he asked.

"Maybe I already have."

He leaned away as if sizing her up, smiling. "I thought so. I hoped so."

New warmth surged through Abby. She said tenderly, "You may kiss me again."

He moved his mouth over hers and reclaimed her lips, embracing her.

Scooter's kisses were surprisingly gentle, not what she expected from a mule skinner. He had gathered her in his arms and was holding her snugly. When he relaxed and without looking away, she backed out of his grasp—not because she wanted to but because she thought it proper. The warmth of his arms had been so bracing, so male. She stared at the ground thinking about the undeniable bridges to be crossed. Just where would their feelings toward each other lead?

Apparently he was thinking of the same thing. "Is the reason you let me kiss you because we talked about religion and you think I might become a Mormon?"

Although his nearness still made her senses spin, she felt compelled to give him an honest answer. She'd already gone down that road before. She'd married Evan before he consented to baptism and lost him. She didn't want that to happen again. It had been a factor in her agreement to offer Isaac her hand in marriage.

"That has something to do with it," she said. "Remember our conversation the first day we met, about Isaac and the Endowment House? When I marry again, it will be in the Endowment House."

He paused, sized her up. "Could you learn to love a teamster?"

"Maybe I already do."

"But not enough to marry? I have to be Mormon first?"

"You don't have to do anything. You have your freedom to choose. You can be a Mormon, or you can refuse. But if you want me . . ."

He finished the sentence for her. "If I want you, I become a Mormon."

She framed him with an intense look. "I've had this feeling for a long time, a feeling that God wanted us to meet. As bad as the battle was back in January, it had a strange way of bringing us together. Some say that everything happens for a purpose. We've met under very unusual circumstances. Now we're locked together in a search for Yahnai. Whether or not this will lead to you becoming a Mormon or lead to us talking seriously about marriage, I don't know. I can't predict. But right now, you occupy a special place in my heart."

"And you in mine," he said. He turned back and embraced her again.

The sky had darkened. The crispness in the air was plummeting toward a real night chill. "It's getting late," she said.

Hand in hand, they began walking toward the campfire.

Chapter 34

WHEN ISAAC JACOBS OVERTOOK ABBY and Scooter's freight wagons earlier that day, he took a wide berth, kicking up a plume of dust. He'd left Franklin on one of the express ponies and had changed horses at every station. When he saw Abby perched on the wagon seat next to Scooter, his heart skipped a beat. He wished he were there with her instead of Scooter. He kicked the horse under him and passed the wagons without a wave. Soon he'd be in Bannack City.

Over Winny and Carl's objections, he'd left as soon as Winny shared Abby's letter with everyone in the settlement. They contended that Abby was safe traveling with Scooter. Isaac had thought of Abby every day since she vanished. It tore him up to think that she'd just disappeared in the middle of the night without telling him and traveled to Salt Lake City to see her parents without him. The longer she stayed away, the more likely she wasn't coming back. When he learned the truth, like a peal of thunder, everything came crashing down on him. The fog in his brain suddenly lifted. He chastised himself for not listening to her. When he heard the news from Sagwitch about Yahnai, he should have thrown supplies on his wagon and taken Abby to Bannack City. He had been selfish. He had been blind. Now he felt fully awakened to his responsibilities to her.

Likewise, a fear gripped him, a fear greater than the thought of his own death—the fear that he might be losing Abby. Scooter might be winning her heart, day after day, mile after mile. If so, she was misguided. He had to save her. It would be wrong for her to fall in love with a freighter, a non-Mormon. He felt his teeth clench in rage at the mere thought. He had to thwart any notion of that. Only one thing mattered now: Beat Scooter and Abby to Bannack City. Find Yahnai before they arrived. Present the boy to her, all cleaned up, happy, and smiling. Then everything would go back to normal, the way things were meant to be. Make the trip to the Endowment House. He'd have a wife again, a young one, one who wanted to have children. He'd have the opportunity to start a second family, a family that would include Yahnai.

His bad leg ached, but he rode hard, leaned forward in his saddle, and spurred his horse on. He had a desperate task before him, but he'd do it even if it killed him. He passed a steady stream of traffic, not only freighters but anxious men on horseback hoping to file claims. He saw a wagon full of elk and deer and buffalo carcasses to provide meat for hungry miners. He saw a wagon full of barley, soon to be brewed into beer.

Covered with trail dust, he arrived in Bannack City under a warm afternoon sun. He twisted his neck to the right and left, getting a sense of the place, trying to get a clear idea of where to start his search. Not in his wildest imagination had he formed a correct image of the gold town in his mind. It was the armpit of Idaho Territory. Sagebrush hills and mountains bordering the narrow valley were dry and bare, almost devoid of trees. Only stumps remained. Men, hundreds of them, were working the hillsides with picks and shovels, like bees in a hive, with each queen bee poised to sting a competing queen bee. Like ants swarming over an anthill. Squatting along the edges of Grasshopper Creek. Panning for gold dust and nuggets, sacking it up in leather pouches. Muddying the waters and trampling the grass with their enthusiasm. Some miners were obvious greenhorns, swarming around other men's workings, gawking and popping questions. Other men, toting portable bars, strolled along the banks of the river selling liquor to the young and callow miners. Several of the men had been too busy, apparently, to build any type of permanent structure to live in. There were several brush huts, shallow caves, and wool blankets where men rested without any shelter at all. Several miners had arrived in Bannack City in small wagons. Now those wagons were abandoned, strewn everywhere. Isaac saw a man forming an ax handle out of a wagon wheel spoke.

Isaac sat in the saddle, indecisive, wondering where to start. There were swarms of people to talk to, enough to befuddle the eye. He felt like a mariner trawling in a sea he hadn't charted. All he could do was dart around randomly and hope he bumped into someone who would know something.

A map he'd seen showed two main roads leading into town, one from the south and one from the east. He had come in from the south, through what was called Horse Prairie. The first section of town he passed had a wooden sign spiked to a post. It read *Yankee Flat*. Union flags, dirty and tattered, flew from several of the tents and huts. He scratched his cheek, amazed that the tentacles of the Civil War stretched all the way to this part of the country. Based on their apparel, many of the men looked as though they had been soldiers for either the North or South. That meant they were probably deserters. They wore an assortment of mostly worn-out and ill-fitting clothing crusted with dirt and sweat from the diggings. There were Union-blue and Confederate-gray frock coats, shell jackets, vests, shirts, and trousers—often mixed with buckskins.

Freighters were locked into the business of auctioning off their wares, and store owners and miners were bidding for them. He heard not only Southern and Northern accents in the bidding but foreign accents as well. He heard the exasperating heaviness of German; the strange rhythms of Russian and Polack; the good-natured mispronunciations of the Swedes, Norwegians, and Danes. Mexicans, prancing on their mustangs for the edification of the crowd, shouted their bids in Spanish.

Dodging building sites, litter, and manure, Isaac meandered along a row of log buildings. A few Indians caught his eye. Some mingled with whites. Others pressed their noses against window panes, begging for food. He decided against going near the saloons. The smell of a forged fire and heated iron from a blacksmith shop caught his attention, but when he heard vile cursing, he avoided it. He passed a small goldsmith shop; the smith was fashioning gold watch chains, earrings, unique nuggets on a conversation stick piece, and other jewelry out of the miner's gold. On nearly every shop were posted the words, *Help Wanted*. Isaac gasped at the wages offered.

Earlier in his life, Isaac had watched as Salt Lake grew from nothing into an impressive city. Despite all the talk, he had a hard time envisioning Bannack City materializing into anything similar. It really didn't deserve the title of "city," and it wasn't much of a town either. Except there were a lot of people crowded into it and around it. Three thousand souls? Four thousand? Five?

None looked like the men of Franklin settlement. Too wild. Too unkempt.

There were teepees and wickiups above the creek. He took a drink from his canteen, ate a few strips of jerky, and rode toward the Indian village. There were barefoot children staring at him, their fingers in their mouths, until they were snatched by anxious mothers who wouldn't meet his eye. He questioned one of the Indian women. She spoke adequate English. Yes. She knew about an Indian boy that had been given to a white woman. She directed him to a little Indian village farther up the hill, just above the creek. He rode there and questioned another woman. She looked kind and welcoming. She spoke good English too. She pointed to a wickiup.

There he found an Indian man with leathery skin. His eyes glistened, black like oil. His wife was roasting a rabbit over a fire with three children watching. Isaac dismounted and talked to them. It took them a long moment to register the fact that he was searching for a Shoshoni boy named Yahnai.

Pay dirt! He was amazed that he'd found Yahnai's trail so easily. They acknowledged that Yahnai had lived with them since April. But where was he now?

The woman said another white man took him.

Isaac felt his face fall. The answer deflated him, and he grunted in disgust. Given to a white man? Incredible! Who would know about Yahnai? Who would be searching for him? And why? It mystified Isaac. He almost refused to accept the preposterous thought that Yahnai *had* been here but now wasn't.

Think, Isaac told himself.

"Who was the white man?" he asked.

They shrugged. They didn't know. Nor did they care. Isaac got the impression they were glad to get rid of Yahnai. The couple had three children of their own to feed.

What about the white man? What did he look like? When was he here? How was he dressed? What color of horse did he ride?

In their limited English, it proved difficult for the Indians to provide a proper description. But within a few minutes, Isaac drew out a few key facts about the white man who now had Yahnai. Red hair. Red facial hair. Long moustache. Funny hat. Buffalo coat. Black horse. Where the redheaded man took the boy, they didn't know.

How was Yahnai dressed? Nearly naked. Breechcloth. No shoes.

Blue sweater?

Yes.

Isaac's eyes watered. Yahnai was tantalizingly close. But where? There was only one thing to do. Wander the town and ask about the redhead.

❃ ❃ ❃

The town bulked around Main Street, which ran straight as a string east to west. It boomed with new buildings, most with false fronts, but none with any aesthetic triumph as in Salt Lake City. Stores, saloons, and commercial establishments on the north side were matched by similar establishments on the south side. Several more buildings were under construction. Isaac heard the bang of the hammer and the buzz of the saw. He tied his horse to a hitching post and ventured a few cautious steps. He propped his back against one of the buildings and took it all in for a few minutes. People were coming and going, not in big crowds, mostly in twos and threes.

Think, he told himself again. He tried to assess the situation logically.

What else should he be looking for, aside from red hair and a red beard?

Number one, there had to be some kind of motive for a stranger to take Yahnai. Possibly extortion. So Yahnai most likely wouldn't be with the man right now. It would be pointless to look for a man walking the streets hand-in-hand with an Indian boy.

Number two, the redheaded man would be behaving differently than anyone. He wouldn't be digging for gold. He wouldn't be selling goods from a freight wagon. He wouldn't be buying goods. So what would be some of the telltale signs? He'd be looking for Abby. And he'd be nervous, sweating, and perhaps even irritable.

Someone in Bannack City had to have seen the redhead. Isaac calculated how many hours he had until Abby and Scooter arrived. He looked at the sun. Inch by inch, it would move in the sky. Time wouldn't stand still. *Find the redhead*, he told himself. *Find Yahnai. Find Yahnai, and you'll have Abby. You'll get rid of Scooter. Find Yahnai.*

He began walking again along an unstable boardwalk until he came to a log structure with a false front. It looked like a good place to start asking questions. The sign read, *Chrisman Store*. Near it were unloaded crates. Chrisman had been buying from freighters. The store had small, dirty windows. Through them he saw a lame display of goods, but when Isaac walked in, the store was crowded with miners and freighters. The store was even more crowded with half-empty shelves. Isaac smelled coffee beans, spices, oatmeal, dried fruit, honey, molasses, cheese, syrup, dried beans, cigars, and tobacco. Rifles, revolvers, and pistols had their own smell, so did ammunition. He saw bolts of cloth, pins and needles, thread, ribbon, silk, buttons, collars, undergarments, suspenders, dungarees, trousers, dresses, hats, and shoes. There were lanterns, lamps, rope, crockery, pots, pans, and dishes. An apothecary section offered patent medicines, remedies, soaps, toiletries, and elixirs. He saw coffee grinders. He saw a scale, a scale to weigh gold for payment.

It was evident that a few freighters had beaten Scooter to Bannack City, but goods were flying out of the store.

Chrisman was a stocky man of medium height with a shock of curly brown hair. A man like Chrisman probably knew a little bit about everything in Bannack City. If anyone had seen the redheaded man, Chrisman probably had. At the post office section of the cramped and dusty store, the proprietor was helping a young mule skinner.

When he was done, he turned to Isaac. "Now, mister, what can I do for you?"

"I'm looking for a redheaded man," Isaac said.

"I can think of a couple dozen redheads around here. What's his name?"

"I don't know."

Chrisman began to laugh. "Come back when you know."

"Wears a funny hat and a buffalo coat. Rides a black horse."

Chrisman furrowed his brow. He looked a little puzzled, but he wasn't hiding anything. "Could be any one of the redheads in town. Now what can I sell you? A bucket or two? A shovel?" He touched his scales, ready to accept payment in gold.

"Maybe the hat was a bowler. Or a circus barker hat."

"Look, I've got customers to tend to."

"He might have a young Indian boy with him."

"Check the saloons. Or the streets." With that, Chrisman turned his back to Isaac and began helping another customer.

Isaac went out of the store and looked to his left and to his right. To his left, down Main Street, a sign caught his eye. *Skinner's Saloon.*

When he got to the door, Isaac opened it and went in. One hinge squealed, and one hinge moaned. He wondered how often mayhem erupted here and how often it spilled out into the street. With a vigilant look, just in case, he surveyed the interior. The air was smoky and smelled of liquor and sweat. There were several men crowded around a bar, drinking bourbon from chipped glasses, drinking beer from bottles, and smoking cigars and roll-your-own cigarettes. Others sat at tables, playing cards, leaning in, leaning back, some talking loud, some saying nothing at all. Here or there a man looked a little pinched and wary compared to the others, which most likely meant they weren't doing too well at their gambling. There was plenty of buzz, but Isaac sensed no outward hostility.

None of the men had red hair.

Isaac approached the closest man at the bar, a burly fellow, with a dark beard, quaffing whiskey. Up close, he looked sullen and unhelpful.

"Can I talk to you for a minute?" Isaac asked.

"Why, I reckon you can," the man said.

"I'm looking for a man. A redhead. Red beard. Funny hat."

"Old or young?"

Isaac flinched. That was a question he hadn't asked the Indians. "Probably young. He wears a buffalo coat. Rides a black horse."

"Cain't help you. I'd buy you a drink. Had a good day at my claim."

"No, thanks."

The whole place dripped in money, literally. Gold money, practically the only medium of exchange. The men seated around the closest table looked too drunk to talk to, so Isaac threaded his way around it. The men playing cards at the next table weren't so glassy-eyed, but there was a lopsided tension in the way they held themselves, as if the card game were a life-or-death ordeal. They sat tightly together, looking damaged, uncomfortable, and querulous, as though they wanted to rob the outgoing stagecoach.

One big man was round and smooth and heavy, like a steer being fattened for slaughter. He struck Isaac as being a professional gambler, too lazy to work his own claim but preying on those who had. He'd just won a hand and was raking in coins and gold nuggets, laughing, all swelled up like a toad in a churn.

Isaac interrupted the men and repeated his line about the red-headed man.

They reacted the same way.

Which redheaded man? How old? What was his name? Why are you looking for him? Why would a redheaded man be toting around a young Indian boy?

The big man took a long swig from a bottle. He wiped the neck of the bottle with his sleeve and then thrust the bottle at Isaac. "Drink?" There was one empty chair at the table. The big man kicked it out with his foot and gestured for Isaac to sit.

Isaac said, "No. But thanks anyway."

The man sprinkled one hand with the contents of his bottle, set the bottle on the table, smoothed his hair with both hands, and said slowly, "Deal another hand, boys. No sense wasting more time."

As Isaac turned to go, a tall and spindly miner entered the saloon, threw a poke of gold dust on the bar, poured out a generous stream of the yellow stuff, and announced, "Drinks for everyone in the house."

The bartender scooped up the dust, ignored the balancing scales on the bar, and began pouring drinks.

Isaac shook his head in disbelief and went back out onto the street, discouraged. He questioned men on the street. He questioned men in other saloons and in stores and in stables. He looked for men with red hair. He saw one or two. But they were not the right redhead. Soon, long shadows were cast by buildings and men walking along them. The sun had reached the western mountains.

At a hotel, a butcher shop, and a bakery, the answers were the same. The conclusion, he feared, was that he didn't have a good enough description. There were four or five thousand men in Bannack City. How many were redheads? Odds were forty or fifty. Maybe a hundred.

He'd ridden hard the past two days. His body ached. He felt a thickening shroud of fatigue settling over him. After he questioned a few more men, he remounted his horse, rode to the edge of town, ate some more jerky and corn dodgers, spread his bedroll, and settled down for a night of rest.

Tomorrow he'd continue his search. If he asked enough questions of enough men, perhaps the redheaded man would find him.

He hoped so.

Chapter 35

When Abby and Scooter reached camp after their walk, they squeezed each other's hands and parted. He went to join his men around the campfire. She went inside her tent and spread her blankets out. She wondered if she should sever her relationship with Isaac and marry Scooter. There was a magnetism that was pulling them together as sure as day is light and night is dark. She pictured Scooter dressed in white, being baptized. She pictured kneeling at the Endowment House altar with him—and Yahnai kneeling with them—to be sealed. Rosy-cheeked children fathered by Scooter. Bedtime stories. Living in Salt Lake in a home large enough for many children. Expanding his freight business.

She thought about his gift, the half eagle gold coin. For some reason, she had the desire to have that coin in her hand, to confirm that everything was real. The coin reminded her of Evan, and she wanted a feeling of confirmation from her former husband as she thought about marrying Scooter. She made a beeline toward the wagon that contained Scooter's lockbox, trying to stay out of sight. She hid behind one of the wheels, held her hand on the hub, and peered through the spokes. No one had noticed her.

The box was located under the seat. It wasn't as wide as the wagon but was nearly as wide as the seat. She stood on the wagon tongue. She would have to take the chance that the box wouldn't be locked. It wasn't. She peeked in and saw leather pouches. All but one were empty. One was about a third full. She hefted it for a second. It was heavy. She guessed it was gold, Scooter's spending money. She saw a set of scales to weigh gold as he sold his freight. She saw the coin box, sitting on top of some letters. Letters from his mother in Virginia, she guessed. She held one in her hands, wondering what a mother would say to a son so far away in the west, a son she had told to hide until the war was over. She rummaged through a few of them but thought it inappropriate to read any. They were private letters. Her eye caught a small pile of letters with monogrammed envelopes. She picked one up and looked at it. The handwriting was different. There was the faint hint of perfume. She couldn't help herself. She opened the letter. It was written on monogrammed stationery. It was from a girl in Virginia. A girl named Millie.

My Darling Scooter, The war rages on and my longing for you grows. I remember our days together beneath our magnolia trees festooned with blossoms, and I look forward to the day when we can walk those paths together again—to the day I'll be your wife.

Abby stood at the lockbox in silence, stunned to the core, enduring the sharp pang of another loss in her life. Her eyes stung with humiliated tears. Why hadn't he told her the truth? If he lied about his past, would he lie about his future? Was he merely feigning interest in the Church? Feigning interest in her too? Deep down, perhaps he was worse than the other mule skinners he employed. Disillusionment and betrayal shattered her.

She glanced in the direction of the campfire. She could hear Scooter's laughs.

She tried to shake cobwebs from her mind. They wouldn't go away. They told her that Scooter had deceived her. But why? The conclusion was diabolically simple. He was manipulating her until she gave him what he wanted. A conquest. In this regard, he was no better than Cadmus Arbuckle. Just the use of different tactics. In fact, Scooter's method was more sinister and cruel, like trapping a frog in a kettle of water and then heating it gradually until the frog is boiled to death. Giving her gifts, whispering in her ear, luring her to take one more step. She should have seen it coming. She felt sheepish and gullible. She detested him for his sinister ways.

The devil didn't have a long red tail and horns. Yes, sometimes he had red hair and a walrus moustache. But sometimes he had long golden hair. Often more subtle and clever than she'd ever imagined. She thrust the letters back into the box. She fondled the coin box for a few moments then returned it as well. A gift from Beelzebub. As she made her way back to her tent, the wind picked up and her dress danced in the breeze. She felt dirty.

All this brought an intricate dilemma to her. What to do? Should she give him a tongue-lashing like she had Colonel Connor? For Yahnai's sake, should she continue to travel with him and pretend she hadn't read the letters from Millie? Or should she strike out on her own, like she'd done when she'd left Franklin? That was it. She'd leave in the middle of the night, undetected. She still had her horse and saddle. She still had Evan's clothing and hat. Bannack City was only two days away. Only a few hours by horseback. Find Yahnai.

But what then? How could she and Yahnai make it all the way back to Franklin without exposing themselves to danger? Was it a lousy idea? Not if there were a safe way to travel. There was only one answer—the stagecoach. But it would take money. Her mind drifted again to the gold coin. She couldn't tear her thoughts from it. It was hers. Despite the source, she had to have it. She didn't know how much a stage-coach fare from Bannack City to Franklin would be. If the coin wasn't enough, she could pay the remainder of the fare when she reached the settlement. Isaac could help her. Winny and Carl could help.

She opened the tent flap and peeked out. She listened. Scooter and the men were still sitting at the campfire talking. Long shadows encroached everywhere, making her uneasy. Night insects had started up their crazy chants. She could hear the howl of wolves, the cry of coyotes, the scream of a cougar, the invisible beating of bats' wings, and the hooting of owls. She crept out, taking tiny steps, one foot in front of the other, very slowly, making no noise. She felt as though the earth were tilting beneath her feet. So far, so good. No one looked her way. She kept going. She made her way to the wagon and the lockbox and retrieved the coin. She also took a sheet of writing paper. Then she returned to the tent the same way—total stealth. None of the mule skinners noticed.

There was barely enough light in the tent to write a note, with Riddle standing right next to her. She wrote it with chilling precision. She told Scooter not to follow. It was over between them. She had seen Millie's letters, and she did not want to spend the rest of her life with a liar.

Chapter 36

ISAAC AROSE AT THE CRACK of dawn. The mountain air was cold and a little damp. He got ready for what he hoped would be a successful day in terms of finding Yahnai. The redhead first and then Yahnai. He ate more jerky, washed it down with the waters of Grasshopper Creek, and rode toward the mining area.

Under a big sky whipped clean by a steady light wind, he continued to ask his question of the rough-looking miners. There appeared to be little point in brushing hair, trimming beards, using soap, or changing shirts in the camps.

He quickly learned that miners were not lazy. There were no flabby men. They had been worn down to pure muscle and sinew by the rigors of their labor. He got a sense of their urgency. They had left their makeshift camps early, surprisingly sober, gum boots on, ready to work hard. Men were whipsawing logs into boards for sluice boxes, diverting the creek into the sluice boxes, shoveling gold-laden gravels, discharging the tailings back into the gulch, collecting the heavier black sand and gold in the riffles.

He saw a redheaded miner striking the earth with his pick. Isaac approached him and said, "I'm looking for a redheaded man."

"As you can see, I'm redheaded," the man said without looking up.

"Are you the one that's been looking for a lost Indian boy?"

"Do I look like I'd be wasting my time doing something like that?"

"I suppose not," Isaac said.

The miner rested from his work and looked at Isaac. "Want a job, old-timer?"

The question insulted Isaac. He didn't consider himself old. Not unless he compared himself to the man he was talking to, who looked younger than thirty. He gave his answer tersely. "No. I don't want a job."

"My partner and I will pay you six dollars a day in gold."

"Not interested. Do you know of any other redheaded men?"

The man pointed downstream. "Try those pumpkin pilers down yonder."

"Pumpkin pilers?"

"Farm boys. They know more about pilin' pumpkins, gatherin' cranberries, diggin' ginseng, or raisin' wheat then they know about using the pick and shovel. But they tell me that, even for them, diggin' gold pays better. I reckon it does. Miners that know what they're doin'—like them Pike's Peakers and us Californians—average anywhere from sixty to six hundred dollars a day. Them farmers down yonder are lucky to average a dollar or two a day. Don't know what they're doin'."

Isaac said nothing.

"You look seasoned enough," the man said. "Good workers are hard to find. How about eight dollars a day? I've hired men who didn't know much about mining. Just wanted to earn enough to last them until they could get somewhere else. They left more gold behind than they were worth. How's about it? Eight dollars."

"No, thanks," Isaac said.

"Tell you what. You work for us for a month at eight dollars a day. You prove your worth, we'll make you a partner. I don't know why I'm even sayin' that. We've turned down offers to buy part of our claim, but none of them had a face we could trust. Now, you. You're different for some reason. I don't know why. But the offer stands."

"No, thanks."

"Dollar to a doughnut you'd transport twenty-five pounds of gold back home by the end of the year. Do you know how much twenty-five pounds of gold is worth? More than five thousand dollars. How many years of labor anywhere else would get you that much money? Probably ten years or more. You'd be fixed for life."

The insinuation that he would be tempted to accept the offer further insulted Isaac. Brigham Young had said not to mine for the riches of the earth, so the man's offer made Isaac bristle. He wanted nothing more than to remain true to his goals. Find Yahnai. Reclaim Abby. Make that trip to the Endowment House. After this life, end up in the celestial heavens.

Isaac asked again, "Any other redheads you can think of?"

"I've seen one or two amongst the Confederates and the Union boys."

This registered with Isaac.

The Californian added, "But be careful. Southerners and Northerners are clannish bunches. They don't abide each other. Now myself, I try to stay out of that North and South stuff. Gettin' gold out of mother earth is what concerns me. Sure wish you'd stay on, but if you find an unemployed Chinese in your travels, send him this way."

Isaac thanked the man and moved farther downstream, to territory yet unexplored. He shook his head in disbelief at what the miner had offered. He wondered how drunk the Californian would get tonight at one of the saloons, which dancing girl he'd proposition, and where he and his partner hid their gold. He wondered if the man would actually make it home before someone stole his gold and killed him.

As he walked, he saw men hunched over a drift, debating how far down they'd have to dig. Farther still, he saw men removing the body of a miner who'd been buried in a cave-in. He saw long sluices, some as long as fifteen feet. He saw miners placing mercury in the riffles to aid in the collection of gold particles. Others were boiling off the mercury; the fumes gave off a noxious smell. He saw diviners leading greenhorns up the sides of gulches where they drove stakes into the ground when the forked stick twitched.

He saw more redheads and questioned them, some wearing Union-blue, other Confederate-gray. But none who knew anything about an Indian boy.

Discouraged, he led his horse away from Grasshopper Creek, north along a busy street, past a new jail built of logs, not far from Chrisman's store.

Behind him, he heard a voice. "I hear tell yer lookin' fer me."

Isaac whirled to find a man wearing a dusty circus-barker hat over curly red hair. His eyes were screwed tight against the bright sun. He had a greasy red beard and a walrus moustache. The redhead radiated subliminal *stay away* signals, but he knew something. Isaac could see it in his face. He had reddened eyes that jumped around in his head like he was about to be struck with lightning.

"Why, I might be," Isaac said.

There was something else different about the redhead. He showed missing teeth in an ugly, smug smile, scarred lips, and a bruised face. "Who are you?" the man asked.

"Isaac Jacobs, from Utah Territory."

"Well, strike me blind. I expected the woman or Scooter or both."

"Abigail?" Isaac asked as foot and horse traffic threaded past them. He felt his skin crawl. Who was this man? Theories went through his head—none comfortable—but he had to ask the question. "Where's the Indian boy? Do you have him?"

The redhead pointed east, between two rows of buildings that faced the streets. "We need to parley. In private. Right over there."

Isaac followed willingly. The redhead walked slowly and tenderly, as if he were nursing an injury of some kind. He didn't go very far, and when he stopped, Isaac spoke again. "Where is the Indian boy? I'm here to take him back home."

The redhead returned a deadly glint in his narrow eyes. "I took 'im. That's true. He's not far from here. I reckon he's worth a lot of money to someone."

Isaac grunted in disgust. Had he heard correctly? Had Yahnai's disappearance turned into a kidnapping? "What do you mean?"

The redhead inched closer, staring at him, giving off a corrupt unwashed smell. He posed the question, "How much gold do you have?"

Isaac held up a rigid palm. "I'm not a miner."

"Don't fun me. All men up here are either miners or freighters. Or businessmen."

"I told you. I'm from Utah Territory. Franklin settlement."

The redhead furrowed his brow, and his expression clouded. He went quiet, like he was profoundly disappointed. "You're not the man with the broken leg . . . ?"

Isaac stared at him, confused. Slowly it came to him. It was beginning to make sense. "Were you with the freighter that day? With Scooter?"

As the redhead nodded and pooched his lips out, Isaac's heart raced. He recalled things Abby had told him about that day. Things he couldn't remember himself. A redhead who threatened to shoot his horses being jerked to the ground by Scooter.

The man touched his six-shooter. "I want a pouch of gold. A big one. Or I blow a hole in the boy's head. And one in his chest, for good measure."

Isaac felt a knot tighten in his stomach. If he partnered up with the Californian, he'd have gold. But it would take too much time— weeks, maybe months. "I'm just a poor farmer from the settlement. You've been there. How could you expect gold from someone like me?"

"Scooter will have gold. Just as soon as he sells his freight. Lots of gold."

"What does Scooter have to do with this?"

"I hate 'im. He's done me a lot of wrong. Months of wrong. Now he's fired me. Nothing left. I need money. I need gold."

Isaac took a deep breath, trying to take stock, assessing the anger in the redhead's eyes, this grudge against Scooter, this hate. What kind of man was he? Evil? Crazy? Lazy? What was more important to him? Gold? Revenge? Both? A desire to ruin Scooter? "What's your name?"

"Not important."

"Is the boy alive?"

"Yep. Alive and kickin'. He don't like me too much."

Isaac thought it conceivable that the redhead had the wrong boy. So he began a new line of questioning. "How tall is he?"

The redhead held out a meaty hand like a measuring stick. "Right to here."

"What's he wearing?"

"Near naked. Totin' a blue sweater."

For Isaac, that confirmed everything. He had Yahnai. An idea came to him. He hoped the redhead had room to reason. "If you go through with this, you'll be hung."

"I ain't plannin' on gettin' caught."

"You don't like Scooter?"

"I told you. I hates 'im."

Isaac related to the remark. To be honest, he sort of hated Scooter too—the kind of hate that existed between two men courting the same girl, especially when it looked like one had lost. "Why do you hate him so much? What happened?"

The redhead narrowed his eyes. "He never treated me right, not from the beginning. Goes clean back to St. Louis. He put Hagen over me. I wanted to be foreman. Hagen didn't understand. I wanted to marry the girl. She came into our camp. She wouldn't have me. Stuck me with a knife. Hagen chained me up. The men laughed at me."

"Was Scooter there? Did he chain you up?"

"No. His men did. Scooter was one day behind us. Scooter is puppet master."

Isaac put two and two together. Abby had ridden out alone and caught up with freighters. The redhead propositioned her, and Abby fought him off. The mule skinners banished the redhead, and he blamed Scooter. Now Scooter was protecting Abby. Gaining her favor. Abby fell for a gentile once, and now she might be doing it again. A gentile. A deserter. This realization filled Isaac with fear. *Think,* he told himself. *Think.*

"Gold," the redhead repeated. "A big pouch. I want gold."

A thought came to Isaac. "What about making a deal?"

"Any deal, as long as I get gold."

Isaac smiled. "How about trading me the boy for some information that will lead to more gold than you've been thinking of. Maybe two or three big pouches."

"Information? I don't care beans for information, not a single red-eyed bean or a string bean. I ain't budgin' one hooter. I want gold."

Isaac waved a hand in the redhead's face. "There's a better way for you to get what you want. I have information. Information that could ruin Scooter."

"I don't think so," the redhead said. "Gold is better than information."

Isaac tried reasoning with him. "Sheriffs and judges hang kidnappers. You'll be a wanted man forever if you go through with this. Think about that rope around your neck. Being buried in a shallow grave. Wolves digging you up."

The redhead said nothing.

"Where you from?" Isaac asked.

"Ohio."

"Union man?"

"Yep."

"Can we make a deal? Information for the boy."

The redhead went blank. He said nothing.

"If you follow my plan, you'll get more than just gold. You'll avoid the hangman's noose. You could end up with Scooter's business. And Scooter's gold. You've got an opportunity right under your nose. Can't you smell it yet?"

The redhead looked wary.

"It'll work this way. You give me the boy. I give you information that will ruin Scooter. Scare him off. You take over his freight wagons. Sell the freight for gold. Not only that, but you'll end up with Scooter's wagons and mules. You end up a respected businessman. You won't be hunted down and stretched by the neck until dead."

The redhead looked incredulous. "Are you sure? Me ending up with all of Scooter's gold? And his wagons and mules? How will that work?"

"First, I need to know if the boy is alive," Isaac said.

"If yer funnin' me, I'll kick ya so far it'll take a bloodhound six months just to find yer smell."

"Trust me. This plan will work. Now take me to the boy."

"Tell me details."

"Not until I make certain the boy is alive."

"I have partners, invisible to you. So no funny business."

Isaac looked to the left and to the right. The saloons and streets had been full of suspicious, crafty-looking men. What the redhead was saying could be true. "I agree," Isaac said. "No funny business."

"I need to search you."

Isaac stood as still as a statue while the redhead took his knife and removed the rifle from his scabbard.

"I've got a horse down at the corrals," the redhead said. "We'll be ridin' out of town a ways."

Isaac crossed his fingers. He felt he was doing the right thing.

❊ ❊ ❊

Isaac followed the redhead as they rode west, away from busy roads that led east toward Alder Gulch or south toward the Snake River crossing. The redhead rode a black mare with burrs infesting its mane and tail. After two or three miles, he veered off the main trail into the mountains, following what was no more than a path made by deer and elk. When they had ridden another ten minutes along a hillside thick with trees, Cad stopped the horses and dismounted.

"Why up here?" Isaac asked, tying his horse to a tree.

"Injuns don't need no hotel room. I feed 'im some. Water 'im regular."

Isaac focused his eyes on boot prints and barefoot tracks leading up the hill toward an outcropping of rocks. He followed the redhead through the sparse timber, brush, and rocky terrain. At length he saw a shallow cave embedded in the rocks.

"Yahnai?"

The redhead laughed. "I've got 'im gagged. He can't talk, but he's there."

As Isaac approached the entrance of the cave, his eyes pooled with waves of abhorrence. There in the shadows, Yahnai lay bound hand and foot, gagged, and blindfolded; his legs were drawn behind him, secured to the back of his neck. He looked pale and washed out. Had a wolf found him, he would have had no chance.

"Cut him loose," Isaac said.

The redhead touched his six-shooter again. "Tell me the plan, a plan better than a pouch full of gold. If I like it, I'll cut 'im loose."

Isaac took another pitiful look at Yahnai and thought about what he was about to say. He grappled with it. Late last winter or maybe early spring, Abby had blurted something out. Something about Scooter. Something that she perhaps had not intended to say. But she said it anyway. Perhaps she said it as a result of her fits of deep depression. She spilled everything. Afterward, she acted as though she had made a mistake, but she couldn't take the words back. Instead, she made him promise not to tell anyone else. He made the promise. But right now, he was going to break that promise. For a good reason. To save Yahnai's life. Isaac reasoned what he was about to do was for the good of everyone. It would get Yahnai out of the redhead's custody unharmed. It would reunite Yahnai with Abby. The collateral damage would be Scooter and his business. But he was from a wealthy family, or at least he had a wealthy mother. Scooter could always write her for more money and another start.

It seemed there was no other way.

He took a deep breath, let the air out, and rubbed his hands together. "Your old boss, Scooter, is not from wherever he told you. He's from Virginia. He lived on a plantation there, a big one. Not only that, he admitted to me that he's a deserter from the Confederate army."

The redhead squinted in thought and returned a wily look. "He told me he was from St. Louis. Why would he tell you somethin' like that?"

Isaac shook his head. "He told Abby, and she told me. It's the truth. I swear it is."

"She's a feisty one. That Abby."

Isaac nodded, recalling Abby's flaws. "Yes, she's feisty."

The redhead scratched his head. "You must have a big imagination if you think I'll get Scooter's gold. How's that gonna happen?"

With a burst of confidence, Isaac asked, "How many miners wear either Confederate-gray or Union-blue?"

The redhead shrugged. "Dunno. But lots of 'em."

"Back at the crossing of the Snake River, I heard that President Lincoln had sent a couple of men out here to make certain that Bannack City gold ends up in the federal treasury to help fund the war. What if you spread the word that all the profits from Scooter's business are sent back to Virginia to help fund the war for the South?" Isaac said the words with shameless falsehood. Justified by the chance to free Yahnai and return him to Abby.

The man's eyes brightened a bit, a sign his skepticism was melting.

Isaac added more spice to his argument. "What if you went back to Bannack City and spread that rumor to every miner wearing Union-blue? Won't be long till they'll be mad enough to run Scooter out of town. You'll be a hero with the Yankees. If you do this right, they'll confiscate Scooter's wagons and his mules and his freight and give them to you. You could end up with everything. The Yankees wouldn't want the wagons and mules anyway. They're more interested in their gold diggings."

The redhead's eyes brightened. "Go on."

"Think of it. You'd end up a wealthy businessman. You could hire your own men. You could make your own decisions. I won't say anything to anyone." Isaac paused, letting the words register. He could tell that he had tickled and nursed the man's delusions. In reality, however, he didn't regard the redhead clever enough to actually pull off such a stunt.

"I've told you everything," Isaac said. "Now cut the boy loose, and I'll take him off your hands."

The redhead bit his lower lip as his last shreds of doubt withered away. His rigid posture finally relaxed. "I reckon it might work. I know where Scooter is. His wagons are gettin' close to town. That ain't leavin' me much time."

"If I were you," Isaac replied, "I'd get started right now. Cut the boy loose. Then head back to town and start spreading the news."

The redhead unsheathed his knife and waved it at Isaac. "This'd better work. If it don't, I'll slash your throat."

With those words, he stepped toward the boy and removed the blindfold. Yahnai blinked and squinted, trying to adjust his eyes. As the redhead cut the cords and ungagged him, Yahnai widened his eyes with joy and surprise.

"Uncle Isaac!" he said.

"Yahnai! Come here, son. Everything will be fine from now on."

Yahnai skipped toward him, staggering some, his muscles not working quite properly yet, crying his name over and over. Isaac smiled triumphantly. He wrapped his arms around Abby's son and drew him in. They stood there in a prolonged embrace. Tears came to his eyes and to the child's.

The redhead walked to his black horse, threw Isaac's rifle and knife to the ground, and mounted. Isaac watched as he galloped off down the trail. He wondered what the redhead would do with the information. It may have been a risk, but Yahnai was safe with him. It was worth it. Yahnai for Scooter any day of the week.

"How'd you like a clean hotel room, a nice meal, and a warm bath?" Isaac asked the boy. "And a long talk?"

Yahnai shuffled in place a little. The ordeal hadn't cured him of his bashfulness, but he gave Isaac an enthusiastic nod and held on as though he'd never let go.

Chapter 37

ABBY'S GETAWAY FROM SCOOTER'S CAMP had been clean. She had avoided detection by the night herder or anyone in the tents. Snip stole away as if she'd been trained to, with Riddle following along obediently. No lonesome neighing, snorting, blowing, or nickering. She just put herself into a slow, steady, obedient walk. The moon was nothing more than a quarter of its full size, high in a black sky. She relied on her mare's night vision, vision as good as a cat's. She followed the road, deeply rutted with wagon tracks. She put the mare into a gallop for a ways. Evan's pants flapped against her legs like sails.

It was daylight when she crossed a creek. She assumed it was Horse Prairie Creek. Scooter had described it to her. A half mile from Bannack City, she saw more freighters waiting for their turn to occupy space on Bannack City's main street so they could auction off their freight.

A low rumble echoed from the direction of the town. Scooter had mentioned that too. Blasting powder. Miners getting at gold-bearing quartz.

The town was just as Scooter had described it. It glowed like a promise. Yahnai was here somewhere. The town sat in a little valley. Miners swarmed all over around tents and makeshift cabins. Yankee Flats, where the Northerners lived, flew Union flags. Confederate flags were flying elsewhere. She wondered if miners sang "Yankee Doodle" in that section of town and "Dixie" in the other.

The blue in the Union flag reminded her of the blue sweater she'd knitted for Yahnai. She said a prayer in her heart. *Please, God. Lead me to Yahnai.*

She crossed Grasshopper Creek and thought of how Scooter had told her its original name—Willard Creek.

Why couldn't she get him out of her mind? It was like he was everywhere: in the freighters she'd seen just outside the town, in the men she saw working at the creek, in the men riding and walking around the streets. It had been that way when Evan died. She saw and felt Evan everywhere she went. Everything and everyone reminded her of him. Now it was the same. Scooter's memory shadowed her every move, her every thought.

Tousled and weary, she headed for the first teepee that caught her eye and began her questioning. She questioned Indians one by one. All looked at her as if they'd never seen a white woman in men's clothing. And perhaps they hadn't. Eventually one of them, a woman, pursed her lips like she was trying to search her memory, trying to be helpful. The woman pointed to a village on the hill overlooking town, above the creek.

Indians there directed her to a family living in a wickiup. Abby saw an Indian woman standing inside the doorway. She was easily Isaac's age, maybe older. She was short and thick and heavy, with braided black hair, plain and blunt. She was wearing an ugly dress made of deerskin, well worn and greasy. She had sad, sallow eyes. The woman told her that Yahnai had lived with her for several months. But no more. She had given him to a white man. She said she was happy to give him up. It had been a burden to feed and care for him.

As the blood drained from her face, Abby stared at the Indian woman in astonishment, trying to force herself to accept what she had heard. So close to finding Yahnai, but he wasn't here. Given him to a white man?

Yes, she said.

"Tell me about the white man."

The first thing the woman said was that the man had red hair. She went on to describe other things about him as well. Funny hat. Buffalo coat. Riding a black horse. Abby's gut reaction was one of stark disbelief. A knot came to her stomach. Sudden chills. Shattered emotions. The description fit Cadmus Arbuckle. Not only that, but another white man, an older one, had inquired about the boy.

"Where did the man take Yahnai?"

The Indian woman shrugged her shoulders as if it didn't matter and without emotion pointed toward town.

Confused and disappointed, Abby rode off the hill. Where had Cad taken Yahnai, and why? And who was the other white man?

She also felt anger. Anger at herself. Had she discovered Millie's letters a day or two earlier and ridden out then, perhaps she would have found Yahnai before Cad. Strangely enough, she found herself thinking about Isaac. If she would have had more patience and asked Isaac to go with her, she would have found Yahnai. Safe with the family. Easily. She would have never met Cad. And Scooter would have never broken her heart. Eyes welling with emotion, she kicked herself for her lack of restraint and patience. And proper judgment.

But how to find Cad? What was his motive? She wished she had a knife. She might have to stick him in the other shoulder. Or worse.

As she came to Main Street, her eyes searched every stranger she saw. They stared back at her, a woman wearing a man's clothing soiled with mud, dirt, grease, and blood. She didn't care. She saw fleets of huge freight wagons, enough to practically block the street. She saw mule skinners, bullwhackers, and swampers unloading freight. Auctioneers worked the crowd with rhythmic cries. Miners and store owners bid on flour, salt, dried vegetables, shovels, picks, buckets, clothing, and more.

But no sign of Cad.

Black discouragement came over her. She was fatigued, running on no food and no sleep, and traumatized by Millie's letters. Her lips were parched—she hadn't taken a drink since crossing Horse Prairie Creek—and her stomach growled. She hadn't eaten since Scooter's camp. Her body ached. She'd ridden all night and all morning.

She turned up a side street and dismounted.

As Riddle licked her hand, she leaned against her horse and began to cry.

Chapter 38

SCOOTER AWOKE AT DAWN TO an almost silent world. His blankets were warm, but the morning air was brisk. He peeked out of his tent. Murky silhouettes of trees and wagons emerged in the early light. He wondered if Abby was awake. He glanced at her tent and thought of the previous night, her kisses and her sweetness. He closed his eyes again, savoring the memory.

A few minutes later, the meadow where they had camped seemed to burst to life. The night herder was bringing the mules in. Scooter heard their braying. He heard the crackling of a campfire and the rattle of iron pots; he smelled the coffee.

He put on his britches and a green plaid shirt. He pulled his leather boots on and stepped outside his tent. He didn't see Abby. *Let her sleep*, he told himself. He ate his beans and bacon, filling his plate twice and adding a few prairie chicken eggs the cook had gathered. While he ate, he bantered with Oscar and his men. Still no Abby.

He stepped toward her tent and called her name. "Abby?" No answer.

Alarmed, he bent his head and walked to her tent as though he were bucking a high wind. He rattled her tent. "Abby? Time to get up. Big day ahead of us."

Nothing.

He opened the tent. Abby was not there. He just stood there speechless for a moment. The empty tent was so unexpected that he could not think clearly. He put a hand to his chest. The gesture made him look like a guilty man proclaiming his innocence. The dress she wore last evening was neatly folded on top of her blankets. On top of the dress, a piece of paper. He staggered forward to pick it up. He hadn't sensed anything wrong. Yesterday had been perfect. Last evening, wonderful. Beyond wonderful.

His jaw dropped as he read the short, terse note. He felt his face go pale. His skin felt like wax. The words hit him like a hammer.

I know about Millie. I read her letters. Don't follow me.

He burst out of the tent, kicking himself for not telling her about Millie. He couldn't shake the sensation that Abby was riding into some kind of danger in Bannack City. "Oscar, saddle two horses! And be quick about it!"

Oscar jumped to his feet. "What's wrong, boss?"

"Abby's gone!"

Scooter ran to the night herdsman. "Did you see her leave?"

"No, boss. Am I in trouble?"

Scooter didn't answer. Abby had left Franklin without being detected. She'd done it again. But this time there was no question as to where she's gone—to find Yahnai.

He knew the answer to the next question before he asked it. "Is her horse gone?"

The men scattered. They looked in the meadow, along the creek, in the trees, and everywhere. The mare was gone.

Scooter's eyes found Hagen's. "Hagen, you get the wagons to Bannack City. I'm taking Oscar with me. I'll find you when I get there. I've got to find Abby."

"I won't fail you, boss," Hagen said.

❉ ❉ ❉

Scooter dashed toward Bannack City, reeling with heartache and gloom. His better judgment screamed at him. He should have told her the whole truth about his background. He should have told her about Millie. He should have told her about his conversion and baptism. Had he done so, Abby would know he was on the verge of asking her to marry him. He'd had his fun teasing her, stringing her along, and now it had cost him. But he wanted her to love him *for him,* not just because they were of the same faith. Now she was gone. She was at least six hours ahead.

Ghastly images thrashed through his mind, crushing him, stabbing him. Images of her rummaging through riffraff miners and Indians looking for Yahnai. Doing it without him. He should be helping her with the search. Together they could find the boy. Alone? He didn't want to think about it. She'd had a bad experience with Cad. There were men far worse than Cad in Bannack City: gamblers, thieves, escaped convicts, killers—all looking for female companionship. Not enough women to go around.

It gave him the shivers just thinking about it.

If something bad happened to her, he'd carry the regret the rest of his life.

He spurred his horse. The sooner he could get there, the better.

Chapter 39

ABBY WIPED HER TEARS AWAY and girded herself. Now was not the time to be weak. She had to be strong. She tied her horse to a hitching post and patted Riddle on the head. If Cad were still in Bannack City, she aimed to find him. Her most basic fear kicked in. The fear of the unknown. Cad was out there somewhere. With Yahnai. But *why*?

She glanced up and down the wagon-rutted streets. She quickly understood why she'd been warned not to come here alone. If any frontier city deserved the palm for hardness, this was it. The wild license of the town was unspeakable. Streets were crowded with truculent, armed men seemingly in search of trouble. Revolvers flashed, bowie knives flourished, and foul oaths filled the air.

Main Street was filled with an assortment of businesses, tents, brush shanties, and log cabins. Not one church. Not one school. Where were the judges, lawyers, doctors, teachers, and clergymen? The only respectable men she saw either walked or rode side by side for their own protection. She saw nothing that reassured her.

There was only one way to do it. Search systematically, every street, every building. She mashed Evan's hat down on her head and tried her best to look like a man. "Come on, Riddle. Stick close."

Scooter was right. Gold was everywhere. Everyone toted some—in leather pouches, tin cans, and sacks. It was the medium of exchange, evident as she peeked into hotels, saloons, bakeries, meat markets, grocery stores, a restaurant, a brewery, a billiard hall, blacksmith shops, and stables. Every business had a set of scales to weigh gold.

Hours passed. No Yahnai. No Cad. She'd been told to try bachelor's row, a grouping of small cabins and shacks that lined the hill behind Main Street. She faced that direction. From behind, a husky voice not only startled her but unraveled her as well.

"Well, butter my butt and call me a biscuit. If it ain't the sheriff's wife."

Abby whirled to find a man grinning at her through a greasy red beard. Her blood went cold. Cadmus Arbuckle. One of his ears was just a big scab. His face was still discolored. His split lip hadn't healed completely. And behind Cad stood two men. One wore sky-blue trousers with a vertical stripe, the other a Union forage cap. Like Cad, they laid lusty eyes on her.

Riddle growled.

She fought a wild urge to unsheathe his knife and thrust it once again into his shoulder. He still favored the shoulder, obvious in the way he carried himself.

"I reckon yer lookin' fer me. Change yer mind? Want me ta marry ya?"

"Where is my boy?" she said in a steely voice. She planted her feet apart. "I know you took him. I found the Indian family."

There was conflict all over Cad's face. "I don't know," he said. "How's about going back to Ohio with me? You and me and the boy."

"Just tell me where he is." She said it in a tone that discouraged further useless conversation.

"An ole boy from Utah Territory beat you to 'im."

"What do you mean?"

"Sleepy-eyed ole boy. Broke his leg in the creek."

It couldn't be, she told herself. "Isaac? Isaac Jacobs? Where?"

"Said he was gonna take the boy to one of the hotels and wait fer ya. I don't think he was expectin' ya 'til tomorrow."

Abby was puzzled. It made no sense that Cad would take Yahnai and then willingly give him up to Isaac. No sense at all. She refused to accept the preposterous thought that he'd done it as an act of goodness. She had the impulse to dig deeper. But right now the impulse to reunite with Yahnai was stronger. "Which hotel?"

"He didn't say."

Abby didn't know whether to thank Cad or not. She turned on her heel, wondering which hotel to try first.

"Where's Scooter?" Cad asked.

"Your guess is as good as mine," she said as she walked away.

"Soon," Cad said with a laugh. "He'll be here soon."

❋ ❋ ❋

The hotel she picked was all wood, so new it practically smelled like a sawmill. It was two stories high but built as if wood were more valuable than gold. Narrow staircase. Small lobby. Stuffed with people. How Isaac got a room in any hotel, she didn't know.

The clerk was a tiny, feisty fellow. At first, when she asked if a man by the name of Isaac Jacobs had registered, he didn't look up. When he did, his eyebrows shot up with surprise, delight, and curiosity. He didn't answer her question. "Are you lookin' for work? Dancing girl, or what? Take off that hat. Let me have a good look at you."

Abby took an unconsciously defiant stance. Her words shot back at him. "Just answer my question. Do you have an Isaac Jacobs here? He'd be with an Indian boy."

"They left the hotel just a while ago."

"Which direction?"

"Chrisman's store. Something about buying clothes for the Injun boy."

Abby began blinking rapidly, fighting tears. *Injun boy.* That confirmed it. With damp eyes she bolted out of the hotel, crossed the street, and made a beeline to Chrisman's store. She'd been there earlier. Somehow too early. She'd missed them.

❋ ❋ ❋

Isaac had outfitted Yahnai head to toe. The selection of clothing for children Yahnai's age hadn't been all that good, but he now wore new leather shoes, tan britches, and a red shirt. He'd insisted on wearing his blue sweater over the shirt, and that's the way he was dressed when they left the store.

He and the boy were only a few yards from Chrisman's store when he saw the slim figure of a person walking toward him along with a brown-and-white dog. A person with a distinct woman's walk but in the clothes of a man—soiled trousers and shirt and felt hat. He did a double take. It was Abby! He knew why she was here. She was looking for Yahnai, maybe even looking for him. She had probably questioned the same Indian family that he had. But it was her, no doubt about it. Yahnai had been walking along with his head down, as he often did. Isaac squeezed his hand to get his attention and pointed. "Yahnai, look," he said. "Who's that?"

Yahnai looked up. The recognition was instant. "Mama!"

Yahnai broke the grip Isaac had on his hand. He ran toward his mother effortlessly, as though his feet weren't touching the ground. She ran toward him, squealing his name, equaling his speed and energy. Yahnai jumped into her arms. There was shrieking and crying and laughter all at the same time. They staggered around together in the sunlight. Miners walking the street stared at them. They backed off, giving the mother and her son room to celebrate. Isaac guessed they'd never seen a white woman so excited about an Indian boy. Abby scooped Yahnai off his feet in a wild hug, spun him around and around, and kissed him. Yahnai's feet windmilled outward.

Riddle remembered the boy. He licked at Yahnai's hands. Abby said, "Yahnai, oh, Yahnai. How I've missed you." She whirled him in the air again and hugged him. She kissed his cheek again, danced him around in another circle. Tears had flooded her eyes and Yahnai's.

Isaac just watched from the shadows of the buildings along the street. He didn't want to intrude on their happy reunion until it felt right.

Yahnai buried his face into his mother's chest. "Can we go home now?"

She sobbed her answer. "Yes. Soon." She held on to the boy as though he were more precious than all the gold in Bannack City, which in Isaac's view, he was.

Abby caught Isaac's eye. "You found him. Thank you."

"There were complications," Isaac said, taking cautious steps toward her, assessing her feelings.

"A redheaded man," she said.

"Yes."

She nodded as though she understood. She extended a hand toward him. He took it. He drew her in. She allowed him to embrace her. And then she drew back. Yahnai stuck to her like glue.

"I didn't have a hard time finding the family who had Yahnai," he said. "The thought that they had given him to a total stranger was a shock. It took me until this morning to find the man. In fact, he found me."

"I know who he is," Abby said.

"He told me that he'd been one of Scooter's men. That there had been trouble."

Abby lowered her eyes. "Lots of trouble."

"Let's get off the street," Isaac said. "You can tell me more back at the hotel. We can leave for Franklin tomorrow if there's room on the stage."

"We can go home?" Yahnai looked at Abby hopefully.

Abby ruffled his hair. "Yes, we can go home. All together."

"The hotel is over there, Mama," Yahnai said, pointing.

"I know," she said. "I found it already. The man said you had gone to the store. You look nice in your new clothes. Handsome." She turned her eyes on Isaac. "Thank you for what you've done."

"We'd better go back," he said, gesturing to the store. "They have a few nice dresses."

"I don't want to shop right now. I just want to enjoy being together."

Abby and Yahnai led the way to the hotel. Isaac thought they looked perfect together. Yahnai was hopping with energy, and Abby looked peaceful and radiant and beautiful, even in Evan's old clothing. Why she was wearing those clothes was a question remaining to be asked. She was sure to have a lot of questions of her own.

❀ ❀ ❀

In the hotel room, Abby feasted her eyes on Yahnai constantly. She couldn't quite believe they had found each other. She treasured his touch and the sound of his voice.

The muslin-ceilinged hotel room was no larger than eight feet by twelve, and there wasn't much inside—only a bedstead made of rough lumber, a straw mattress, a straw-filled pillow, and two wool army blankets with no sheets. Isaac explained that the sheets were used in the daytime for tablecloths in the restaurant next door. The sheets would be on the bed following dinner. There was one rough stool to sit on. The mirror consisted of just one piece of a broken looking glass. No lock on the door.

"There's a washbowl in the hotel office if you want to wash up," Isaac told her.

The walls were thin. She could hear conversations on both sides. In one, she thought she heard a man saying something about taking chunks of raw beef to bed with him so the bedbugs had a chance to feed on something besides him.

Isaac radiated pride from every pore as he told his story. He sat on the wooden stool, and she sat on the bed with Yahnai. They talked in hushed tones. He told her how bad he had felt when Winny shared the letter with him.

He'd left the settlement immediately, trading horses at every relay station, just like an express rider. His leg bothered him, and he didn't ride quite as fast as a relay rider, but he made good time. He admitted seeing her sitting next to Scooter as he passed. They talked for a couple of hours, sharing stories about their separate travels, about worries and concerns. The most important thing was that they ended up together. Still, somewhere out there, Cad lurked, his motives and plans unclear.

"But how did you get Yahnai?" she asked Isaac. "You didn't have any gold."

"Cad didn't expect someone like me to show up," he said. "He knew you would come along. He knew Scooter would have a lot of gold once he sold his freight. So it was simple. He'd force Scooter to give up his gold for Yahnai."

"And he thought he could get away with it? How did you change his mind?"

"Cad's not very bright. I just told him he would be a hunted man for the rest of his life. That he'd be caught and hung by the neck until dead. In reality, I don't think the sheriff would take much notice to the kidnapping of an Indian boy. You can just imagine what the sheriff here has on his plate. But what I said did the trick."

"Just that simple?"

Isaac swallowed hard and looked away. "Nothing's that simple, of course, but don't worry about it. I'd give my all for you. What I've sacrificed is my concern."

Abby shook her head. She saw pain in Isaac's familiar, tired-looking eyes. But she saw joy there too. And love. Isaac had wrested Yahnai away from Cad. Yahnai was here in the hotel room with her. They'd be going home on the stagecoach. Whatever sacrifice Isaac referred to had somehow left him and Yahnai intact, safe, and together. Isaac had proven his love for her. She let go of her questions, her infatuation for Scooter, and her fear. She breathed a sigh of relief. It was over.

"You told me Indians stole your packhorse," Isaac said, "but what about Snip?

Abby sat up straight. In the excitement, she'd forgotten all about Snip. "Oh, dear," she said. "My horse is still tied to a hitching post out on the street."

"I'll take care of her for you in a bit," Isaac said. "I'll take her to the express station. They can use her until she makes it back to the settlement. After we're married, I'll put her in the express string. Your mare is a good runner. She'll be a valuable addition."

Abby blinked her silent opposition. She didn't want Snip anywhere but in the settlement corrals or out to pasture. Snip was *her* horse. Not his. She decided it best to talk about it later.

Isaac took her hand and squeezed it. "You've been through a lot," he said. "I'm glad it's over. And I know you are too."

She pulled away and embraced Yahnai again. "It's your turn, Yahnai. I want you to tell Mama about everything. Everything since I saw you last. When Sagwitch took you away to the winter camp."

Yahnai told a frightening story. The day of the battle, he wore both his blue sweater and his sheepskin coat. Just before dawn, he and other children had been shooed to safety behind the warriors. He had been put to work pouring hot lead into molds for bullets. Even so, the Shoshoni warriors ran out of ammunition quickly. That allowed the soldiers to overrun the village just before dawn.

The child had seen much of the killing. Even in the dense willows of the camp, there was no place to hide, but before the soldiers closed in on him, he was rescued up by a warrior on a gray horse. Three warriors took him north, to the head of Marsh Creek. He stayed there for several days in the care of Indian women and the remnants of families. There was little to eat. The warriors told him it was wrong for him to live with white people and that Sagwitch should not have given him to a white woman. He was then moved farther north in stages and given to a band of Bannacks who brought him here to Bannack City and found a family for him. The family was nice to him but not loving. They had little to feed him. Sometimes he went into town and begged for food with other Indian children. He said he'd cried every night after the battle, wondering if he'd ever see her again. He had nightmares about remaining Shoshoni raiding Franklin and killing all the settlers. Then the redheaded stranger showed up. He convinced the family that he was there to take Yahnai back to Franklin. Yahnai believed the man, and the family gave him up willingly. They kept his sheepskin coat for their other children but let him have his blue sweater. The redheaded man had a camp just outside town. For two days he watched every freight wagon that came into Bannack City.

Abby was overcome with images from Yahnai's story. Witnessing that much killing, being evacuated in such cold weather, living among strangers near Bannack City—people who didn't love him. All of this reinforced the idea that she was better off with Isaac. At such a young age, given all that had happened to him, Yahnai was going to need a stable home and a lot of love.

She began to feel the fog of wonder and adrenaline dissipating. She was exhausted. She rubbed her eyes hard with her thumb and forefinger. Isaac looked at her as if he understood. "I need to rest for a while," she said.

Isaac took her by the hand again. His eyes were tired too. For the first time, she realized the stress she had caused him. He'd probably been up all night too, maybe several nights, trying to get here to Bannack City. Trying to find Yahnai, making everything right.

"While you rest, I'll take Yahnai back to the store and buy you a new dress. You can wear it to the dance tonight."

"Dance? What dance?"

"I've seen some posters around town. Actually there are several dances. It's what these people do after working all day. There's a new dance hall, just built. The poster says children are invited. No alcohol allowed in that one."

She nodded a preliminary approval.

"We can celebrate being back together again. Celebrate our engagement." There was a ring to his voice. A self-satisfied tilt of his head. A bright, puckish gleam in his eyes. It all showed his satisfaction in bestowing his generosity. He stood up, leaned over her, and kissed her. She didn't resist.

Yahnai groaned and buried his head in a pillow.

"I'll be back after a while," he said.

"Don't let Yahnai out of your sight," she said.

"I won't," he said as he closed the door.

Abby laid her head on a pillow and stretched out. She thought about Winny walking Ellen to school. Carl in the fields working. Her parents in Salt Lake City. She thought about Scooter for a minute, in random flashing images. She imagined him reading her note—hanging his head, regretting his lies, sitting on his wagon seat, slowly making his way to Bannack City.

Chapter 40

$\mathcal{I}$T WAS AFTERNOON WHEN SCOOTER and Oscar arrived in Bannack City on their worn-out horses. The last time he'd seen the town the air had been thick with flakes of snow. Spring had brought bright greens to the hills and valley.

Spring had also brought an unexpected challenge. He had to find Abby.

Scooter slowed his horse to a walk when they reached Yankee Flat. It was more crowded than he remembered it. He recalled a rift that developed here during his first visit, a rift between the boys of the North and the boys of the South. One night some boys in gray struck down one of the Union flags in Yankee Flat. Boys in blue quickly replaced it but not without some scuffling. The Southern boys chopped it down as well. The affair developed into a free-for-all. Eventually the boys in blue mended the pole again and won the day. Both sides went back to work. No serious injuries.

To find Abby, he knew he'd have to throw some caution to the wind, even among Yankees. He turned to Oscar, who looked at him, ready to do anything.

"Let's split up," Scooter said. "You start here. I'll ride to the east end of the main part of town and work west. I hope by the time we meet we'll have found her. I swanny, if we don't, I'll feel guilty the rest of my life."

"Yes, boss," Oscar said.

Scooter spurred his horse across the creek and turned east. He rubbed his right hip with a free hand. He'd ridden so hard his Colt-filled holster had bruised his hip. He saw Main Street glittering in the sun. It too was far more crowded than he'd remembered. Fleets of wagons lined both sides of the street. A narrow corridor in the center of the street remained open for horse and foot traffic, but even at that, the crowds of people bidding on wares practically blocked that corridor. At the eastern edge of town, he turned around, dismounted, and faced the street that had become a jungle.

There were many men about. He picked out a lanky, loose-built man wearing Confederate-gray trousers. He looked sullen and unhelpful, but Scooter began with him anyway. "I'm looking for a woman dressed in man's clothing, riding a bay mare."

"Cain't help ya," the man said. "I'd like to have a woman in any kind of clothes. Or dressed in somethin' so skimpy you could barely dust a fiddle."

Scooter turned away, disgusted. He repeated his line to men on both sides of the street, but no luck. He crossed the street. In a desperate, hooded squint, he saw someone who almost seemed to be tracking him. The man wore a soiled Union forage cap. He came to a stop face-to-face with the man and repeated his questions.

"I ain't seen such a woman myself," he said, "but I know someone who has."

Scooter counted himself lucky. Perhaps the search for Abby was going to turn out to be a short one. "Who?" he asked.

"Follow me. I'll take you to him. Down by the ditch, beyond the corrals."

He came close and took up a position alongside Scooter. The man was in his twenties, his face youthful and his coffee-colored eyes dark and wide. He had an oily brown beard and fingernails black as tar. The man walked shoulder to shoulder with Scooter, ahead of Scooter's horse, as if he were an old friend.

Soon Scooter saw several horses tied to corral poles and a cluster of men huddled together as if they were making plans to take over the world. They were young, sinewy miners, their bodies built up by working the earth. They had walnut knuckles, thick wrists, and knotted forearms. Dirt was ingrained in the folds of their skin and clothing. Their boots were muddy and creased. All wore ragtag remnants of Union uniforms, one man in sky-blue trousers, another in a sky-blue great coat, others in blue fatigues. Some were short, some were average, but one was a giant. Even without the black felt Hardee hat he wore—a hat favored by Union officers—he towered over the others.

The man in the forage cap pointed at Scooter. "This is him, lookin' for the woman."

"I'm looking for a girl named Abby," Scooter said. "She's wearing men's clothing, riding a bay mare. I understand one of y'all has seen her."

All the men fixed their eyes on Scooter like he was some kind of celebrity. They began to twitch and rock back and forth. They looked like trouble.

"Have you seen her?" he asked again. Scooter saw the hands of the man in the forage cap move. One second the man's hand was empty; the next it was full. He had a revolver. He clicked the hammer back—a small but ominous sound—and pointed it at Scooter's nose.

Instinctively, Scooter touched his six-shooter.

"I wouldn't," the man said.

Scooter heard the rustle of metal against leather. All the other men had drawn their revolvers as well. They were pointed straight at him, on a line between his chest and his navel. Scooter had seen plenty of these revolvers. They were Colt .44s, widely used by Union soldiers. They had a six-shot rotating cylinder and fired a lead ball propelled by a thirty-grain charge of black powder. Muzzle velocity of nine hundred feet per second. One ball was capable of blowing a hole in him big enough to see daylight through.

Scooter staggered backward, shocked that his status had been reduced to prisoner. He raised his hands in a small, abbreviated gesture of surrender. Surely there must be a misunderstanding. What social outrage had he committed to deserve staring down the barrels of a dozen weapons? Clearly he was trapped. He shouldn't have followed the man in the forage hat. He should have been smarter. "What's this all about? I just want to know about the girl. That's all."

"Very slowly," the forage-cap man said, "unbuckle your gun belt."

Scooter drew a breath and looked at the man. His finger was bone white on the trigger. The weapon was coming closer, right at Scooter's nose. The gun came to rest with the muzzle on his forehead.

"Do it now," the younger man said.

The others had grouped themselves in a tight formation, surrounding him. Several had glassy eyes, an obvious buzz going on. It was oozing from their pores. Scooter could smell it. Whiskey for breakfast; whiskey for lunch. They were capable of craziness; that was certain.

Sweating, leaning backward, Scooter unbuckled his belt. "Who are you?"

The forage-cap man took Scooter's gun belt and revolver. "Just miners," he said.

"What do you want?"

"You," he said with cold clarity, nodding at the giant with some kind of consent.

The giant came into perspective. He stood nearly as tall as a horse—when a horse had its head in the air—and he was as broad as a bull. His neck was thick, and his hands were the size of dinner plates. He was Goliath. Scooter felt like David without a slingshot. The giant put one of those big hands into a saddlebag and pulled out a dark bottle.

"Know what this is?" he asked. He asked it with distaste on his face.

"Whiskey," Scooter said.

"Yes. Whiskey I bought from you last winter. It's my last bottle."

Scooter shrugged his shoulders. "So?"

The giant's voice was deep and authoritative. "I don't think much of this bottle."

Scooter shrugged again.

The giant tossed the bottle on the ground. It was full. It hadn't been opened. The seal was still good. The giant stooped low to the ground. With one dinner plate–sized hand, he picked up a rock. A large one. The giant stood again and held the rock directly over the whiskey bottle. He dropped the rock. The bottle shattered.

Scooter blinked his surprise. He could smell the rich bourbon as it wet the soil.

"That's what I think of that bottle you sold me. That's what we think of everything you brought up here: whiskey, barrels of beans, bacon, shovels, buckets, clothes, tobacco. Everything." The giant's revolver was practically swallowed in his big meaty hand. He laid the muzzle against Scooter's temple and looked beyond Scooter's shoulders at the forage-hat man, waiting for a sign, maybe hoping for a sign. His trigger finger twitched.

"I don't understand," Scooter said helplessly. "I'm just a freighter. I provide a service. Without freighters like me, you men would starve to death."

The forage-cap man had a rope. He looped it over the neck of Scooter's horse and then secured the other end to his own saddle horn.

"What did I do to offend you boys?" Scooter asked.

"Ask him," the giant said, pointing behind Scooter. "He exposed you."

Scooter twisted at the waist. He saw a man behind him, a man he'd hadn't noticed before, a man with red stringy hair, like cats had been sucking on it. A man he'd hired. Cadmus Arbuckle. "Cad! What are you doing here? What's this all about?"

Cad smiled a lopsided, evil smile. "Feel a little uncomfortable around these Union boys? You should. They know what you've been up to."

"What are you talking about?"

Cad's smile disappeared. His mouth flattened. "These boys know everything. They know where yer profits are goin'. They know you've been hauling freight up here, selling it for big profits—big pouches of gold—sending the gold back down South. You've been helping fund the Confederate war effort."

"That's ridiculous."

"Oh, is it? Why didn't we hands know more than just a smatterin' about you? You ain't from St. Louis. You're from Virginia."

Scooter felt his jaw drop. Where did Cad get his information?

The giant pressed his revolver into Scooter's ribs and spit out a curse. "We promised Mr. Lincoln's men we'd do everything possible to make certain all gold shipments out of Bannack City end up in Washington D.C.—in *our* government, not yours. Besides that, your money helped kill my brother. I ain't happy about that."

Scooter bit his lip. Now was not the time to mention that he'd lost a father and two brothers on the Confederate side. He turned his gaze back to Cad. Galling was the fact that he'd attacked Abby in the black of night. Unsuccessfully, thank the Lord. Sent down the road by Hagen, Cad should have been arrested. Locked up or hung.

Scooter said, "I'm here looking for Abby."

Cad shot back a quick answer. "She's with the man with the lazy eyes."

Suddenly restless, Scooter blinked and blinked again. "Who do you mean?"

"From Utah Territory. The man with the broken leg. Isaac Jacobs."

Scooter had a hard time believing Cad. Why would Isaac be here? He scratched his head and thought. The answer came quickly. Winny had shared Abby's letter with Isaac. Isaac's reaction must have been immediate. He'd lit out for Bannack City immediately with one purpose, to find and win Abby. "What about Abby's Indian boy?"

"Easy to find. They act like a happy little family now."

Through a mist of insanity and darkness Scooter tried to make sense of what he was hearing. The giant still had a revolver pressed into his ribs, making it hard to think, but the answer came to him. Cad had been in Bannack City for days and found the boy. Abby arrived, looking for Yahnai. Somehow Abby ended up with him. Perhaps Isaac had something to do with it. A payoff? But where would a poor farmer from Franklin get the kind of money Cad would demand?

A puzzled look came upon the giant's face. "Who's Abby?" he asked. "And who's Isaac Jacobs? And what's this about an Indian boy?"

"Don't matter," Cad said.

The man in the forage hat aimed his revolver at Scooter's nose. "That's enough questions. We're gonna ride along the ditch for a ways, then south to Yankee Flat. You'll ride in the middle. As you can see, there are more than a dozen of us."

Scooter said nothing as he considered his options. That didn't take long—he didn't have any. He was surrounded by a dozen men. Their Colts were still pointed at him. Another Yankee tied Scooter's hands behind his back. The men calmly reholstered their .44s as if it were the natural thing to do. They had rendered him helpless.

The forage-cap man spoke again. "If you try anything, one of us will shoot you. We all know how to shoot. One more dead man in this town means nothing."

"Time for a hanging, boys," the giant said.

Scooter recoiled at the words. *Hanging?* Ever since his mother had talked him into leaving the army, he'd feared hanging. He sank lower and lower in the saddle. His head began to split with ache. He felt an urge to massage his temples but couldn't. His hands were tied behind his back. Cad had turned this trip to Bannack City into a nightmare. Cad had muddled the waters. Scooter's hopes of finding Abby had dimmed to black. For that, a profound wave of failure shuddered through his core. Tension tore into his body. Where was she? Already on her way back to Utah Territory with Isaac and Yahnai? If these men were serious, Scooter realized he'd never see Abby again. Or his mother. At least Isaac would take care of Abby and her son. Maybe that's the way God intended it to be. Just like in the beginning on that day he'd rescued them from the creek crossing.

His horse obediently followed as if there were nothing wrong.

The Yankees began a short trek from the corrals. The steady *clip-clop* of the horses' hooves was unnerving. With relentless determination, the Union boys moved the procession along the street, macabre silhouettes rising and falling against buildings. The procession turned south, toward Yankee Flat, threading right and left through freight wagons, bullwhackers, mule skinners, and miners. To Scooter's dismay, no one gave the blue-clad men a second look. Nor him.

The talk about a hanging continued. *I'm going to die,* Scooter realized. *Here and now.*

As he rode, unwillingly plummeting toward death, emotions knotted in his chest. Twenty-two years of his life were about to disappear like the little wisps of dust kicked up by the horses ahead of him. Surreal strands of memory sifted back into his consciousness. For a moment he relived the last time he saw members of his family. He saw his father riding away from the plantation, proud to be in the Confederate army, to fight for what he believed in. He saw his two brothers. He saw Billy dying in his arms. He saw his mother pleading for him to leave. He saw her standing there as he rode away on the horse she'd brought him. He saw Abby, all drenched with cold water at the creek crossing. He saw the way she looked when he kissed her for the first time. All this came back to him vividly. He imagined arriving in heaven. Everything white. A blinding, pure light. At least he'd found the Church. He knew there was an afterlife, a resurrection. A hope not only for salvation but for exaltation as well. He saw no hope of escape.

He hung his head in resignation.

Chapter 41

ABBY AWOKE WHEN SHE HEARD Yahnai, Isaac, and Riddle return from the store. Still groggy, she wondered for a moment if she were dreaming. Yahnai jumped on the bed and wrapped his arms around her. His touch was better than any dream.

"Oh, I've missed you!" She sat up to soak in his warmth, the smell of his clean skin, and the sight of his bright eyes.

"We bought you a dress," Yahnai said.

Isaac held up a maroon-colored gown, which was far nicer than anything she owned. It was almost as nice as the yellow dress she'd worn while with Scooter.

"Uncle Isaac bought me some paper and a pencil!" Yahnai said, and he promptly plopped down on the floor and began drawing. She remembered the last time he'd drawn that way—before the winter camp and all of the horror. It melted the tension and fear in her heart, and she felt that spring had surely come. In that moment, it occurred to her that she'd never have to give Yahnai up again, even for winter camp.

"I'll bet you're hungry," Isaac said. He wore a new, crisp red shirt.

"Famished."

"Is famished the same as hungry?" Yahnai asked without looking up.

Abby laughed. "Yes. Famished is the same as hungry."

"Change clothes, and we'll eat," Isaac said. "The restaurant is next door."

"Not there," Abby said. "Not with my bedsheets on the tables."

He laughed. "There's another restaurant up the street."

"I have money," she said, retrieving the gold coin from her pocket. "I can buy."

He looked surprised. "What money?"

"Scooter gave me this," she said with a trace of malice. "Just like the one Carl and Winny have. It was a gift. But now I'd like to get rid of it. It'll just remind me of him." She fought the urge to run her fingers over it, to think of Scooter's kisses.

"Very well," he said happily as he took the coin. He gave her a thin-lipped grin and winked his sharp hazel eyes. "Now, you put on that dress. I'll wait outside."

Abby changed her clothes while Yahnai continued to color. She noticed that he was drawing a picture of their home in Franklin. Straightening her hair as best she could, she tried not to remember Scooter and focused on Isaac's kindness. Her family was together again because of him. Nothing else mattered.

After the languor of the hotel room, the warm spring air was bracing. Freight wagons passed along the street as the trio walked to the restaurant. Abby thought about Scooter. His wagons wouldn't be here until tomorrow.

Horsemen clad in various articles of Union-blue clothing clomped past. Abby took scant notice of them as they descended toward the creek, but suddenly something caught her eye. One man, seemingly surrounded by the others, had his back to her. Hair the color of the sun streamed from beneath a dark felt hat, just like Scooter's. It couldn't be him, of course. He was probably preparing to come into town the next day and sell his wares, lamenting the fact that his conquest had escaped his clutches.

The blue-clad men's coarse talk and laughter reminded her of Cad. They passed along a brown bottle, taking long swigs. A few of them seemed to speak louder with every swig. One said, "We should have left a big tree instead of cuttin' 'em all down."

"We don't need a tree. We'll build our own gallows."

"We could just shoot 'im and get it over with."

"Naw. I want to see a hanging. A genuine hanging."

Abby felt a chill. The level of civilization in Bannack City certainly wasn't very high. The men had to be deserters. Worse men than those under the command of Colonel Connor. Was there no law here? Why the men were intent on hanging the man with blond hair was beyond her. Had the blond jumped one of their claims? Stolen gold? Cheated in a card game? In this lawless town, it could be anything.

Behind them, another man followed on a black horse. Red hair, matted, stringy, showing from beneath a funny hat. Cad?

Abby found the restaurant plain and unappealing. It was smoky and overcrowded. She could smell the sweat of the hardworking miners mingling with the smell of roasted and fried meats. There were kitchen noises and the sharp sounds of silverware on plates and the thump of cups going down on wooden tabletops. Customers had settled in at every table, like they were happy to linger over their meals despite the line of people waiting to be seated. Germans sat at one table, telling stories and singing about the Fatherland. Painted ladies sat at another, giggling. The other tables were full of miners and freighters. As soon as a table emptied, a little man with an unruly mass of dark hair cleared the wreckage of plates, cups, and utensils and sat impatient patrons there.

In a corner Abby caught the sight of seven men crowded around a table meant for four, all leaned back expansively on their chairs, enjoying themselves like they owned the place. They were all a little red in the face from the liquor they were consuming. Six of them were listening to the seventh. Abby saw why. The seventh man had a star pinned to his black shirt, easy to see—it had to be either the sheriff or one of his deputies. The other six men hunched forward, elbows on the tables, conspiratorial, nodding back and forth. A few minutes later, all seven men left. She wondered if she should warn him that a group of men was preparing a hanging just yards away. Somehow she doubted he would care.

Her food was served on a thick china plate. Maybe Scooter had brought them here. Each plate held a medium-sized steak, a pile of beans, a large mound of potatoes, and a smaller mound of fried onions. She drank water from a chipped glass. Her steak was tough, the beans average, but the potatoes and onions, from Utah Territory, were tasty. All in all, probably much better than the meal miners were getting in their grimy camps.

The sun was still out when they finished eating. But it was low in the sky, and the streets were in shadows. The dance hall was close to the creek, not far from Yankee Flat. Most miners walking toward it wore red, blue, or green flannel shirts with soft collars and neckties. A few wore suits, dragged out of trunks, aired, and pressed. Even fewer sported white shirts with stiffly starched fronts. Abby saw a few husbands and wives, even a few children. Everyone shuffled along at a happy pace.

"Do I have to dance?" Yahnai asked.

"Only if you want to," she said.

"We're going to celebrate," Isaac said. "We're all together again."

Abby allowed Isaac to wrap his arms around her and give her a tight hug. She didn't pull away. Locked arm in arm with Isaac and Yahnai, she floated toward the dance hall bounding with the rhythm of fiddle, banjo, and tambourine music.

"Why, hello. Are you folks new in town?"

The voice behind Abby was female and pleasant. Abby twirled to find a young lady wearing a brown calico dress. The man with her sported a blue suit foxed with buckskin. A silver badge reflected off his chest. She gave him a quizzical little glance. It was the same man she'd seen in the restaurant. He had changed clothes and expressions. There he'd been conniving. Right now he was relaxed, eyes full of fun.

Abby smiled her answer. "We're from Utah Territory."

"Why, I declare," the young woman said. "We have to thank folks like you for freighting us goods. I'm Electa. This is my husband, Henry Plummer."

"I'm Abigail. This is Isaac Jacobs. And my adopted son, Yahnai."

"An adopted Indian boy?" Electa looked surprised.

The sheriff shook Isaac's hand and asked, "Is this young lady your daughter?"

"No," Isaac said, gritting his teeth. "We are engaged to be married."

"Oh," said the sheriff. "That seems unusual. You must be twice her age."

Electra scrutinized Yahnai. "So this is your boy."

"That seems unusual too," the sheriff said, as if Indians were a scourge.

"Oh, Henry," Electa said, "that means Abigail has a big heart. He'll fit in just fine. There are other children here tonight."

Plummer tipped his hat. "Shall we go in?"

Abby nodded, told Riddle to say outside, and stepped toward the hall. The brief conversation seemed like something she'd have to get used to when she married Isaac—the questions, the defensive flexing of Isaac's jaw. There had always been raised eyebrows about Yahnai. She'd adapted to that, so she could adapt to this.

As Abby entered the hall, she was hit with a wall of sound and warm air. Dancers jostled around her. Most were men dancing with men. The sheriff's silver badge had its magical effect. The miners parted in a courteous manner, as if they were all wanted men.

"Your dress is darling," Electa said.

"Isaac bought it for me just today. Yours too."

"It's the dress I wore at my wedding," Electa said. "Just a short time ago, up north at my parent's place, not far from Fort Benton. Any dance you favor?"

"The quadrille," Abby answered. It was a lively dance with four couples facing each other and forming a square. "I've danced it in our meeting house in Franklin." With a pang, she remembered that Evan had died just before the building was complete.

Electa tapped the sheriff on the shoulder and spoke in his ear. Plummer threaded through the dancers and spoke to one of the fiddle players. When the current dance ended, the fiddle player announced a quadrille. The sheriff and his wife made one couple, Abby and Isaac another. Electa selected three other children. With Yahnai, that made eight people.

The dance began. Miners whooped and hollered, turning silly and glib.

Midway through the quadrille, with everyone shifting partners often, another man with a badge on his chest rushed into the hall. He didn't look smart, and he didn't look pleasant. He pulled on Sheriff Plummer's arm and whispered in his ear. Whispered primly and smugly with a degree of certainty, as if he had access to insider information. Plummer's eyes calculated. He nodded often. Once, he pulled out his pocket watch and looked at it. He whispered into Electa's ear, and the two men immediately left.

Abby assumed trouble. She wondered if it had anything to do with the string of men she'd seen riding past the restaurant, ready to lynch their prisoner. Almost without skipping a beat, Electa found another partner. Apparently such interruptions for her husband were common. She acted like they were. The dancing resumed.

When the quadrille ended, the fiddle player announced a Virginia reel. As the music took up again, Abby unconsciously thought of Scooter. But she was startled out of her thoughts when she saw a familiar barrel-chested man jostling his way through the dancers. He was coming straight at her, his strides resolute and quick. It was Oscar. Surprised, she put a hand to her heart. "Oscar. What are you doing here?"

He looked like he'd seen a ghost. His face was grim, sallow, and stern. He began pulling on her arm more urgently than the deputy had tugged on the sheriff. "Lord a-mercy, Abby! Scooter's in danger. They're gonna hang him."

She stared at him in disbelief. *Hang Scooter?* Then he *was* the man she'd seen riding away with the group of Yankee soldiers. Panic charged through her as she realized she'd put him in danger by not alerting the sheriff earlier. "You weren't due to be here until tomorrow," she said, still refusing to believe.

"We realized you were gone, and we hurried here. But they found him first."

She felt Isaac go quiet beside her. She exchanged uneasy looks with him and with Yahnai. It took her a few seconds to respond. In a shaky voice, she asked, "Who's 'they'? Who's going to hang him? What for?"

Oscar spoke the words half out of breath, in short, rapid clips, with a worried twist to his mouth. "Union guys, a peck of trouble. A dozen or more of them. Maybe two dozen by now. At Yankee Flat. Not far from here. They think he's a Confederate agent sending his profits back to the South. For the Confederate war effort. I heard the sheriff was here, but I don't see him. We need him or one of his deputies or all of them."

The explanation left Abby weak and dizzy. Her head swam, and her throat seemed to be choking shut.

"I'm the sheriff's wife," Electa said. "Can I help?"

"The sheriff needs to come quick," Oscar said.

Abby wrung her hands together. "A deputy dragged him out a few minutes ago."

"I'm sorry," Electa said.

"Maybe he's already at Yankee Flat," Abby said hopefully.

Electa shook her head. "No, some kind of trouble at Alder Gulch."

A strangled sob escaped Abby's throat. "What shall we do, Electa?"

Electa said, "Things like this happen all the time. More than my poor husband can handle. The best thing for you to do is fight force with force."

Abby grasped Yahnai's hand, motioned at Oscar and Isaac, and then took her first uncertain steps toward the door. "How far is Yankee Flat?" she asked.

Chapter 42

ISAAC FOLLOWED ABBY OUT OF the dance hall warped with remorse. He felt sweat forming on his brow. What had he done? He'd meant to scare Scooter away—to push him on to California or back to St. Louis. It had been a horrible mistake to suggest that Scooter was an agent of the South, a mistake that was about to have irreversible consequences. Isaac's desires were not worth a man dying. Not even Scooter.

He should have expected this. Yahnai's rescue had come too easily, with no exchange of gold and no bloodshed. Hadn't Isaac seen the hatred in the greasy man's eyes? *If you wallow with pigs, expect to get dirty.* That's how he felt. Dirty. He wiped at his forehead. He wiped at his cheeks. He pulled at his chin. He rubbed the back of his neck. He shrugged. Relief would not come until Scooter was safe.

Oscar led them across the footbridge, up the road, east on Yankee Flat's main street, and then up a gradual hill. Isaac hurried behind the rest of them, wincing as his weak leg began to stiffen. Riddle ran alongside Abby and Yahnai as Oscar explained how he and Scooter had hurried to the city and then split up to find Abby. Their plan to find her and meet up in the center of town had ended with Oscar alone at their meeting place. Then Oscar finally spotted Scooter near Yankee Flat, surrounded by former Union soldiers and spurred on by a smiling, victorious Cad. Talk of hanging. Talk of revenge.

Oscar held Abby's elbow, his voice thick with concern. "Miss Abby, those men are wrong. Scooter ain't sending no money back to the Confederacy."

"Of course not. Where did Cad even get such an idea?" Abby asked. "He was there with you, wasn't he? He saw how Scooter expanded his business last winter."

Isaac closed his eyes to fight the burning sensation of shame.

"There they are," Oscar said, pointing to a knot of men clad in various bits of Union-blue. Twenty or more, like rats in the mulch. They had a prisoner. He was hard to see, but there was no doubt it was Scooter. He sat on the ground, hands tied behind him. Gagged. Someone had taken his hat, or he'd lost it. His golden hair was tousled, falling free over his shoulders.

With looks of wolfish satisfaction on their faces, Scooter's captors were passing a bottle around. Laughing. Cursing. Making threats. Casting long shadows.

If they were going to hang Scooter, they appeared to be in no hurry.

Isaac quickly determined why. He heard the familiar sound of a saw. They were building something. No doubt a gallows.

If you wallow with pigs, expect to get dirty.

Isaac looked straight at Abby for the best part of ten seconds, unable to speak, but she wasn't looking back at him anyway. She was staring at Scooter, her face flushed and her eyes flooded. She had the same fighting expression she wore when she'd burst into Isaac's home and verbally torn into Connor. Isaac hung his head, realizing he'd earned the right to be on the receiving end of her wrath. He didn't know what to do.

❀ ❀ ❀

A lump formed in Abby's throat. As danger surrounded Scooter—in the form of drunken and angry men—the fact that he had lied to her didn't matter anymore. He didn't deserve this.

She felt an overpowering urge to wade right into middle of Scooter's accusers. Surprise them. Give them a tongue-lashing like she'd given Colonel Connor. Perhaps it would work. Perhaps it wouldn't. Talking to Colonel Connor certainly hadn't improved anything—he'd still gone ahead and slaughtered innocent people. This situation felt so similar her bones ached.

"Isaac, what shall we do?" she asked as she stroked Riddle's head.

Isaac shrugged and looked up as if surprised she'd spoken to him. "I don't know," he said in a neutral, toneless voice, as if he were more shocked than her.

She took a few more steps toward the mob of men, slowly, cautiously. Her head felt as though it would burst. Oscar threw a stiff arm at her, holding her back.

"Don't get any closer," Oscar warned. "Those Yankees are drunk, all outta kilter. They're trigger happy. They might shoot you—even if you are a woman. We need the sheriff and a posse."

"I don't want them to hurt Scooter," Yahnai said. "I like Scooter."

"I like him too," Abby said, kneeling down, holding Yahnai's little face.

Oscar spoke, his voice pulling Abby away from a confused stupor. "Scooter loves you, you know. His heart was broken when he found out you left. His lips were all pooched out. He'd meant to tell you somethin', somethin' very important. He was going to tell you just before we entered Bannack City. But he waited too long."

"What was he going to tell me?" she asked, her heart aching at the thought of the letters from Millie—the truth about Scooter's past. Was he going to tell her the truth?

"He got baptized. In Salt Lake. Just before we left. He's a Mormon."

Abby gasped. "What?" In her mind she replayed all of their discussions about religion, and didn't know whether to be angry or to laugh. "Why didn't he tell me?"

"Because he has a hankerin' for you. He's fallen in love. He wanted you to fall in love with him, but he didn't want his baptism to influence you. We stopped by the settlement to see you, but you had left. After you found us on the trail, he was fixin' to tell you, but he decided he had plenty of time—time to see how things would work out. He wanted to see if you could love him because of who he was. Who he is. Not just because he joined your church. I think you can see he's a changed man. He's had an influence on us all, especially me. I was thinking about joining your church too.

Abby hung her head. Once again she'd been too judgmental, too limited by the blinders she chose to wear. Everything she wanted had been within her grasp, and she couldn't see it. Then she remembered the other woman—the reason she left Scooter's camp. "But I read letters, letters from a girl named Millie."

Oscar shook his head like a horse fighting off flies. "Old history. In the past. She may still love him, but I'm certain he doesn't love her anymore. He loves you."

She fell to her knees, still holding Yahnai's shoulders. "What'll we do? It won't be long until they finish their gallows."

When she needed advice, she usually turned to Winny. Or to Isaac. She turned toward him, and he stood silently looking at the ground and rubbing his weak leg. Rarely had she seen him so withdrawn and so silent. Perhaps he saw the truth of the situation. Perhaps in the last few minutes, as Oscar explained everything, Isaac realized that he had lost her. Even if the worst happened and Scooter didn't make it through this, Abby could no longer imagine herself at Isaac's side. In a moment her world had changed, and she knew what she needed to do.

"Do we have time to find help?" Abby asked Oscar.

"If we hurry. It looks to me like these Union rascals are just as interested in their skunk oil as they are in hanging Scooter. It's a neck-tie party, and they don't want it to end too early. Once the hanging is done, the party is over."

Abby's mind churned, and finally an idea began to form. "There are as many Confederates in Bannack as there are Union men, wouldn't you say?"

Oscar's eyes widened. "Why, yes. Yes, there are!"

"I saw a few of them at the dance."

Oscar spoke as though hit by a bolt of lightning. "Before I found you, I wandered into a dance hall farther up the street. It was a dance put on exclusively for Southerners, or so the sign said. I'll go there. We'll raise our own posse. I'll bet I can be back here with two dozen men quicker than the shake of a lamb's tail."

Clouds of doubt began to evaporate for Abby. A light of possibility shone through. With a painful but determined expression, she nodded at Oscar. "Go. We'll meet back here with a few extra men for support."

Oscar turned on his heel, took off in a quick sprint, and disappeared.

She stepped toward Isaac, who didn't even turn to watch Oscar leave. "Will you help me save Scooter's life?" she asked, hoping he'd be able to put his own hurt aside to prevent a horrific act.

Isaac coughed a little and didn't look up at Abby when he spoke. "Abby, I will help you any way that I can."

If they'd had time, Abby would have embraced him. Isaac had always been willing to help her. In fact, she owed him more than she could account, and to have her ask this of him must have been a dagger to his heart. The men behind her erupted with raucous laughter, and the sounds were like a spur in her side.

"Come," she said. "Let's hurry."

With resolute strides, Abby led Isaac and Yahnai back to the hall. The flow of early evening revelers had increased to a tide. Miners were streaming into not only the hall but all the saloons and restaurants. When she arrived, she posted Isaac and Yahnai at the entrance. Both wore red shirts, easy to see. "Isaac, I'll send men to you. You gather them outside, and then we'll take them to Yankee Flat with us."

"How will you know which ones to ask?"

Abby scanned the dance floor. "Electa is still here. She can help. We'll ask all the men, one at a time. We'll ask where they're from. If they say one of the Southern states, I send them to you. All of them that look young enough to fight."

After enlisting Electa's support, the two women began with the men loitering along the walls. Straightforward question, no introduction, no small talk.

"Where are you from?" Abby asked a man in a blue suit that smelled like moth balls.

"New York," the surprised miner said, hoping for a dance partner.

She left the New Yorker standing there baffled and approached a man with thin black hair wearing a yellow shirt. "Sir, where you from?"

His eyes rounded in pleasure. "Why, South Carolina, if that makes a difference."

"See the man in the red shirt over there by the door? Go see him. It's urgent."

The man shrugged his shoulders and swam through the crowd toward Isaac.

For the first time, Abby found her status as a pretty young woman an asset. Within minutes nearly twenty men were hanging around in the shadows near Isaac, just outside the door, puzzled looks on their faces. Wondering why they'd been called out and assembled. Just about every Confederate state was represented: Texas, Louisiana, Arkansas, Florida, Mississippi, Alabama, Georgia, and North and South Carolina.

"Thank you for your time," Abby said. "I'm here to ask for your help. A good friend of mine, a Virginian, is about to be hanged in Yankee Flat."

Eyebrows lowered in anger. Eyes narrowed. Fingers wagged. Voices turned gruff. Though others wondered why that was any concern of theirs.

"He's a freighter named Scooter. He is accused of sending money back to the Confederacy to support war efforts, but he is only trying to make a living." She swallowed as emotion tightened her throat. "These Yankees are going to kill a Virginian for no good reason—with no proof of any crime. I want to win back this man's freedom!" She let her voice swell, and she punched the air with her fist. The voices surrounding her grew angrier, stronger, and more engaged. Most of the men began to rally, but she hadn't won all of them over yet. They needed only a bit more encouragement before they became a weapon in her hands to fight back against Scooter's enemies.

"I've seen what men can do when they are misguided and led by lies. They spill innocent blood. Well, you can help me protect the innocent tonight. Together we can stop these Yankees from robbing a mother of her loving son. This innocent man is a good leader of a group of honest men. He is a man who is tender and loving with children, and he respects women like no other man I've ever known." Her throat tightened, and she realized in a rush just how much she loved Scooter and how desperately she wanted to be with him again.

"Well, let's go get him!" one man said.

Elated, Abby clapped her hands together. She could see it in their eyes now. There was no way they would allow this travesty to happen. And neither would she.

Chapter 43

ABBY'S PESSIMISM REVERSED. HER TRIGGER finger was now set. Nothing could stop her from saving Scooter. Her enlistment of gray boys would be a nightmare for the blues. If the smart money was to bring a gun to a knife fight, she was doing one better—she was bringing a stick of dynamite. The Southern boys were nearly ready to explode.

As she thought of the impending confrontation, she remembered the last time she'd fought herself out of a bad situation. She looked down at Riddle. He greeted her with a wagging tail. Energy buzzed in the air as she began to lead her little army off on their rescue mission.

She turned to Isaac, sensing the awkwardness between them. Still, she trusted him completely. "Will you take Yahnai?" she asked. "Protect him if things go wrong."

Isaac nodded. "I hope there's no bloodshed," he said. His eyes looked bloodshot in the fading light. She hadn't seen him look so old and fragile since that day in the creek.

"I'll go ahead of them," Abby said. "I'll plead for justice, for rational thought. And I'll trust in God." She did her best to sound strong and faithful, though fear pierced through her for a moment.

"Things have already gotten so . . . complex and dangerous," Isaac warned. "Abby, you don't know what could happen."

Abby knew Scooter's life hung in the balance. She knew she had potentially orchestrated a small war between North and South. At the worst, she'd lose everything. It could be the Battle of Bear River all over again, only worse.

"Stay behind the crowd," she told Isaac. "Don't let him see if anything goes wrong. He's seen enough war."

Isaac nodded and then looked at the ground again.

Abby walked to Yahnai and took his hand. "Go to Uncle Isaac," she said. "Stay with him until we rescue Scooter." She kissed his head, holding on to that moment with all of her energy. Yahnai moved to Isaac's side and took him by the hand.

Ignoring her throbbing heart, Abby rushed back to her little army. "You men know why you're here, correct?" she said.

They responded with a chorus of shouts, some drawing their weapons.

"Put your weapons away for now," she said. "You are joining me to add to my strength, to show that they cannot overpower us without a fight. All I want is to gain the release of one man. He's one of yours. I don't want anyone killed or even injured. You understand? We don't want blood. We want the innocent to be free."

The men holstered their six-shooters and nodded. Their enthusiasm had been dampened a little. She hoped not too much. "Follow me," she shouted. "Hopefully we will meet reinforcements along the way." She wondered if Oscar had been successful and how many men he had gathered.

Like a herd of angry oxen, like a pack of ferocious wolves, the men followed her toward Yankee Flat. At the footbridge, she saw Oscar. He had a dozen or so men waiting with him. Angry men, their lips curling into hard grimaces. Their arms were down by their sides, their hands tense and poised to grab a weapon or throw a fist.

Oscar approached Abby. "I've fetched a dozen men. You've fetched even more. We'll match them dang-nabbed Yankees, or close. They ain't finished the gallows, but they've made progress. They're drunked up and rowdy, which has slowed their ability to work, so that's in our favor. A few of the men have passed out, so our only concern is the mean ones—the drunks who get bloodthirsty."

Abby nodded. Those were definitely the kind of men she worried about.

Oscar said, "The scalawags are holding Scooter smack dab in the middle of the clump to the side of the gallows. They're well armed.

They're apt to see us as soon as we hit that point." He pointed near the creek, drawing an imaginary line. "Scooter is tied and gagged, but he ain't blindfolded. Still, the gallows will make it hard for him to see what's happening. They're holding him on the ground."

Abby looked at the camp and caught a glimpse of Scooter as a man brought his rifle butt down on Scooter's back. He sat on the far side of his captors, his hands tied behind him, and his feet tied too. She drew a sigh of relief. The blue boys hadn't seen their approach yet. The element of surprise was still with them. She quickly counted heads. The Union forces had multiplied since she'd been there, but she still had them outnumbered. The soldiers had started a fire near the gallows to provide more light as the sun began to set, and the flames cast eerie shadows across the earth.

Oscar turned his back to Abby, assessing the camp once more, an itching finger caressing his six-shooter.

"Keep a safe distance," Abby warned Isaac one last time. He nodded and seemed to grip Yahnai's hand a little tighter. She smoothed her new dress, ready for action.

Abby led her Confederate army across the footbridge and then toward the former Union soldiers. Oscar's assessment of the men who held Scooter captive, and of their collective mood, turned out to be correct. They were still hammering on their makeshift gallows. Still passing bottles from one lip to another, laughing and cursing. Pointing at Scooter, who sat staring at the scene with wide-open, fearful eyes. The noise masked Abby's approach.

Soon they crossed Oscar's imaginary line. Swallowing her apprehension, she glided toward Scooter's accusers. The crowd of gray boys bunched behind her.

One of the blue boys saw her and her little army. And then another. And another. The hammering stopped. The passing of bottles stopped. Abby smelled the pungent liquor and heard the roar of Grasshopper Creek. She turned and held up a hand to stop her gray army. All alone, she took a few more steps. She'd thought about having Oscar be the front man, but he was just that—a man. She was a woman. Perhaps the blue boys would reason with her or at least be distracted enough to let Scooter get away somehow.

"Who goes there?" one of the men said. He tipped a Union-blue forage cap back and gripped a hammer tightly. He'd been working on the gallows. Debate was on his face and in his narrowed eyes. Behind him stood a giant of a man, tall and wide. He had hands big enough to crush the head of a boy like Yahnai. Both men scared her. She took a deep breath and let it out. The knot in her stomach tightened.

"There's a man you are holding prisoner," she said. "He's my friend. I came to get him."

"And just who are you?" the man in the forage cap asked.

"Abigail Butterfield Browett. From Utah Territory."

"This is none of your business, little lady. Best go back to your kitchen in Utah."

Abby stood her ground. "I'm not alone," she said.

"I see you brought a crowd with you. They're just grays. I'm not impressed."

Abby heard her reinforcements rumble their anger. "My friend's name is Jesse Kemp. We know him as Scooter. He's from Virginia."

"His name means nothing. His deeds say a lot. And if you're friends with him, that makes you our enemy as well. And coming here makes you a foolish girl, a bad judge of character."

"I can prove what I know about him, and back up my testimony with that of several other witnesses. All you have is the word of a redheaded scoundrel."

The sticky conversation had drawn the blue boys closer, as if they couldn't believe their leader was conversing with a woman. The giant who hovered behind the spokesman stood to his full, intimidating height. In his crumpled Hardee hat, he looked like the kind of guy who ate two dinners and was still hungry afterward.

The leader yelled at an unidentified man in the crowd behind him. "Did you hear what she called you? She called you a redheaded scoundrel." He looked into the crowd, and Cad lowered the bottle in his hand.

Abby flinched at the sight of him. She'd wondered somewhere in the recesses of her mind how she would feel when she saw him again. She recoiled at how awful he looked. Though he had always been repugnant, he showed the remnants of the beating Abby and Riddle had given him. His ear was one big scab, red and full of puss. Though his black eyes had healed, they were framed with green and yellow remnants of bruises. The swelling on his cheeks had gone down. His split lip had almost healed. She didn't know if his teeth were still loose. He walked gingerly, as though the stab wound she'd inflicted on him was still a little painful. He took slow and precise steps, left and then right, as though thoroughly buzzed by the drinking he'd done. He sucked on a big cigar as though he were already celebrating Scooter's demise. Slowly, he walked toward her, avoiding eye contact.

"Well, she would know whether I'm a scoundrel or not," Cad said. "You remember, don't ya, Abby? That night under the wagon?"

Riddle began growling as Cad approached.

"You keep that dog away from me!" Cad said, and he stopped his advance.

Abby grinned. "See, even my dog knows a criminal when he sees one."

"Cad is the one who ought to hang," Oscar said. "For trifling with Abby. How do y'all think her dog knows him? Riddle done chewed off Cad's ear."

The blue boys began buzzing—groaning and bombarding Oscar and Cad with accusatory gestures.

Abby held out her hands to try and quiet them. "Yes, Cad did try to trifle with me. And now he's lying to you. He only wants to punish Scooter for firing him. And Scooter fired him to protect me. Scooter used his money to expand his business, and Cad was there the whole time. He knows the truth, and he's using all of you to get something."

The forage-cap man said, "Well, forgive me if I don't believe your yarn, little lady. Southern men have a way with women. They make a business of deceiving little girls like you. Cad here may be an ugly cuss, but he's a patriot. And after we hang the freighter, it's only fair that Cad gets to take over the wagons and animals. No more gold from the sale of freight will be funneled off to the South."

Abby gave the man an incredulous stare. The facts were so obvious to her.

"Now," said the man, "why don't you take your growlin' dog and the other mutts you brought with you and skedaddle." He approached Abby until she could smell stale, hot alcohol on his breath. "I'd hate for anyone to get hurt."

"Back away from her!" Oscar said.

Abby couldn't look at the man who walked around her so closely, smelling so terrible. Instead, she looked out at the crowd of men—blue and gray, divided by only a few feet of tense air. Near the gallows, Scooter watched the scene before him, his blue eyes full of rage and desperation. Scooter began to fight, to kick against his restraints and to bite at the cloth in his mouth. The guard nearest him slammed him with the butt of his rifle until he doubled over in pain.

"No!" Abby said, lunging toward Scooter. It gave Oscar an unintended opening. Oscar slammed a hooked punch into the man wearing the forage cap. The man fell to the ground behind Abby, and Oscar wrenched the hammer away and threw it out of reach.

A room full of gunpowder only needs a spark to explode. Oscar was that spark. Blues and grays joined in the melee. Grabbing arms, big strong hands on elbows, pushing one, pulling the other. No one touched the giant. Big, red-faced, meaty, he crouched like an ape between Abby and Scooter, daring anyone to touch him.

Abby heard foul oaths escape Cad's lips. He threw his cigar to the ground and bunched his hands into fists. Cad approached Abby with an apparent mission in mind—his eyes burned through her, and Abby knew he wouldn't hesitate to hit her.

"Riddle! Sic him!" Abby shouted, and the dog obeyed. The approaching, growling animal distracted Cad long enough for Abby to launch her fist into his shoulder just before Riddle attacked. Cad flinched and screamed in pain. With one hand he clutched at his injured shoulder. Riddle had the other hand. The dog had sunk his teeth into the flesh and was growling and shaking his head back and forth.

There was dread in Cad's eyes. Abby knew that if Cad lost his balance and fell to the ground, Riddle wouldn't hesitate to go for his other ear or throat. She saw the fear in his eyes, and as he struggled to keep his balance, she realized he knew it too.

"Git that dog away from me!"

Abby looked at Cad. He'd caused far more trouble than he was worth. She actually felt sorry for the pathetic man. In a glance, she could see everything escalating around them. Men were reaching for

weapons—knives mostly, but the guards stood over Scooter with their
rifles pointed at the crowd. She guessed most, if not all, of the men
probably had a firearm. She'd lost control. Perhaps she'd never really
had control to begin with. Isaac had been right to caution her—to tell
her she didn't know where her dangerous choices would lead.

"Down, Riddle!" Abby commanded. "That's enough. Back off."

She reached at Oscar's hip and jerked his revolver from its holster.
Then she climbed up on the scaffold for the gallows and fired the
weapon into the air.

At first, only a few men stopped fighting and looked up. Instantly,
she realized her plan would backfire. Those who didn't stop fighting
grabbed at their guns and took aim at the nearest enemy.

"Stop!" Abby yelled, her voice strong and shrill. "No more
fighting! Put your weapons away!" She fired the gun once more, and
more of the men stopped. Still, not all of them were ready to give up.
"You came here for gold, not blood!" Abby continued. This stopped
more of them, until only a few men on the fringes of the group were
still tugging at each other, trying to wrestle their enemies to the
ground. She smiled and felt another surge of hope.

"Gold!" She yelled the word loudly, as if she were yelling fire in
a public place. The men stopped fighting and looked toward her.
"That's right. That's what all of you want. Gold."

She paced along the scaffold, the weapon still hot in her hand.
"Even Scooter came here for gold. And what good does it do to die
for gold? I would hope that you'd all agree there are more important
things than that."

Some of the men were listening. And some of them agreed.

"Well, I didn't come here for gold. And I didn't come here for a
fight. Love for a child brought me to Bannack City, and love for a
man brought me here. I suppose we've all done some insane things
for love." She looked behind her where Oscar held Cad's arm behind
his back. Cad was bleeding from his shoulder, and Abby realized
she had reopened the stab wound with her punch. "You ever done
anything insane for love, Cad?"

He growled at her. Abby leaned closer to him and did some
growling of her own. "You tell these men the truth, or I'll sic my dog
on you again."

"I only did . . . what old man Jacobs told me to do," Cad drawled, slurring his words badly. "Scooter spent the money . . . to grow his business, just like she said."

Abby took a step back. "Old man Jacobs?" she asked. "You mean Isaac?" Suddenly it all made sense—how easily he seemed to get Yahnai from Cad's clutches, how he avoided telling Abby about the sacrifice he had to make, his odd behavior since they found out Scooter had been captured. Isaac must have known all about Scooter's past, as she did. How did that happen? A memory assailed her. She vaguely remembered telling Isaac about Scooter back at the time she felt so depressed. If that were true, this had to be her fault! She was to blame for Scooter's misfortune. She had betrayed a trust, and Isaac had revealed Scooter's secret in exchange for Yahnai.

Looking out at the fringes of the group of men, Abby realized that the fighting would have encouraged Isaac to take Yahnai far enough away to keep him safe. She couldn't ask Isaac to offer confirmation, but she knew that this information was true, even though it came from Cad.

She turned toward the guards. "See, you heard Cad. He lied. Let Scooter go."

The Yankees guarding Scooter didn't move.

Abby took her plea to the giant of a man, who had hovered nearby, waiting for a fight and reeking with authority. If he consented, the other men would agree. "Let him go," she pled, ready to drop to her knees and beg if necessary.

He folded his arms across his thick chest. "We've been planning on a hanging for the better part of a day. I'm not sure we'll want to leave without one."

Her heart sank. She was at a loss. "What can I tell you more about Scooter? I know everything about him, and you can have your proof tomorrow when his foreman gets here with his wagons. Scooter has a mother in Virginia. He deserted because she told him to leave." Abby blinked until her eyes cleared, and she wiped the nuisance tears from her cheeks. "His father died in the war, and his brother died in his arms. He still has bad dreams about it. He told me."

She turned toward the group of men and continued speaking, desperation swelling in her chest. "He rescued us at a creek crossing last fall and probably saved Isaac's life. He took care of me when Yahnai was taken. He was there with me during the battle at the Bear River, and he helped me wash the blood from my hands. Innocent blood. And so help me, if you kill Scooter, I'll have blood on my hands again."

She ran for the giant, fists raised. The man caught her wrists and held her like irons. In her rage and fear, the tears dried quickly, and she fought against his grip until her arms ached. He watched her fight with a small grin creeping across his face.

"Abby, stop," Scooter said. "Please stop before you hurt yourself."

His voice was scratchy and dry, but Abby could hear him. She looked around the tree of a man and saw that Scooter was standing on weak legs. Not only had his guards removed the gag from his mouth, but they were cutting the ropes from his hands.

The giant let Abby go, and she ran to Scooter's side. His legs were weak, and she nearly knocked him off balance with her embrace. "I love you," she whispered.

He brushed her hair away from her face. "I can see that."

Abby relished feeling his arms around her, even though his grip was weak and shaky. He was bruised and winced when she touched him. "I'm so sorry Isaac did this to you," she said. "He did it for me, to rescue Yahnai from Cad. Isaac knew something about your past that he shouldn't have known, and it was all my fault. I must have let it slip out during one of his visits. I'm sorry. Please forgive me."

"I forgive you. I'm just glad it helped get Yahnai back," Scooter said as he kissed her forehead.

Somehow, Abby doubted it, but it didn't really matter. She held Scooter—Jesse—in her arms. She loved him. He loved her. He was free.

The world was new.

Chapter 44

THE GIANT STEPPED OFF OF the scaffold and strode toward Oscar. "If we try to hang the freighter now, I'll get my eyes scratched out."

Chuckles erupted from the crowd, whether they wore blue or gray.

"Still," the giant said, "I see no reason to let our gallows go to waste."

The man with the forage cap—the one Oscar had knocked nearly unconscious when the fight began—groaned as he slowly pushed himself off the ground. "I agree," he said. "Let's hang the redhead." Still woozy, he collapsed again, and again the crowd chuckled, a little louder this time as more tension began to dissipate.

The giant walked over to Oscar and Cad, knocked off Cad's hat, and grasped a fistful of the grimy red hair. "I think the noose will fit your neck just fine."

The gray boys cheered. Slowly the blue boys nodded their heads in agreement. Oscar let go of Cad, and the giant walked toward the scaffold, tossing Cad to the ground like a sack of potatoes, right in front of Abby and Scooter.

Abby had let Cad go once, when his life had been in her hands. He'd only caused more problems for her. No doubt he was a treacherous villain melting in Satan's hot grasp. Still, she felt sorry for him. He kneeled before them, whimpering and frightened. Beat up and bleeding. She'd never seen a more miserable man.

"No," she said. "Don't hang him. He has someone somewhere who loves him, I imagine. His mother, at least. Just let him go."

She looked out across the crowd again and saw Isaac and Yahnai approaching in the moonlight, aware the danger was over. Yahnai skipped along, and Isaac seemed to be trying—without much luck—to hold the boy back.

"Yes," Scooter said, nodding his agreement. "Let him go. We all make bad choices. So we all need a little forgiveness. Don't you think?" He turned toward Abby.

"Without a doubt," Abby said, wondering if it were possible for her to love Scooter more. "Forgiveness all around." She smiled.

"Here, here!" Oscar said as men raised their bottles high in the sky.

"They'll drink to anything," Scooter said, smiling, one of his eyebrows raised.

Abby laughed and then watched as the giant picked Cad up by his hair again and pulled him off the ground to lock eyes with him. "If I so much as catch a whiff of you in Bannack City again, you won't find mercy. You lied to us and tried to use us because you're too plumb lazy to work your own claim. You're nothin' but a thief." He threw Cad to the ground again. If Cad had a tail, it would have been between his legs as he turned his back on the group and ran off into the night.

"You're quite a woman." Scooter shook his head. "I just don't know if I can handle a wildcat like you."

"If anyone can tame me, it's you." She kissed him then, and many of the men cheered. With a glance, she saw that Isaac had reached the back of the crowd. He smiled at Abby, though his smile was weak.

Yahnai pushed through everyone until he could jump up on the scaffold and throw his arms around Abby and Scooter.

She saw surprise on the faces of the men. "This is my adopted son, Yahnai," she said. Yahnai turned, saw everyone looking at him, and promptly slipped behind Abby. She laughed and thought about explaining the situation, but the details didn't matter. The only explanation was love.

Chapter 45

ABBY FELT HIGH, AS THOUGH she were riding on a cloud. High as the eagles that soared above Bannack City. She shook with fatigue, but the imminent danger was over. Scooter would not be hanged. He was very much alive—tired, exhausted, drawn out, but still functioning. The area around the half-built gallows had gone quiet. The sudden quiet was more noticeable than the previous noise had been. The blue boys and the gray boys were starting to disperse. The party was over.

Hat in his hands, Isaac approached. "Abby, can I talk to you? In private?"

Abby looked at Scooter, who nodded with understanding. She jumped down from the scaffold and followed Isaac closer to the fire.

"Abby, this is all my fault," he said. He still couldn't look her in the eye.

Abby watched him struggle and felt like her heart might break for him. Everything had worked out all right. He really had no reason to tell her the truth, yet she saw the guilt burning in his eyes—the shame of it hunched his back.

"The truth came out, Isaac. Cad confessed where he got his information."

Isaac stared at the fire for a moment. "I will never forgive myself," he said. "I can't believe I put Scooter's life in danger that way."

"I imagine there was no other way to save Yahnai," she said. "Cad would have killed him if he'd felt like it."

"That's true," Isaac said. "I'm glad you didn't see how bad it was, Abby. When he showed Yahnai to me—"

"Thank you, Isaac." She didn't want to imagine the particulars. "Thank you for saving my boy. Thank you for taking care of me. Thank you for being exactly what I needed after Evan died."

Isaac looked at her and smiled, the firelight reflecting in his wet eyes. "I have something of yours," he said, reaching into his pocket.

"My gold coin," she said, taking it from him. Somehow it meant even more to her now.

"Promise me you'll marry him in the Endowment House?" Isaac asked.

Abby smiled. "I promise."

Isaac turned and walked quietly away, alone. Not far down the road, he began to whistle. It comforted Abby in a way she couldn't quantify.

She returned to Scooter, who was talking to Yahnai.

"Is the old man all right?" Scooter asked.

"Yes," Abby said. "I think he'll be fine."

"Well, Yahnai and I have been talking, and we think it's best if we become a family."

Abby felt butterflies fill her stomach. "You do?" she asked Yahnai.

"Yes." He smiled.

"Well, I agree."

Scooter took her by the hand. "And he taught me a wonderful word."

"Oh, what's that?"

"*Suuntsaa'.*"

Notes

CACHE VALLEY. In 1860, hundreds of wagons carrying settlers streamed into Cache Valley from other Mormon areas to establish not only Franklin but Hyrum, Millville, Paradise, and Hyde Park. This swelled the valley's total population to more than 2,600 souls—which included Logan, Wellsville, Smithfield, and Richmond as well. Brigham Young toured the valley that year, finding that more than five thousand acres had been plowed and planted that spring. The *Deseret News* ran an article, calling it "Cache Valley fever."

Franklin was the first permanent settlement in Idaho, founded by thirteen Mormon pioneer families in 1860, led by Thomas Smart. The town received its name after Franklin Richards, one of the Apostles at the time. The founders believed the town site was in Utah Territory, but in 1872, a survey revealed that it was actually in Idaho Territory, about a mile north of the Utah border. As of the 2000 census, there were 641 people living there.

BANNACK CITY. At the time gold was discovered in 1862, Bannack City was in Idaho Territory. Montana Territory was created in 1864, and Bannack City served as its capital for a brief time. The capital was later moved to Virginia City (Alder Gulch). Bannack City, located on Grasshopper Creek, approximately eleven miles upstream where Grasshopper Creek joins with the Beaverhead River south of Dillon, continued as a mining town for several years, though with a dwindling population. The last residents left in the 1970s. Helena is Montana's capital today.

At its peak, the city had a population of about ten thousand. Some sixty historic log and frame structures remain standing, many quite well preserved. Most can be explored. The site, now the Bannack Historic District, was declared a National Historic Landmark in 1961. The town is presently the site of Bannack State Park, and visitors are welcome.

CHARACTERS. All characters in this novel are fictional except the following: Colonel Patrick Connor; Porter Rockwell; Preston Thomas, the first bishop of Franklin; Henry Plummer, the Bannack City sheriff; Electa Plummer; and all the Shoshoni chiefs such as Sagwitch and Bear Hunter. (Often the name of the Indian tribe is spelled *Shoshone*; the author has chosen to spell it the older, more traditional way, *Shoshoni*.)

COLONEL Connor. Colonel Patrick Edward Connor established Camp Douglas in Salt Lake City in August 1862. Previously he had fought in the Mexican-American War before heading to California, expecting to make a quick fortune mining gold. When the Civil War broke out, he left his business and political interests and volunteered to serve in the Union army. He offered to raise volunteer troops. Once he was made a colonel, he was put in charge of the volunteers to prevent California from being cut off from the rest of the United States. Hoping to eventually fight rebels, he received instructions to establish Camp Douglas. He and his volunteers begged to be allowed to fight in the war back East, but the War Department turned them down.

Following the Battle of Bear River, Colonel Patrick Edward Connor was treated as a hero by the US Army. He was quickly promoted to general. After the Civil War, he stayed in Utah and carried on a war of words with leaders of The Church of Jesus Christ of Latter-day Saints. He considered President Brigham Young to be a tyrant who flagrantly disregarded federal authority. Connor had a goal to overturn Mormon dominance in Utah Territory and considered it his duty to encourage Gentiles to settle there. While President Young discouraged Church members from mining precious metals, Connor promoted mining as a means of attracting Gentiles and decreasing

Mormon influence. In fact, Connor's troops were instrumental in discovering mines in the Bingham area in 1863.

When the Civil War ended, Connor's men were mustered out and regular troops took over. Crude wooden buildings and tents at Camp Douglas were replaced with stone barracks and administrative buildings that still stand. The post became one of the most picturesque and sought-after assignments in the army.

Connor remained in Utah after his military career ended in 1866. He stayed involved in a variety of mining and business interests, including railroads and steamships, but fortune eluded him. In 1870, he joined with Mormon apostates and Gentiles to found the Liberal Party, which vied in local elections against the Mormons. He died on December 17, 1891, and was buried at Fort Douglas.

CHIEF SAGWITCH. Sagwitch and about one hundred of his people joined The Church of Jesus Christ of Latter-day Saints in 1873. Sagwitch was ordained an elder. In 1875, the chief and his wife were sealed in the Endowment House. Wilford Woodruff performed the ordinance. In 1880, Sagwitch and his band settled in Washakie, Utah, and operated a farm. They contributed large amounts of labor toward the building of the Logan temple. A biography of Sagwitch was published in 1999 by Utah State University Press, authored by Scott R. Christensen, entitled *Sagwitch: Shoshone Chieftain, Mormon Elder, 1822–1877*.

SHERIFF HENRY PLUMMER. Henry Plummer, born in 1832 in Maine, served as sheriff of Bannack City until January 10, 1864, when he was hanged by vigilantes. Plummer had organized a gang that robbed gold shipments in late 1863 and killed, by some estimates, a hundred people. He was hanged along with twenty-three other men for their crimes. Electa left him in September and returned to live with her parents in Ohio. Plummer is portrayed in this novel about the time he would have been organizing his gang but perhaps just before the gang's first notorious deeds.

About the Author

DARRYL HARRIS IS THE AUTHOR of six previous novels—the series of five Light & Truth historical novels (*The Field Is White, The Gathering, The Nauvoo Years, The Mormon Battalion,* and *The Journey Home*), and another novel entitled *Finding Zarahemla*. He lived his childhood in southeastern Idaho, served a mission to South Korea, and graduated from Brigham Young University with a degree in communications (emphasis in advertising and journalism). In 1972 he founded Harris Publishing, Inc., in Idaho Falls, Idaho, which today publishes several national magazines, including *SnoWest, Houseboat, Pontoon and Deck Boat, Dirt Toys, Diesel Tech, Potato Grower, The Sugar Producer,* and a local publication, *Idaho Falls Magazine*. Harris Publishing owns Falls Printing. He is married to the former Christine Sorensen. The couple has five children and nineteen grandchildren. Darryl and Christine presided over the Korea Seoul Mission in 1997–2000.